SLAVE O

FRANCESCA LEWIS

CHIMERA

Slave of Darkness first published in 2000 by
Chimera Publishing Ltd
PO Box 152
Waterlooville
Hants
PO8 9FS

Printed and bound in Great Britain by
Caledonian International Book Manufacturing Ltd
Glasgow

Copyright © Francesca Lewis

The right of Francesca Lewis to be identified as author of this book has been asserted in accordance with section 77 and 78 of the Copyrights Designs and Patents Act 1988

SLAVE OF DARKNESS

Francesca Lewis

This novel is fiction – in real life practice safe sex

Chapter One

'I simply can't believe it's ours, can you?' Marianne asked Steve, as she watched the removal van drive away.

'It's going to take some getting used to,' replied her lover. 'It's damn quiet here.'

'But don't you see? That's just what I need,' she exclaimed excitedly. 'It was incredibly generous of Great-aunt Dorothy to leave me this house. Just think, it's only three miles away from Haworth.'

'What's special about Haworth?' asked Steve.

'It's where the Brontë children grew up. Don't you know anything?'

'You're the literary one,' he reminded her, slipping an arm around her slender waist. 'I'm afraid books and computers don't mix that well.'

'You do like it, though, don't you?' persisted Marianne. 'I couldn't bear it if you didn't. I've got this feeling I'm going to be so happy here.'

'I take it you mean we?'

Marianne laughed. 'Of course I do. I wouldn't want to live here if we weren't going to be together, and I do know how much you like London. But this will be a wonderful place for me to write my new book. I mean, look at the views.' Marianne waved her arm in the direction of the Yorkshire Dales, the purple and yellow colours of the heather clear even from the courtyard of the house.

'I can see that,' agreed Steve. 'I suppose as I'm away so much it's more important the place suits you than me. It needs a lot doing to it, though.'

'Luckily the advance on my new book will see to that,' said Marianne. 'It couldn't have come at a better time, and it's wonderfully atmospheric here. What better place could there be for writing a romantic novel about destructive passion?'

'I'd have thought destructive passion was the same whether it took place in London, Manchester or the wilds of Yorkshire,' said Steve.

Marianne shook her head. 'That's where you're wrong. From the moment we walked into the house I felt quite different. It was almost as though I was back in the old days.'

'Then it's a pity you're not writing an historical novel.'

Privately Marianne agreed. It was strange, but what she'd said to Steve was true. When they'd first looked round the house, long before they actually moved in, she'd been able to picture every room as it might have been two hundred years ago. Not only that, she'd felt as though she belonged there, as though the house suited her and welcomed her. She realised she was being fanciful, that it was probably the result of an overactive imagination, but it was still comforting. She'd really felt as though she'd come home.

'It's damn cold here, too,' said Steve, wrapping his arms around himself. 'This house is so exposed. I had no idea your aunt lived in such an isolated place. Come to that, I had no idea the house would be this large. Quite honestly, we don't need all the rooms.'

'Not now,' Marianne agreed. 'But in the future we might.'

'You mean when we get married and have a family?'

Marianne's pale blue eyes widened. 'No! When we have

servants.'

Steve looked at her in astonishment. 'What the hell do you mean, servants?'

Marianne felt as astonished as Steve looked. She had no idea why she'd said such a thing. 'I don't know,' she confessed awkwardly. 'It must be the atmosphere here; you can tell some of the rooms were originally for servants.'

Steve shook his head. 'I think I liked you better in London. At least there you kept your imagination in check.'

Angry at herself, Marianne glared at Steve. 'But for my imagination we wouldn't be able to afford to decorate the house. Don't knock it, Steve.'

He sighed. 'Maybe it would have been better if we couldn't afford it. The house would fetch a fair bit if we sold it. God, I'm freezing.'

Marianne felt a sense of disquiet. Steve worked as a self-employed computer analyst/programmer, travelling round the country helping develop programmes for small businesses. Together they had always made a good pair, his common sense and her imagination fitting together to make one complete person. Suddenly their differences were working against them. She caught hold of his hand. 'We'd better go in if you're cold.'

'At least we brought our own bed with us.'

'We can't go to bed yet; there's too much to be done,' protested Marianne.

'I don't want to sleep.' Steve's voice was heavy with meaning.

Marianne hesitated. The truth was she wanted to get busy on the house, wanted to start arranging the furniture and making lists of all the things that needed doing, but that made no sense. Normally she'd have wanted Steve, too. 'You're insatiable,' she said, sounding far too sharp.

'I thought that was why you liked me.'

'Not always.'

'I'd never have guessed,' Steve remarked, leading her across the courtyard and through the front door of the L-shaped house. Their bedroom was one of four, and the largest. It was the only bedroom that had enough room for their king-sized bed.

'I wonder who used to sleep here?' said Marianne, as she started to take off her clothes.

Steve looked surprised. 'I don't suppose anyone did. The second bedroom's where your aunt slept, isn't it?'

'Oh, I didn't mean then,' said Marianne.

'So when did you mean?'

'When the house was first built.'

Steve stared at her. 'What on earth made you think of that?'

Marianne blinked. She wondered if she was going mad. 'I don't know,' she said slowly. 'The thought just suddenly came to me.'

'When was this house built?' asked Steve.

'Seventeen ninety-something, I think.'

'In that case, a lot of people have slept here over the years. I hope you're not going to try and find out the names of all of them?'

'Of course not.'

'Look, do you want to make love or don't you?'

Marianne didn't know what was the matter with her. Steve was already naked, lying on the bed, his eyes on her as she stood in her jeans and bra on the other side of the room. She could see he was aroused but she was finding it difficult to get in the mood. 'Of course I do,' she assured him.

'Come on then,' he said encouragingly, patting her side of the bed. 'It's not the thought of this house belonging to your great-aunt that's putting you off, is it?'

'Nothing's putting me off,' she said hastily. 'I suppose I'm a bit tired, that's all.'

'I'll soon change that,' Steve told her.

Marianne finished undressing and lay down next to him. As usual, Steve started by caressing her breasts. Within a few seconds his hand was moving between her thighs, and she knew it wouldn't be long before he entered her. She often wished he was a more imaginative lover, that he'd spend more time over foreplay, but he always made sure she had an orgasm, and in that respect she knew she was lucky. In any case, she wasn't as keen on sex as Steve and it didn't bother her too much if it was over quicker than it should be.

To her surprise, Steve seemed to realise she wasn't fully aroused and he moved down the bed a little, his hands under her hips, and started to kiss her belly and the tops of her thighs. He hardly ever did this, but she loved it when he did, and she started to squirm with rising excitement. Encouraged, Steve spread her legs wider and Marianne reached down to caress his hair in a gesture of tender affection as his tongue began to trail along the creases of her thighs.

Marianne's breathing grew more shallow and she felt herself becoming damp. Then, as Steve's fingers parted her sex lips, she gave a low moan of delight as she felt the first stirrings deep within her. Soon, as Steve continued to use his tongue on her damp flesh she was gasping and groaning, the tension growing within her body…

But then, just as the first delicious contractions were

threatening, she saw someone standing in the corner of the room!

With a cry of horror she twisted away from Steve, burying her belly and breasts in the bed as she tried to hide her nakedness.

'What the hell...?!'

Marianne lifted her head and glanced nervously over her shoulder. There was no one there. The room was quite empty and all she could see was Steve, a look of astonishment on his face. 'I-I'm sorry,' she mumbled. 'I... I thought there was someone here.'

'Here? In this room do you mean?'

'It must have been a trick of the light.'

'For God's sake!' Steve sounded thoroughly annoyed.

'I've already said I'm sorry,' said Marianne miserably. 'It gave me a terrible fright.'

'You gave me a terrible fright, twisting away like that. I thought either I'd hurt you or you were annoyed with me.'

Marianne didn't know what to say. She sat up, wrapping her arms round her knees. 'I don't know what happened,' she confessed.

'Use your common sense; how could anyone have got in?' he asked incredulously. 'I thought you were enjoying yourself.'

'I was,' she assured him.

'It doesn't seem to have taken much to distract you.'

'I'm sorry,' she said again. 'Look, let's leave it for now and try later on.'

'Oh, great,' said Steve. 'And what am I supposed to do with this?' He touched his erection.

'I don't know,' retorted Marianne.

'What you mean is you don't care,' Steve sulked. 'You didn't really want to make love in the first place, did you?'

'Not at first, no, but what you were doing was gorgeous,' she said quickly. 'Look, Steve, I really am sorry, but I was sure there was someone standing there.'

'Probably the first person who ever slept in the room,' he said sarcastically.

Marianne got up and started to pull on her clothes. 'I'm going to put the kettle on,' she said shortly. 'Do you want a cup of tea?'

'No, I don't want a cup of tea. I want you.'

'We'll make love later, when we go to bed,' said Marianne, attempting to placate him. Steve didn't reply but she knew there was no point in their continuing now. The mood had been broken and, anyway, she still had the peculiar sensation that they were being watched.

Marianne made herself a mug of tea and ate a large slice of chocolate cake, but even when she'd finished Steve hadn't come down to join her. She realised he was sulking and wished she could turn back the clock and make things right again. It was so important that he liked their new home. Right from the start, from the moment she'd heard about her inheritance, Steve's lack of enthusiasm had been clear, but although he'd initially suggested selling the house he'd accepted Marianne's wish to live there with very little argument. Just the same, she felt it was important to make him as happy as possible, and this had been a disastrous beginning.

She still couldn't work out what had happened to her. Everything had been going perfectly. In fact, she couldn't remember when she'd last been as excited – and yet the figure in the corner had been so clear. It wasn't even as though it was night and she could blame shadows. It was true that the corner of the room in which she thought she'd seen the figure was in shadow but now, refreshed by the tea and with her common sense returning, she simply didn't know how she could have thought anyone had been watching them.

'You'd better get a grip on yourself,' she said aloud, starting to move some of the boxes around, glancing at the labels on them to see what they contained and where they needed to go. Despite what had happened, she didn't think it would be long before Steve joined her, but half an hour passed and there was still no sign of him.

As it was a lovely April afternoon she decided to go outside and take advantage of the wonderful view. The house took up two sides of the courtyard with a wing on the right-hand side. On the left-hand side, slightly separate from the house, there was a grey brick outhouse and also a stable where she assumed that at some time horses had been kept, probably in order to provide transport in such an out of the way spot.

It was surprisingly cool because of the wind, but as she crossed the courtyard to the outhouse she realised that the brick building offered some protection, and the rays of the sun were warm on her face. Marianne loathed spiders and she peered through the single tiny window to see if the place was full of cobwebs. It wasn't; indeed, it looked as though her aunt might have used the place for storage and so she lifted the latch on the wooden door and pushed it open.

As her eyes adjusted to the gloom she moved into the centre of the room, wondering what it had originally been used for. The door swung to behind her and, as she turned to leave, she felt something pricking at her ankles. Glancing down, she was startled to realise there was straw on the floor and she bent down to brush it away from her feet. It was damp and smelly. She wondered how on earth she'd missed it when she first walked in. Opening the door to let in a little light, she returned to see exactly how much mess there was, and felt her jaw drop in astonishment because the floor was now clean. There was no straw anywhere.

'I must be going mad,' she said aloud, looking around to see if there was anything at all that she could have mistaken for straw, but there was nothing. The place was immaculate, having at some point been swept clean, with all its shelves dusted and only a small box of gardener's tools remaining.

She remembered her great-aunt mentioning her gardener and how he'd helped her create the wonderful display of flowers at the back of the house, which needed far more attention than an elderly lady would have been able to give. 'But there was straw,' Marianne said to herself. 'I felt it.' And yet the building remained resolutely clean and comparatively modern.

Turning to leave, she noticed something strange. In the wall, set in the brickwork about eighteen inches off the floor, were two metal rings approximately two feet apart. They looked very old and she couldn't imagine what they'd been used for. Hesitantly, she reached out and touched them, terrified that these, too, would prove to be an illusion, but the metal was cold beneath her fingertips and definitely existed.

Outside in the courtyard again, Marianne felt totally disorientated, unable to make out what was happening to her. She looked at the large rambling house with its narrow windows and flat, rather unprepossessing front. The lace curtains at the windows were filthy; they were at the top of Marianne's list for things that needed replacing. As she stared at them, to her terror, they started to change. Slowly they vanished and in their place were dark crimson drapes of a heavy material. The windows themselves looked different, darker and dirtier. She looked away, blinked, and then looked back. The dingy lace curtains were there once more and the crimson brocade curtains had vanished.

Marianne was very scared. She wanted Steve, needed to feel his comforting arms around her, but she knew she couldn't tell him what had happened to her while he'd been upstairs. He'd think she had gone completely mad and she wouldn't be able to blame him, because she couldn't think of any sane explanation herself. She ran into the house and up the stairs, then gave a cry of fright as she collided with Steve, who was standing at the top.

'It's only me,' he said, still sounding irritable. 'Not the stranger in the corner, I'm afraid.'

Marianne pressed herself against him. 'Please don't keep talking about that,' she begged him, her hands moving over his chest.

'Hey, what's this?'

'Take me to bed,' she begged, desperate for something to blot out the terror of what had happened to her.

'I've only just got up.'

She pressed herself hard against him, squashing her breasts against his chest, and he reacted as he always did to any advance she made. 'If you insist,' he laughed and, picking her up, he carried her into the bedroom. Hurriedly they both took off their clothes and this time it was Marianne who was initiating everything.

She pushed Steve on to his back, kissing him on the lips before slowly circling his nipples with her tongue, something she knew he loved. As the tiny points hardened on his chest she felt him hardening between his thighs. She couldn't wait to feel him inside her now, and lifted herself above him.

'Face the old wardrobe,' Steve urged her. 'That way you can watch yourself in the mirror on the door.'

Obediently she turned away from him, and then guided him into her as she slid down, feeling him ease inside her while her hands started to work at her nipples.

She watched herself move up and down with a gradually increasing tempo that rapidly took the pair of them to the point of no return. She could tell Steve was very excited. It was unusual for her to take the lead like this and he was enjoying it. For Marianne it was an escape, a moment of sensual sanity in the midst of what seemed to be some kind of strange madness brought on by the move.

'I'm coming,' she cried, as she felt the first sparks of desire between her thighs and her muscles began to tighten.

'Wait for me,' Steve urged her.

'I can't,' she gasped, her fingers working even harder at her nipples, rolling them in unison.

Then, just as her pleasure was about to spill, she saw the man.

He was standing in the same place, only this time she could see him far more clearly. He was tall and broad-shouldered with long dark hair that had a few silver threads in it. His eyes seemed to glow like black coals and she knew instinctively she was the one he was there to watch.

There was nothing she could do about it. Her orgasm was so near that even the presence of some inexplicable figure couldn't stop her. With a groan of ecstasy she felt the hot flood of liquid pleasure travel through her veins and her muscles contracted rhythmically, tightening around Steve until, with a cry of triumph, he came as well.

Marianne could feel the sweat between her breasts and on her forehead. She ran her hands through her hair and looked into the corner again, fully expecting the apparition to have vanished. But the man was still there, watching her with piercing eyes, and now she wanted him gone because there was something dangerous about him, something brooding and terrifying.

'That was great!' Steve sighed enthusiastically.

His voice broke the eye contact between Marianne and the apparition. 'Lovely,' she agreed quietly, distractedly, and when her eyes flickered back to the corner of the room the man had gone. Inexplicably, her relief was tinged with a sensation of loss and she realised with shock that his presence had added to the intensity of her orgasm. Once more, she wondered what on earth was happening to her.

Chapter Two

'You're sure you'll be all right stuck out here on your own while I'm away?' asked Steve as he prepared to leave.

'Of course,' said Marianne. 'We've been here a week now and no one's come near the place. Why should I be nervous?'

'Remember, you can always call me on my mobile.'

'I know that, but there won't be any need.'

Steve wrapped his arms around her and kissed her. 'You'd better make a start on that novel while I'm gone. You seem to be putting it off.'

'That's not true,' protested Marianne, but it was. She didn't know why. The atmosphere in the house was perfect but for some reason her characters were refusing to come alive for her. For the first time in her life she found herself wishing she was an historical novelist, and she didn't understand why. 'Okay,' she agreed finally.

'Promise?'

'You do your job and I'll do mine.'

Steve nodded. 'That sounds a fair exchange. Is there anything you want me to bring you back from the big city?'

Marianne shook her head. 'Nothing at all. I've got everything I want here.'

'Personally, I'd go mad if I didn't have the option of travelling round the country,' said Steve. 'This isn't my idea of heaven. Did you know that our nearest neighbours are half a mile away?'

Marianne shook her head. 'No, I didn't, but it doesn't bother me.'

'I met the husband when I went to buy some stuff from the general store. His name's Graham and he seemed a nice sort of chap. He and his wife are about our age. He told me where they live and suggested we call round some time. When I get back, I think we'd better do that.'

'Fine,' Marianne said flatly.

'You don't sound very enthusiastic.'

'Of course I am. Off you go now.'

As Steve drove away, Marianne closed the front door behind him and let out a sigh of relief. It was a terrible thing to admit, but she was glad to see him go. Ridiculously, she felt as though the house didn't want Steve; as though only she belonged there, not him. Also, she wasn't in the least bit interested in making friends with another young couple.

She opened the door into the study where she would be working and glanced at her computer. Steve was right: she really should get on with the book, but at the moment the ideas weren't flowing. This afternoon, she promised herself. Then, feeling guilty but happy, she began to go through the house, moving from room to room and noting down the things that needed to be done.

All too quickly the day sped by and Marianne did no work on her novel at all. By early evening she only had the smallest bedroom to go through. Her face and hands were covered with dirt and she felt hot, exhausted but satisfied. The bedroom was in the east wing of the house, above the kitchen, and at this time of day there was very little light coming in through the one small window. All the same, she was surprised at how very dark it was and, closing the door behind her, reached for the light switch.

To her dismay it didn't work and the room remained dark. 'Blast, it must be the bulb,' she muttered.

She looked across at the window and, to her amazement, realised the net curtains were no longer there. Instead, what looked like a piece of sacking was covering the glass, which she supposed accounted for the gloom. She didn't remember having seen it there before. She was about to move across the floor and take it down, but stopped short.

Suddenly the entire room was different!

There was no carpet beneath her feet, only bare boards, and instead of the divan bed sitting neatly in the centre of one wall there was a small truckle-bed in the far corner...

And she could just make out a shadowy figure lying on it!

Marianne's chest felt tight; it was difficult to breathe and the room felt very cold. As she stood frozen to the spot, unable to move for terror, her eyes gradually began to make out two more figures hunched over the truckle-bed, and she pressed herself back against the door. One of the floorboards creaked, she froze and held her breath, but neither of the figures looked up.

'Wake up, Tabitha,' said a woman's voice. 'The master's home and he's been told of your misdemeanour this afternoon.'

As she was speaking, the woman lit a candle, enabling Marianne to make her out more clearly. She looked to be around thirty years old, with curly brown hair that fell around her shoulders. She was wearing a dark green silk dress with a white fichu and cuffs. The dress was down to her ankles, and round her waist was a chain with a bunch of keys attached.

Candlelight enabled Marianne to see the other figure looming over the bed. She drew in her breath sharply as she recognised the man who had watched her and Steve when they were making love. His hair was longer than she'd realised, and he was wearing knee-breeches and gaiters with what Marianne thought was either a very long jacket or a dark coat over a white shirt with a silk cravat at the neck. Again she was struck by the breadth of his shoulders and the contrast of the occasional silver thread in his dark hair.

'Is she really asleep?' the man asked, his voice deep and cultured.

'Of course not, she's pretending as usual,' replied the woman, and she began to shake the figure on the bed.

Marianne couldn't believe what was happening. It was incredible! Either some locals she'd not yet met thought this a good practical joke to initiate her into the community, or she'd contracted some sort of hallucinatory fever... or she'd gone back in time!

But that was ridiculous – of course.

As she looked more closely, she realised the two shadowy figures didn't seem to see her. The atmosphere was peculiar, tense and frightening, but there was no obvious reason for this. She waited, partly because she couldn't move and partly because she had to know what was going on; who this couple were, and what they wanted with the girl called Tabitha.

'Wake up!' The woman's voice was sharper now and, raising her hand, she brought it down against what was clearly bare flesh, for Marianne heard a sharp slap.

There was a cry from the truckle-bed and immediately the man pulled the blanket off, revealing a slim girl with long brown hair. Her waist was tiny, but her breasts were large with wine-dark areolae and nipples.

'My sister tells me that you spent time with John in the

garden this afternoon,' said the man, reaching out with one hand and grasping one of the hapless girl's nipples between two fingers.

'No sir, it's not true,' gasped the girl, forced to rise to her knees as he tugged at her flesh.

'Are you saying my sister lies?' he asked.

The girl cast a terrified glance at the woman. 'No, sir.'

'It seems to me that you are. What other explanation is there for you contradicting her in this way?'

'It was a misunderstanding, sir.' The girl was crying now, tears rolling down her face.

'What shall we do with her, Edward?' asked the woman.

The man walked across to a small stool, passing only a couple of feet away from Marianne, and moved it to the centre of the room. 'Stand on there, Tabitha.' His voice was low and stern.

'No, please... please don't punish me again, sir,' the girl cried.

The older woman, clearly losing patience, grabbed the girl's slender wrist and dragged her off the bed, causing her to squeal. Totally naked, her body shaking with fear, Tabitha stood between the man and his sister, head bowed in resigned acceptance of whatever punishment was to be meted out to her. The woman handed her brother a thin strip of material, which he used to tie Tabitha's hands together, and then, without any effort, he lifted her fragile body on to the stool. Immediately the girl raised her arms into the air.

Looking up, Marianne saw there was a rope over a beam in the ceiling and at the end of the rope was a round brass ring with a cord through it. The man – Edward, as Marianne now knew he was called – swiftly fastened Tabitha's bound hands with the cord so that she was forced to stand on tiptoe on the stool.

Because Tabitha was so tiny this meant her face was now on a level with her master's, but she kept her eyes on the floor, clearly too terrified to look him in the face. When he glanced across at his sister, Marianne saw a strange expression on his face. It was a mixture of cruelty and excitement and she felt herself tense in anticipation of something sinister, but at the same time highly arousing.

'What do you wish to use on her, Judith?' asked Edward.

'I think the birch,' replied his sister. Tabitha gave a small cry at her words.

'An excellent idea,' agreed her brother, idly running a finger up and down the centre of Tabitha's tightly stretched body. Marianne could see how Tabitha's flesh tried to shrink away from him, but suddenly he gripped her around the waist, his thumbs pressing cruelly into her skin until it turned white under the pressure. 'You really must learn to behave, Tabitha,' he said, his voice almost gentle.

'I didn't do anything, sir,' wept the girl.

'You always say that.' Now his hands were moving to Tabitha's full breasts and his fingers gripped them so tightly that Marianne's own breasts ached in sympathy for the wretched girl in front of her.

'Please sir, you're hurting me,' cried Tabitha.

'You're enjoying it.' His voice was harsh and he flicked contemptuously at one of her stiff nipples. 'Look at that. Have you learned nothing in all your years with us? Your flesh betrays you constantly and is the reason for all your misbehaviour. That's why it must be punished.'

'I can't help it,' wailed Tabitha.

'Be silent now,' he commanded her as his sister returned.

Marianne's mouth was dry. She couldn't understand why she was feeling so aroused, why shivers of excitement were running through her when what she was watching was so terrible and so incomprehensible.

Judith walked behind Tabitha, the bundle of birch twigs fastened tightly together held securely in her hand. For a moment her brother stepped into the shadows, removing some clothing and giving Marianne an even better view of Tabitha.

The girl's whole body was trembling, and as Judith cruelly stroked the length of her spine with the end of the bunch of birch twigs she gave a startled exclamation of fear and strained forward, her feet almost slipping off the stool.

'You must keep still when you're being punished,' ordered Edward from the shadows while his sister readjusted Tabitha's position. 'Still and silent.'

Marianne's hands were clasped tightly together and she realised she was almost forgetting to breathe as she waited for the first blow to fall on the girl. She watched as Judith raised her right arm before bringing it down sharply, causing Tabitha's hips to jerk forward as a moan escaped her.

Marianne could almost feel the shock of the blow, could imagine the dreadful sensation of being so helpless, naked and at the mercy of this couple. But as Judith continued to beat Tabitha, working her way down over the girl's buttocks and the backs of her thighs, so Marianne's excitement grew and her cheeks felt hot and flushed.

After a time Tabitha started to scream with every blow, begging for the beating to cease, but her wishes were ignored and Marianne saw that, despite her protests, Tabitha's nipples were rigid, standing erect, while her breasts were firm and tight.

'Please, Sir Edward, please don't let her hit me any

more,' cried Tabitha suddenly, after a particularly savage blow had caused her whole body to shudder.

Her master stepped forward from the shadows, running his hands over her sweat-streaked body. He was entirely naked now and Marianne gazed in admiration at his tightly muscled buttocks and thighs.

Slipping a hand between Tabitha's legs, he then drew his fingers across her belly. 'Feel your juices,' he said harshly. 'How dare you complain when you're so aroused?'

'It's because of what you keep doing to me,' whimpered the girl, and Sir Edward's free hand closed around her breast, gripping it tightly.

'You love it,' he hissed. His sister was standing motionless behind Tabitha, awaiting her brother's command. For a few seconds Sir Edward stood with his back to Marianne, staring at the girl hanging suspended in front of him. Then, with one swift movement, he snatched Tabitha's thighs and pulled them around his waist.

It was only now that Marianne realised how cleverly they'd positioned Tabitha, because her master was able to thrust into her without any effort, rutting his hips against hers so that she groaned, though whether in pain or ecstasy Marianne couldn't tell. At that moment Judith resumed the beating, and Marianne watched in amazement as Tabitha jerked forward on to her master's erection every time the birch twigs hit her. The girl was crying out helplessly, her anguish clear, and yet, as Sir Edward continued thrusting fiercely into her, her cries changed until Marianne could hear the rising excitement despite the terrible things the couple were doing to her.

For what seemed to be several minutes Tabitha moved

back and forth in her bonds. Marianne tried to imagine what it must be like to be filled by a man like Sir Edward while at the same time being abused by his sister, and her own flesh began to feel hot and needy. Just then Tabitha became rigid and the tempo of her breathing changed. She was gasping and crying, twisting frantically until Sir Edward's hands held the lower half of her still and he moved with fierce efficiency in and out of her in a rhythm that had Marianne gasping too, covering her mouth with a hand to try to muffle the sounds.

She watched as the muscles of Sir Edward's buttocks grew even tighter and then, in a series of swift jerks he came. As he did so Tabitha uttered a strange keening sound as her body heaved in what was clearly a moment of ecstasy.

Only when Sir Edward had withdrawn and Tabitha's slight figure was finally still did Judith cease beating the wretched girl. As she started to unfasten her bonds, her brother turned and looked directly at Marianne.

For a brief, heart-stopping moment they stared at each other, his eyes shining with excitement, and something else that Marianne could have sworn was desire. Despite her utter confusion she felt herself drawn inexorably towards him, but then, without any warning, the entire scene vanished and she was once more standing on carpet in the bedroom, with the divan bed back in place and the net curtains at the windows.

Tentatively, she rubbed her hands over her breasts and was shocked to discover that her nipples were hard beneath her blouse, while between her thighs she knew she was wet. She could never remember feeling so aroused before and found herself wishing Steve was coming home that evening. Staring around the room, she wondered what on earth was happening. Why was this man and his life so real to her? How was it possible for her to see him and for him to see her? She was certain he'd seen her, just as he'd been watching her when she'd first moved into the house. Despite the terrible things he and his sister had been doing to Tabitha, she envied the girl; envied her the knowledge she had and the incredible sensations she must have experienced, although for Marianne the concept of pain mixed with pleasure was difficult to understand.

Later that evening she tried to concentrate on her writing but, to her dismay, her hero kept changing, becoming more and more like Sir Edward. In the end she abandoned the project, deciding instead to take a bath and have an early night. Whether it was because of what she'd seen or the work she'd done in the day she didn't know, but she fell asleep the moment her head hit the pillow.

After her terrifying experience, Marianne spent the next three days trying to work on her book. She felt that if she could only become immersed in it, using her imagination to bring her characters to life, then perhaps the history of the house would lose its strange power over her. However, she quickly realised that it didn't work that way. No matter how hard she tried she simply couldn't make her novel come to life in the way she'd expected.

She took regular walks on the moors, enchanted by the clear spring water and revelling in the feeling of the dark green turf beneath her feet, while around her birds sang as they darted to and fro over the heather. Even outside her thoughts wandered to the past as she realised that the young Brontë children had grown up only a few miles away and that they, too, had spent their time on these very moors.

Originally, her intention had been to write a modern version of *Wuthering Heights*. She'd felt certain that living in this beautiful house, in exactly the same setting as Emily Brontë had lived, would make her task simple. But it seemed to be working in the opposite way. It was proving more and more difficult for her to live in the present because everything about the house and the moors reminded her of the past. She couldn't understand it, and neither could she understand her obsession with the man known to her only as Sir Edward, whose brief, supernatural appearances had had more effect on her than any man she'd met in real life.

The day before Steve was due back, Marianne finally decided to give her book a rest and went up into the attic to sort through some of the boxes that were still unopened from the move. Beneath the sloping eaves, tucked away in a corner, she found an old wooden chest. For some reason the discovery of the chest excited her and she opened it with trembling fingers, certain that within she would find something important, something she needed to know.

There was a lot of old letters and photographs that had belonged to her great-aunt, along with lengths of material and some old shoes. But finally, buried beneath all this, she drew out a book. Glancing at the jacket, she saw it was a history of her new home, Moorhead House.

She opened it carefully, her eyes scanning the pages. The house had been built by Henry Holland in seventeen ninety-four, designed specifically for the original owners, a local industrialist and his wife. After but a few moments it was clear to Marianne that this had been before Sir Edward's time and she moved hastily to the next chapter. It was here, at last, that she was able to read about Sir

Edward.

'In eighteen twenty-six Moorhead House was purchased by one Sir Edward Sharpe, for his widowed sister, Judith Fullick. Sir Edward appears to have spent a great deal of his time in London while his sister looked after Moorhead House for him, with only a couple of servants and her companion, Miss Marianne Clifford, for company. Very little is known about Sir Edward Sharpe apart from the fact that he had inherited money from the wool industry and spent quite a lot of his time at Moorhead hunting and fishing. It appears that he and his sister were considered strange, and local gossip about them was considerable. During the years Sir Edward owned the house there were very few visitors, and his death in eighteen thirty-eight in London meant that the house passed to his nephew, one Richard Broadbeck. It is not known what became of Judith Fullick or the other members of the household.'

Marianne closed the book and hugged it tightly. Now it made more sense, and the words had confirmed what she'd suspected – namely that Sir Edward and his sister really had lived in this very house some hundred and seventy years previously. The reason she was able to see and hear them as they were at that time must be connected to the fact that she and Judith Fullick's companion, by some strange twist of fate, shared the same name. This was the key, the reason behind everything, and she felt almost elated.

The words she'd read emphasised that there was something bizarre about the couple. There'd been an air of danger surrounding Sir Edward Sharpe from the very first time he'd appeared to her. And after the scene she'd witnessed a few days earlier involving the girl, Tabitha, she'd become even more certain that, despite a strange charm, he was a man of dark secrets. Local people at the time had been aware of this, but she doubted if anyone could have known what had really gone on in the house.

'Perhaps I'm the first person to know apart from them,' she said to herself. 'Maybe, if I'm lucky, I'll find out all their secrets.'

The prospect excited her to the extent that her real life seemed boring and unsatisfactory. Every time she entered a room or evening approached she found herself half-hoping that Sir Edward would appear to her again.

Marianne wondered if she could use her feelings for Sir Edward in her book by changing the historical setting but keeping the intensity of emotion she was feeling, however ridiculously, for this spectre from the past. Encouraged by the thought, she hurried down to the study and once again sat herself in front of the computer.

Now, at last, the words began to flow, because she could understand her heroine better, even though she herself was obsessed with someone who'd been dead for over a hundred years and the heroine of her book was obsessed with a modern-day man. She lost track of time, pausing only to switch on the light as the words poured out. As she reached a point where her heroine was sitting in her parent's front room, waiting for her lover to arrive, the study became dark, as though the bulb was failing. Stopping abruptly, Marianne glanced excitedly around her and saw that everything had changed.

The walls were now lined with bookshelves, the books on them having real leather spines. The furniture was of the kind she'd only ever seen in antique shops and the walls were papered instead of painted. There was a rocking chair in one corner of the room and a table with a tumbler and a decanter of port on it, while the old fireplace glowed with burning logs. Marianne pushed back her chair, unable to believe she was going to see him again.

'Please sit down,' said the deep voice she remembered so well. 'I'm sorry we kept you waiting but my sister was explaining to me what had occurred today.'

Marianne's hands brushed at her skirt. The material felt different, coarser, and when she glanced down she saw she was now in a long, rust-coloured woollen dress which prickled against her arms. And her blonde hair had grown in length, some of the curls reaching to her shoulders.

'It looks as though Marianne has been asleep,' said Judith Fullick, appearing behind her brother's shoulder. 'I'm beginning to wonder if she's going to prove a suitable companion for me after all.'

Sir Edward's dark eyes surveyed Marianne coldly. 'It will be better for her if she does not disappoint me,' he said slowly. 'I trust you have not forgotten, Miss Marianne, the things we discussed at your interview?'

Marianne shook her head. She had no idea what he was talking about but realised that she was now her nineteenth-century namesake, caught up in the lives of this strange brother and sister and unable to escape because she didn't know how the transformation worked. In any case, she felt different, as though she was indeed nothing more than a companion to the young widow standing watching her.

'I had expected gratitude,' continued Sir Edward. 'Since you are totally alone in the world it is very foolish of you to behave in an indiscreet fashion so early on in your employment.'

'Indiscreet?' asked Marianne.

'I call going out for a walk alone, and failing to return for nearly an hour, indiscreet,' said Judith Fullick. 'It would be different if I'd sent you on an errand or if you'd had any explanation when you returned but, as I told my brother, you failed to give me any satisfactory answer as to why you went out for so long.'

'I simply wanted some air,' said Marianne, acknowledging the magnetic attraction the moors had held for her ever since she moved into this house.

'It is up to my sister when you do and when you do not take air,' said Sir Edward. 'The sooner you start to learn your place here the better it will be for you. Judith, remove her gown.'

Marianne stared at him, suddenly remembering Tabitha and the terrible things this man and his sister had done to her. Instinctively, she put her hands across her breasts and backed away from the approaching Judith, only to knock against a horsehair sofa.

'My dear Miss Marianne, please stand still,' said Judith. Marianne realised she had no choice and, to her horror, the other woman's fingers began to unfasten the buttons until the gown was open from throat to waist.

Sir Edward glanced at the log fire. 'You look a little warm. Remove the gown.'

Marianne shook her head. 'Please don't make me,' she whispered, feeling incredibly shy.

He raised one eyebrow. 'You see, Judith, it isn't difficult to subdue young women like this. She doesn't look defiant now.'

'Remove the gown,' Judith whispered in Marianne's ear. 'My brother has a terrible temper.'

Marianne felt all fingers and thumbs as she fumbled at the coarse woollen dress, finally managing to remove it so that she was standing in an unfamiliar bodice, petticoat and stockings. Her skin felt hot and damp. She'd never been so nervous and yet at the same time she was excited by the expression in Sir Edward's eyes. Reaching towards her, he slowly unfastened the ribbon that was threaded through the front of her bodice, peeling the garment off her. His eyes shone with pleasure as she trembled in front of him.

Judith, who Marianne could tell was no stranger to scenes like this, assisted her brother in stripping her totally naked. She was finally exposed to his gaze, trying hopelessly to cover herself with her hands while all the time his eyes burned into her.

'Such lovely white skin,' he murmured, walking around her. 'No doubt it marks very easily...' She felt him trail a fingernail down her spine. She jumped, and he gave a low laugh.

'I think Miss Marianne has eaten too well since she joined us,' he said slowly. 'There is more flesh on her than I expected.'

'That's because you're used to Tabitha,' explained his sister.

Sir Edward nodded. 'Possibly so.'

The heat from the fire was warm against Marianne's buttocks and back and she could feel a sheen of perspiration on her breasts as Sir Edward continued to walk around her, occasionally running the palm of a hand over her hips. Mostly, though, he contented himself with looking, and his gaze was so penetrating that she felt certain he could tell the effect he was having on her.

'What's this?' he asked sharply. Marianne realised he was looking at her breasts. Glancing down at them she was horrified to see her nipples were erect, a clear indication that his leisurely examination of her body was affecting her.

'It seems I've brought a loose woman into our house,

Judith,' he said quietly. 'No real lady would respond in this way.'

'She must be punished,' said Judith, her voice full of satisfaction. 'Perhaps it's fortunate that she's come to us. At least here she can learn discipline.'

Marianne's legs were beginning to shake but the longer she was left naked with the pair of them watching her, the more her body swelled and tightened with arousal. And when Sir Edward finally ran the flat of his hand across her breasts such piercing pleasure streaked through her that she couldn't suppress a moan.

'Dear me,' said Sir Edward, one corner of his mouth lifting in amusement. 'The first thing we must do is discipline these...' he pinched her left nipple. Pain shot through her and she gasped. 'Hand me your hairbrush, Judith,' he said.

Marianne watched as his sister handed him a silver-backed brush. His eyes locked on to Marianne's. 'This should teach you not to take pleasure from punishment,' he said coldly. 'You are to stand perfectly still and keep looking into my eyes, do you understand?'

'Y-yes,' whispered Marianne.

'Yes, sir,' he corrected her.

'Yes, sir,' she said hastily, and her blue eyes made contact with his almost black ones.

'Remember, you are not to move,' he repeated, and she felt her mouth go dry as the bristles of the brush were drawn around her left breast, circling lightly at first but with increasing pressure.

The sensation wasn't disagreeable to begin with, but then Edward brushed harder until her skin started to burn. 'You're hurting me,' she cried.

'Be silent!'

She tried to flinch away from him but he gripped her waist savagely before starting to brush her other breast. This time there was no gentle start; instead, the bristles were moved briskly over the tender surface of the sensitive flesh.

The sensation was extraordinary. It was a burning feeling that made Marianne's breasts ache. She felt as though she wanted to shrink away from him but, at the same time, her breasts felt tight and her nipples were so hard. She was shocked to discover that she was aching between her thighs as well, and when she saw the expression in Sir Edward's eyes she knew he had guessed what was happening to her.

He continued to torment her breasts with the brush until she felt she could bear it no more. 'P-please, I beg you... stop now,' she cried falteringly. 'I'm truly sorry for whatever it is I've done, and I'll never do it again.'

Edward tossed the brush away and grasped her scarlet nipples between his fingers, squeezing them lightly at first. His touch caused pleasure to flood her body, and she felt her vagina growing moist. 'You're still enjoying this too much,' he said, and his fingers tightened.

Marianne's breath caught in her throat as terrible streaks of pain darted over her flesh, but still the tightness within her grew and she longed for him to cover the sore flesh with his mouth, to cool the burning heat with his tongue...

She shivered, ashamed at her own thoughts.

'Do you think she's learned her lesson?' Edward asked his sister. Judith shook her head. 'I agree,' he continued. 'Should we continue this elsewhere? The outhouse, perhaps?'

Instinctively, Marianne knew she mustn't allow this to happen or her body would be subjected to something truly terrible. She tried to twist away, but his fingers were still holding her aching nipples and she cried out at the pain. 'I've learned my lesson, I have,' she blurted, desperately hoping that this would be enough to appease the couple.

To her relief the pressure on her nipples eased, and he turned to his sister. 'Do you not agree that she has overeaten?' he asked teasingly.

Judith moved closer, reaching out one small hand and enclosing it around Marianne's right breast, which her brother relinquished to her.

Marianne remained motionless, not daring to move without permission, while the brother and sister played with her breasts, their fingers so different in the way they touched her that she found the experience unbelievably erotic.

'She's not as large as Tabitha,' said Judith at last.

'True, but the rest of her body is more rounded,' countered Sir Edward.

'I'll watch what she eats,' agreed Judith. 'Perhaps I have been too generous.'

Sir Edward moved a hand down over Marianne's belly and she whimpered with a mixture of trepidation and desire. 'I think we should visit the outhouse,' he said firmly.

Strange and frightening visions flashed through Marianne's brain. 'No!' she screamed. 'I won't go! I won't go...!'

Abruptly, everything changed again. Sir Edward Sharpe and his sister disappeared. The furniture became modern once more and Marianne was standing by her computer. She was fully dressed, but her emotions still percolated. Now, when it was too late, she wanted to call them back. Her body needed satisfaction, and although part of her had sensed the outhouse she would be a place of punishment, she also knew beyond any doubt that, like Tabitha, she would finally have been allowed pleasure. As it was, she was alone with only her computer for company and she felt totally bereft.

'What on earth's the matter with you?' she asked herself. 'The man's a sadist. How can you possibly respond to him?' She didn't know. She didn't understand anything, certainly not what was happening to her. All she knew at this moment was that she would have given anything in the world to go back to the past and learn the secrets of the outhouse.

The sound of the phone ringing made her jump out of her skin. She sent books and papers flying as she scrabbled to pick it up. 'Hello?'

'Marianne?'

She sank on to her chair. 'Steve! Where are you?'

'In Leeds, of course. Are you all right? You sound strange.'

'I'm fine,' she said weakly. 'You startled me, that's all.'

'Were you asleep?'

'No, writing my book.'

'Glad to hear it.' Steve laughed. 'How's it going?'

Marianne couldn't remember. Nothing seemed real to her now except the incredible scene in the drawing room with Sir Edward and his sister. 'Okay, I think,' she said slowly.

'You don't sound very enthusiastic.'

'Well, it's always difficult to tell early on.'

'I just rang to say I'm missing you and I'll be back by four tomorrow afternoon.'

'Oh, that's great.'

'Well you might sound as though you mean it.'

Marianne could tell that Steve was hurt. 'I do mean it, honestly I do.'

'So you're lonely without me?'

'Not really lonely,' she said carefully. 'There's a lot going on here.'

'I find that rather hard to believe.'

Marianne realised she'd slipped up. 'I've got the book and the house to get in order,' she explained.

'Oh, that! You made it sound as though you'd got a flood of people coming in and out of the place. You haven't met our neighbours yet, have you?'

'No.' Marianne realised she sounded irritable, but she couldn't help it. She wasn't interested in the modern couple down the road, but the bizarre couple from the past.

'I'll have to go, the line's breaking up,' said Steve. 'Miss you lots, can't wait to get back. Bye.'

The line went dead and Marianne replaced the receiver. She wondered why hearing from Steve hadn't been more pleasurable. Only minutes earlier she'd been desperate for someone to comfort her, yet when her lover had rung her all she'd felt was an unexpected surge of irritation with him. She ran her hands over her breasts and realised they were still tender and sensitive. Suddenly she had to have satisfaction, had to reach the pinnacle of pleasure. Hurrying upstairs, she threw herself on the bed.

She didn't even bother to remove any clothing but instead thrust one hand inside her blouse and the other up under her skirt, rubbing at herself through her panties until she could feel the swollen nub of her clitoris. Closing her eyes, she pictured Sir Edward, and immediately her senses tingled as though he was there, caressing her. She moved her fingers in rapid circular motions against the silk material, thrusting her hips upward while her other hand rhythmically squeezed and released her breasts. At the last moment she slipped her hand inside her panties and eased one finger inside herself while her thumb brushed her clitoris so that, with a cry of pleasure, she climaxed.

She supposed she should feel guilty because Steve hadn't crossed her mind once, but she couldn't help it. It was Sir Edward Sharpe who'd triggered her desire and she'd needed to picture him in order to satisfy it. 'I wonder how I can get back,' she muttered to herself. 'If only I knew how to control things.'

All through the rest of the evening she kept hoping her surroundings would change, but nothing happened. The house remained resolutely the way it should be, and finally she locked up for the night. 'Don't stay away too long,' she whispered as she closed the study door, and she sensed that he wouldn't.

She shivered as she made her way to bed, knowing she was allowing herself to be drawn into a dark and dangerous world where sexual perversion was the rule of the day, and where her pleasure would always be earned at a price.

Chapter Three

Marianne was on the phone to her agent when Steve returned home the next day. She was in mid-argument and scarcely had time to acknowledge his arrival as he walked past her and up the stairs. By the time he came down she'd finished talking and hurried over to greet him.

'You're very flushed,' he remarked. 'Who were you talking to?'

'Angela.'

'What were you arguing about?'

'I've decided to change my book,' she said defiantly.

'Change it in what way?'

'I want to make it an historical novel.'

Steve blinked. 'You've always laughed at historical novels. Anyway, you've done the outline and been paid the advance, you can't possibly change it now.'

'Funny, that's what Angela's been telling me. You don't happen to be a literary agent in your spare time, do you, Steve?'

'Hey, don't take it out on me!' Steve protested. 'You must admit, this isn't like you. Anyway, you told me Moorhead House was perfect for writing your book.'

'It's even more perfect for writing an historical one,' retorted Marianne. 'It's not going to be my usual kind of book, either. It's going to be more physical.'

'Physical?'

'Do stop repeating my words,' she snapped. 'It's like having a parrot in the house.'

Steve looked hurt. 'What on earth's got into you? It's hardly surprising I'm finding this difficult to take in. Your books are popular because they deal with emotions. Are you telling me you're going to have explicit sex scenes in this latest one?'

'Do you think I can't write them?'

Steve shrugged. 'How would I know? The point is, do your readers want you to write them? And there's another thing. Without wishing to be rude, a lot of other writers deal with that subject and have far more experience of it, I'd have thought...'

'Perhaps I'd have more experience of it if you weren't away so much,' she sniped.

'I didn't mean real experience. I was talking about your writing.'

Marianne sighed. 'I know that. I'm just being tiresome. I'm sorry, Steve, but this is something I feel very strongly about and Angela didn't understand. I hoped you would, but you're the same as her.'

Steve put an arm round her shoulders. 'I don't know anything about writing, and if you've got a passionate desire to write an historical novel that's more sexually explicit than your books usually are, then go ahead. I just don't understand why you've changed your mind or how you can expect your publisher to accept what you want to do. Why don't you finish the book you promised them and then write an historical one?'

'Because I can't! The original book isn't working. I've got to do this.'

'So, exactly how physical is it going to be?'

Marianne looked away from him. 'Not very,' she said evasively. 'Let's face it, our ancestors did have sex, otherwise we wouldn't be here.'

'Sure, but sex is sex whenever it takes place. If the only thing you want to change is the sex content, why not put a bit more in the novel you've already started?'

'Sex wasn't the same then,' said Marianne, her voice passionate. 'It wasn't all out in the open, something people could read about and watch on television. It was quiet, furtive and...'

'And probably bloody boring,' Steve concluded dismissively.

'Why do you say that?' she demanded. 'Anyway, modern sex can be boring, too.'

'Well thank you very much. This is a nice welcome home, I must say.'

'I didn't mean that personally,' Marianne said hastily, although she knew she did. 'What I'm saying is, perhaps in the past they had more exciting sex lives than we realise.'

'Perhaps they did,' he agreed after a pause. 'But since we'll never know I don't see why you're getting quite this worked up about it.'

'You don't understand what it's like to have a story in your head and know that you've got to get it down.'

'No I don't,' admitted Steve. 'I like my work but I never feel that passionate about it. That's something I envy you.'

'Then you'll support me in this?'

'It's got nothing to do with me. It's Angela and your publisher you've got to talk round.'

'If they don't like it I'll send back the advance for the original book and then show them the finished manuscript for the new one,' said Marianne determinedly.

'You can't do that,' Steve protested. 'We need the money – you know we do.'

'I know, but right now the way I feel about this seems

more important than the money.'

'Bloody hell,' sighed Steve, running fingers through his hair. 'This is a fine homecoming.'

They fell into silence for a few minutes, and then Steve changed the subject. 'By the way,' he said, 'I saw our neighbour, Graham, when I stopped at the local store earlier. I've invited him and his wife over this evening for drinks.'

'Oh no. What did you do that for?'

'Because I thought it would be nice if we got to know some people around here,' he said abruptly. 'I don't want to live in splendid isolation, even if you do. When I'm away you can shut yourself off from the whole world for all I care, but when I'm here I like company.'

'And I'm not enough company for you?' demanded Marianne.

'We're only talking about a couple of hours. We've been together too long now to need to be alone every minute of every day.'

'I'm not in a mood for visitors,' she said sulkily.

'I don't know what's happened to you since we moved here,' he remarked impatiently. 'I'm beginning to wish we'd stayed in London.'

'You never wanted to come here in the first place,' she retorted.

'True, but I did because I knew how much it meant to you. What I didn't expect was that it would change you. I don't think you realise how much you've altered. You've become absolutely obsessed with the past and the history of the house. You're even willing to jeopardise your work for it. It's as though this house has cast a spell on you. If you ask me, it's bloody spooky.'

'Well, I didn't ask you,' she snapped.

Ever since the meeting with Edward and Judith, Marianne had felt constantly on edge sexually. She wanted to be aroused and used in the way the phantom couple had used her, and she'd been longing for Steve to come back, if only to give her some kind of physical attention. After their quarrel she realised this wasn't going to happen and shut herself away in the study to begin work on her new novel, only emerging reluctantly to change thirty minutes before their visitors were due.

When they arrived she knew at once why Steve had wanted them all to become friendly. They were about the same age as them. Sandra was short and slim, her brown hair streaked with highlights and cut in a bob, while her husband was around six foot tall, his fair hair thinning slightly, his face amiable and his eyes intelligent.

'Hi,' said Sandra, holding out a bottle of wine. 'This is a rather belated "welcome to your new home" present.'

'Thanks very much,' said Marianne, smiling back at the other girl. 'Do come through. What would you like to drink?'

'So this is what the house looks like,' said Graham, gazing about. 'We always wondered. It's pretty big for the two of you, isn't it?'

'Marianne's Great-aunt Dorothy left it to her. It's not the sort of place we'd have bought.'

'Do you like living here?' asked Sandra.

'I love it,' said Marianne enthusiastically. 'Steve isn't as keen. He thinks anything north of Watford is foreign territory.'

'But it's so peaceful here,' said Sandra. 'And the countryside's so beautiful.'

'It's always cold,' Steve snorted, with a laugh. 'Doesn't the wind ever stop blowing?'

'You get used to it,' Graham assured him.

The next couple of hours passed pleasantly enough but Marianne found it very hard to concentrate on the conversations. Once or twice she totally lost track of what was being said and Steve had to rescue her. 'I'm sorry,' she apologised. 'It's because I'm writing at the moment.'

'Steve told Graham you're a writer,' said Sandra. 'Is it fiction?'

Marianne wanted to laugh. 'It always has been,' she said cryptically.

'It is still,' said Steve abruptly.

'Yes, yes, of course it is,' said Marianne hastily. 'I just meant that at some time in the future I might want to write something non-fiction.'

'Like what?' asked Graham.

'I don't know. A history of this house, perhaps.'

'That would be interesting,' agreed Sandra.

'God, it's all she goes on about at the moment,' complained Steve. 'Since we moved in here she's become totally obsessed with the house's history. I'm sure nothing very dramatic ever happened here.'

Sandra pulled a face. 'I'm not sure that's true.'

'What do you mean?' asked Marianne eagerly, leaning closer.

'Well, I was born here,' said Sandra. 'And when I was young I can remember there were a lot of stories about this place.'

'What sort of stories?'

'Well, apparently, some time last century there were some rather strange goings-on here. I don't know the details, of course, but it had something to do with a man, his sister, his sister's companion and two servants. Local legend has it that there were some very unsavoury practices being indulged in, and visitors were kept away. After the brother died his sister vanished – terrified, or so they say, that without his protection local people would invade the house and discover her secrets.'

'What kind of secrets?' asked Marianne, her mouth suddenly dry.

'I don't know, I can only guess,' said Sandra. 'But it seems that none of them were any better than they should have been.'

'That's fascinating,' said Marianne.

'Sounds like a load of rubbish to me,' said Steve. 'Probably they just didn't want to mix and that upset the locals.'

'I'm sure that's true,' said Graham. 'It's bad enough here now. God knows what it was like in those days. You wait, Marianne, they'll try and rope you in for all the local fêtes, bazaars, jam-making competitions...'

'Of course they won't,' said Sandra. 'You're lucky, you're too far out to get cornered. Because we live on the edge of the village I'm the one who gets dragged into that kind of thing. Anyway, I'm sure your work keeps you too busy for anything else.'

Marianne opened her mouth to answer but suddenly the room started to grow dark and she gripped the sides of her chair with terror. Surely it couldn't be going to happen now? Not with other people present. 'Shall I put the light on?' she asked uncertainly.

Steve looked puzzled. 'Why?'

'Because it's getting dark.'

'It isn't.'

'Isn't it?'

'You're not used to the evening light here,' explained Sandra. 'Also, your lead-paned windows make it seem darker than it really is.'

'Not that dark,' said Steve. 'You'd better have your eyes tested, Marianne.'

She didn't reply. She couldn't, because right in the middle of the room, between where she was curled up in the comfortable chair and the sofa where Sandra and Graham were sitting, figures were appearing. She felt her pulse quicken. It didn't seem possible that no one but her could see the apparitions. She didn't recognise the young man kneeling on the floor. He was a sturdy, muscular lad of about nineteen with blond, wavy hair. The upper half of his body, which was naked, was tanned, as though he spent a lot of time outdoors. After he'd knelt down, Sir Edward led Tabitha across the floor and Marianne watched with stunned incredulity as, right in front of her and her visitors, he forced the girl to lie across the young man's back.

Tabitha was totally naked and Marianne heard her give a nervous cry as she was stretched back like a bow, with her long hair touching the carpet on one side and her tiny feet scrabbling to keep a contact with the floor. The young man's muscles rippled but it seemed he could bear Tabitha's weight quite easily.

Marianne began to tremble. Her hands shook and she spilt some of her wine down the front of her dress. 'Damn!' she cursed, brushing frantically at it as Sandra, Graham and Steve glanced at her.

'It's not like you to waste wine,' laughed Steve.

'Would you top my glass up, please?' she asked him, trying to control her voice, which was quavering with excitement and fearful disbelief. She was terrified that, by speaking, she'd drive the ghosts away. But they remained there, seeming as real as Sandra and Graham and Steve.

'So do you think that's true?' asked Sandra.

Marianne didn't have a clue what her visitor was talking about. 'Oh, yes,' she said. 'Do go on.' Luckily it seemed the right thing to say because Sandra continued talking, leaving Marianne free to watch the tableau unfolding in front of her.

She realised that Sir Edward was holding a riding crop in his hand. He tapped it impatiently against his leather boots as he watched the quaking servant girl's body with cruel deliberation while she whimpered and trembled. Her large breasts were thrust upward and Marianne couldn't take her eyes off them. Neither could Sir Edward, but he continued his observation of the girl for so long that she started to cry, obviously unable to stand the rising tension as she awaited punishment.

'What about coffee, Marianne?' asked Steve.

Marianne jumped. 'Coffee?' she repeated stupidly, horrified to see that the ghosts from the past had started to blur at the edges. 'I – I don't want any.'

Ignoring Steve and their visitors she resumed concentrating on the figures, and their outline became firmer once more. She let out a small sigh of relief as she realised she wasn't to be deprived of this exciting moment after all.

'I'd better get it,' said Steve. Marianne realised vaguely that she'd put him in an awkward position, but she didn't care. Nothing counted but what she was seeing. She simply had to watch, had to know what Sir Edward was going to do to the wretched servant girl this time.

It wasn't long before she found out. Eventually, having obviously decided that he'd kept Tabitha waiting long enough, Sir Edward raised his arm and, with deadly precision, flicked his wrist so the crop fell over the girl's ribcage, curling round her torso and causing her to cry out with pain and shock. She was unable to move, however, because Sir Edward was standing over her.

Marianne's heart began to pound in her chest and she watched while the crop rose and fell time and time again. Every time it did, it left a bright red mark on Tabitha's flesh. These never crossed each other. Sir Edward's aim was accurate, and as he worked his way down Tabitha's stomach the girl started to tremble violently, and Marianne knew the wretched girl was excited despite her torture.

Plainly Sir Edward knew this, too, because now the end of the crop trailed in a teasing fashion up over the abused flesh and then round each breast in turn. Those breasts had so far been left alone, and Tabitha moaned.

'No... no...' she pleaded, her voice trembling, but Marianne knew the pleas were useless, and her excitement grew.

For a second Sir Edward turned his head and Marianne could have sworn that he was looking directly at her. Then he turned back to Tabitha and she heard the whip crack in the air just seconds before it struck the girl's exposed breasts. This time the servant uttered a piercing scream, but as the scream died away her whole body shook from head to toe and Marianne realised the wicked punishment had actually caused Tabitha's pleasure to spill forth.

'How dare you?' she heard Sir Edward say as he fell to his knees, and then his hands were stretching Tabitha's legs apart and his fingers moved rapidly in and out of her sex, causing her to gasp and groan. 'You're a disgrace... a disgrace,' he muttered, adding a third finger, and Tabitha whimpered helplessly.

Glancing down, Marianne could see the blond boy had

a massive erection, which had sprung free from his tattered trousers.

Sir Edward continued to work between Tabitha's thighs until every tendon in the girl's body tautened. Her hips ceased moving and she became strangely still in what was clearly a prelude to a massive climax. It seemed Sir Edward knew this, too, because he abruptly withdrew his fingers and Marianne heard Tabitha give a pathetic wail of distress.

Marianne felt like crying out as well. She, too, was perched on the edge of sexual release, her thighs clenched firmly together. But then, as abruptly as they'd appeared, the spectral figures disappeared and Marianne was alone once more. She wanted to cry.

'Are you all right?' asked Sandra, sounding concerned. Marianne blushed with embarrassment, not knowing what to say.

'Here's the coffee,' called Steve, walking in through the door. 'I've brought cream and sugar, I wasn't sure who took what.' He looked at the three of them, clearly sensing an atmosphere. 'Is anything wrong?'

'I think your wife may be unwell,' said Sandra awkwardly.

'It's nothing,' gasped Marianne, dabbing perspiration from her top lip. 'Just a sudden pain.'

'Aspirin and a hot water bottle might help,' suggested Sandra.

Steve frowned, but kept silent, and for the rest of the evening Marianne tried desperately to be a good hostess. She thought she'd succeeded, because when Sandra and Graham left they seemed genuinely sorry to go and promised to return the invitation before too long.

'You'd never have behaved like that in London,' accused Steve the moment the front door was shut. 'You were a disgrace. Half the time you weren't even listening to a word that was being said.'

'I'm sorry,' apologised Marianne. 'I know my mind kept wandering, but it's the book.'

'The new one?' Marianne nodded. 'Then the sooner you get it finished, the better. Luckily Sandra and Graham didn't seem to notice, or else they think you're always like that. It's amazing what writers can get away with. And what's all this business about a stomach ache?'

'It wasn't true,' she admitted.

'Well what was the matter, then?'

She didn't know what to say. 'I've missed you so much, I ached for you,' she said at last. For the first time since she'd known him, Steve looked flustered.

'Come off it!'

'It's true,' she insisted. 'I couldn't wait for them to go. Here, feel how damp I am.' She pulled his nearest hand between her thighs.

'Well, we'd better go upstairs,' said Steve hastily.

Marianne shook her head. 'No, I want to do it here.'

'Here? It won't be very comfortable.'

'I don't care! I don't want to be comfortable. I want it to be different.' As she was talking she started tearing off her clothes. Within seconds, she was naked and ran her hands provocatively over her rigid nipples. 'Quickly,' she urged.

Steve undressed as fast as he could, but then he didn't seem to know what to do and stood hesitantly in front of her, looking about for a suitable place where they could make love.

Marianne pressed her body against his. 'I want you to hurt me,' she whispered.

'W-what on earth are you talking about?' he stammered.

'I want a change,' she said urgently. 'Let's do it differently. You can tie me up if you want to.'

'I don't want to.'

Marianne felt like screaming. The sight of Tabitha being tormented as she lay across the back of the muscular young man had turned her on to the point where she was sure she'd explode the moment Steve touched her. But she needed the same sense of fear and erotic domination she'd felt in the room. 'Please,' she begged him.

Steve looked helpless. 'I don't know what to do,' he confessed.

Marianne grabbed his hands, pulling them to her breasts. 'Squeeze me hard,' she urged him. 'Pinch my nipples.'

'Won't that hurt?'

'That's what I want. Don't ask questions, just do it. Please, Steve.'

His fingers closed around her flesh, but it didn't feel the way she wanted it to. Steve's heart wasn't in it, she knew that. She understood why, but she needed more than he was giving her if she was to climax. She laid herself over the arms of the chair in as close an approximation as she could of the scene with Tabitha. She felt her body stretch tight, just as Tabitha's had, and the ache in the pit of her stomach increased, while moisture seeped from her opening. 'Take me,' she begged, spreading her legs. 'Hurry... *hurry...*'

It was clear Steve was very aroused. His initial wariness had disappeared and his erection was impressive. Although he thrust firmly inside her he still wasn't tormenting her breasts enough. He still wasn't causing her even minor discomfort, let alone the strange but exhilarating sensation of pain she'd experienced when she'd been trapped in the study with Sir Edward and his sister.

'Is this what you wanted?' he gasped, his hips slamming against hers, and she didn't have the heart to tell him it wasn't enough. Her body was responding, the pleasure was very near, but although it built steadily she found she simply couldn't climax and writhed helplessly beneath him, wishing there was something she could do to herself to topple her body over the edge of the abyss.

'I'm coming,' Steve grunted, and within seconds he was shuddering violently above her, his face twisted with passion. She couldn't believe this was happening, that she was going to be left in this state of sexual tension with no one to help her, and as Steve slumped to the floor she heard herself give a tiny wail of despair, similar to the sound she'd heard Tabitha make.

As she was about to sit upright she was astonished to feel Steve's fingers between her thighs and gave a sigh of delight as he thrust two fingers inside her and began to move them in and out, just as she'd seen Sir Edward do earlier. 'Yes...' she cried. 'That's right, that's exactly right, don't stop.'

He didn't stop. In fact, unbelievably, he added an extra finger and now he was hurting her. She was too full and his fingers were rough inside her until she started to whimper, but even as she did so the delicious sparks of impending orgasm darted through her. When his other hand gripped her breast and his fingers dug savagely into the flesh, the combination of sensations finally allowed her to come with a shuddering moan, and she could have wept with relief as the terrible tension drained from her body to leave her satisfied and replete.

'God, that was good,' she murmured. 'How did you know what to do?'

'I just followed my instincts,' Steve murmured.

Marianne looked down at her lover. He was lying on the carpet with his arms spread out and his eyes closed. At that moment she realised the truth. They hadn't been Steve's hands at all. They had been Sir Edward's. Somehow he'd been there with her and Steve and, understanding her needs better than her lover, he'd given her satisfaction in the way he liked to, a way she was starting to crave.

'What were you saying just now?' asked Steve sleepily. 'I didn't quite catch it.'

'It doesn't matter,' said Marianne quietly, as she started to put her clothes on. Now the pleasure had gone she was very frightened.

It seemed that the past and the present were beginning to mix and she had no control at all over what happened. She wasn't sure she wanted it to be this way. She wanted to keep her two lives separate, but she guessed that if Sir Edward's wishes were different from hers then his would prevail. He was the one deciding how often she saw him, and she sensed his need for her was as great as hers for him. She wondered how she was going to cope, how she could present a façade of normality if he intended to continue intruding on her modern life. 'Please wait for me to come to you,' she whispered beneath her breath. 'Don't involve Steve. I'll be back with you as soon as I can.'

No one answered because no one was there, but she was filled with a peculiar sensation of well being tinged with fear. She guessed this was how Marianne Clifford had spent most of her days at Moorhead House.

Chapter Four

Marianne found the next few days very difficult. Encouraged by her behaviour on his first night back, Steve had instigated several sessions of lovemaking where he'd attempted mild bondage games, but they merely increased Marianne's frustration. In truth, she would have preferred it if Steve had stuck to his usual routine, because compared with what she'd seen and indeed experienced at Sir Edward's hands, the things she and Steve were doing were so tame as to be almost laughable. As a result, despite regular orgasms, she felt constantly frustrated and on edge, both her body and her mind yearning as much for the atmosphere as for the acts her journeys to the past brought about.

She was relieved when it was time for Steve to leave again, although he made it plain that he'd far rather remain at Moorhead House. 'You were right about this place,' he said as he kissed her goodbye. 'It's definitely good for you. You're a changed woman.'

Marianne didn't know what to say. 'That's a bit of an exaggeration,' she murmured.

'I don't think so. Mind you, it's a good job I'm going. It's time you got back to that book of yours. I must have a look at it when I get home.'

Once he'd gone Marianne roamed around the house, walking in and out of each room, hoping for the light to grow dim – the only visible sign she ever had that a transformation was about to take place. After an hour or so she was forced to accept that it wasn't going to happen and decided to get down to her writing.

A couple of hours later, her fingers aching from the speed with which she'd been typing, she decided to go for a walk on the moors. She needed a break and it was a lovely day. Pausing only to collect a light jacket as protection against the wind, she locked the front door carefully behind her and set out along the track that led from a small gate at the back of the rear garden straight on to the moors.

She supposed she'd been walking for about ten minutes when she heard strange sounds coming from a dip in the ground nearby. Suddenly nervous and aware how vulnerable she was, she started back towards the house, then stopped in her tracks as she heard a familiar girl's voice crying out with pleasure. She knew beyond any shadow of a doubt that it was Tabitha she was hearing. Intrigued, and with a sudden surge of hope, she decided to investigate.

Leaving the path she walked as quietly as she could over the heather until, suddenly, her feet slipped from under her and she toppled down into a small hollow, sheltered from the wind.

Shocked by the tumble, she sat up, rubbing at her left arm, which she'd struck on a stone. Immediately she began to tremble with excitement as she felt rough woollen fabric beneath her fingers instead of her windcheater.

'We weren't doing nothing miss,' cried a girl's voice, and Tabitha was scrambling to her feet, desperately trying to fasten the buttons of her blouse. 'Please don't tell on me. The master will go mad.'

For the first time Marianne realised Tabitha wasn't alone. There was a young man with her, blond-haired and muscular. It was the same man she'd seen crouching on the floor, bearing the weight of Tabitha's body when she was being punished. 'Who... who are you?' she asked him uncertainly.

Tabitha looked puzzled. 'It's John, miss, the gardener. You know how angry the master gets if he and I meet up, but we were that desperate to see each other, and...'

All at once Marianne was afraid for the girl, afraid for all of them. 'Of course I won't tell, but you must get back to the house,' she said.

'What are you doing out here, miss?' asked Tabitha, her timid eyes wide.

'I was simply taking air.'

'That's not allowed, either.' Tabitha sounded a little bolder.

Marianne knew that, she could remember as much from her previous encounter with Sir Edward and his sister. 'In that case we're neither of us in a position to tell tales, are we?' she said, surprised at how crisp her voice sounded. 'We'll hurry back together and let us hope we haven't been missed.'

Out of the corner of her eye she could see that John was pulling on the same pair of ragged trousers he'd been wearing when she'd first seen him. He wouldn't look at her at all and, somewhat ungallantly, fled across the moors the moment he was dressed without even a backward glance for his timid lover and her new companion.

'You won't tell, will you, miss?' Tabitha pleaded again as she and Marianne set off to follow him.

'I've already said I won't.' Marianne gasped, wishing the modern-day path was still there because the heather was catching at the strange shoes she found herself wearing and it was difficult to hurry.

It seemed to take an eternity but, finally, they were back at the house. Instinctively, she followed Tabitha to the back door, the one leading directly into the kitchen. Her heart was pounding so hard against her ribs that she felt her chest would burst as she tumbled into the kitchen behind the servant girl, holding her side because a stitch was paining her.

'Well, well,' said Sir Edward from the opposite side of the room. 'At last the wanderers return.'

'I wasn't doing nothing wrong,' whimpered Tabitha. 'Ask Miss Marianne.'

Sir Edward's piercing eyes moved to Marianne. 'Is she telling the truth?' he asked.

Fatally, Marianne hesitated. 'I-I believe so, sir,' she stammered at last.

'But you're not sure?'

'We only met up on the garden path,' she lied.

'How very strange. I was watching from the upstairs window and could have sworn I saw the pair of you running across the moors.'

Tabitha went white and shrank back against the kitchen door, but Marianne stood her ground, although her knees felt weak and she wrung her hands in anguish.

'Was I mistaken?' he continued.

Marianne didn't know what to say. She'd promised the terrified servant girl that she wouldn't tell on her, but his gaze insisted on an answer. 'Perhaps we met a little earlier,' she conceded quietly.

'How sad that behind such a beautiful face lies a deceitful nature,' remarked Sir Edward. 'Perhaps it's fortunate that your parents are dead and therefore remain unaware of their daughter's true character. How fortunate, too, that you have come into this household where my sister and I can teach you the error of your ways. We try to do the same for Tabitha. Isn't that true, my girl?'

Tabitha made a whimpering sound that could have meant anything, and his sensual mouth curved into a slight smile. 'I shall take that as agreement. However, neither of you have explained where you were, at least not to my satisfaction. I think this time it might be beneficial if you were disciplined together.'

His words, whilst clearly causing Tabitha nothing but distress, excited Marianne beyond belief. This was what she'd wanted, to be here in this time and at his mercy. She waited, her rising excitement mingled with trepidation as he studied her thoughtfully.

'We'll go to the outhouse,' he declared.

Tabitha began to weep, and for the first time Marianne started to panic. She didn't know why, but some sixth sense told her that in the outhouse she would experience things far darker than anything she'd witnessed so far. 'No,' she said defiantly.

As she spoke Sir Edward grew fainter and she realised this was what had happened the last time. Because she'd protested and meant it she'd returned to the twentieth century. If she was going to find out the truth about Sir Edward and his sister's companion, Marianne, then she must stay. 'I'm sorry,' she said hastily. 'If it pleases you, then...'

'It does please him. It pleases him very much,' said Judith, coming slowly into the kitchen. 'I've prepared the outhouse, Edward. Marianne, come with me.'

Obediently, Marianne followed the other woman, but behind her she heard struggling and turned to see that Sir Edward was having to drag the protesting Tabitha out of the kitchen and across the courtyard. Plainly this was not the servant girl's first visit, and she fought every inch of the way. Finally, as he threw her into the small brick building and she fell to the floor, all the fight went out of her and she stared up at him as though hypnotised.

'I know you've not been here before, Marianne,' said Sir Edward. 'It's unfortunate that it's proved necessary, but you are becoming a very obstinate young lady.'

'Remove your clothes,' said Judith, and Marianne obeyed without question. Her fingers were once more clumsy and after a few seconds Sir Edward lost patience. Reaching out, he hooked two fingers in the neck of her dress and tugged, tearing the material apart with ease. 'Hurry,' whispered Judith. 'You don't want to annoy him further.'

Marianne certainly didn't. Tabitha was already naked, her slender body shaking, and when Marianne had finally divested herself of all her garments, Judith pushed her hard in the back so that she stumbled and fell to the floor next to the servant girl.

Because there was only one small grimy window in the outhouse it was gloomy despite the sun, and Marianne's eyes took a little time to adjust. She was constantly aware of Tabitha whimpering next to her and wondered what was causing her such distress. What did the servant girl know that she didn't?

'Did you bring the candles and the cotton?' Sir Edward asked his sister.

Tabitha's tiny hands clutched at the top of Marianne's arm. 'Don't let them do this to us,' she pleaded. 'It's terrible, terrible.'

'What happens?' Marianne whispered back urgently.

'Be silent,' snapped Sir Edward swiftly. 'Tabitha, we've already attempted to teach you discipline this way, and I expect you to show Miss Marianne how things are done. Get yourself in position.'

Marianne stared as Tabitha, her head drooping, squatted awkwardly on the floor, putting her hands behind her back. Only then did she remember the strange metal rings she'd discovered when she and Steve had first moved into Moorhead House. Quickly, Tabitha's hands were fastened to the rings and she squatted with her legs slightly apart, her breasts straining forward. Now Judith approached the servant girl, holding what looked to Marianne like sewing cotton. Carefully she snapped off two short lengths, licked and then wound them tightly around Tabitha's puckered nipples.

'Please mistress, I beg of you, don't do this,' whimpered Tabitha, but she was ignored.

Marianne's stomach felt hollow, her muscles clenching tightly with fear but also, undeniably, desire.

'Marianne, position yourself in the same way over there,' said Sir Edward, indicating with a nod of his head where she should go. Hesitantly, scarcely able to believe what was happening, she did as she was told. When Sir Edward fastened her hands to the second set of metal rings, however, she gave a tiny sound of protest as her arms were pulled painfully behind her back, her thigh muscles starting to ache because they were unused to her squatting in such a position.

'What are you protesting about?' he asked in amusement. 'We haven't begun yet.' As he spoke, his fingers lingered on her bare shoulder for a moment, then she felt them move up through her hair in a soft caress that ended abruptly as he tugged sharply at the roots and her head jerked back. 'It is fortunate indeed that you fell into our hands,' he murmured, almost to himself. 'I can tell how badly you need this discipline.'

At that moment Judith approached and proceeded to tie a thread of damp cotton around Marianne's nipples, just as she had with Tabitha. Marianne couldn't understand why Tabitha had protested so much; the cotton wasn't too tight.

Sir Edward and his sister stood back and surveyed their two victims. Marianne could feel her leg muscles trembling with the strain of remaining in such an awkward position, but Sir Edward gave her a fierce stare that stopped her from daring to protest. As his eyes roamed over her body, her excitement grew. She'd never before been physically helpless, literally at the mercy of a man's desires, and she was astonished to discover how much it was exciting her.

'You know what you have to ask for, Tabitha,' said Judith.

Marianne could see by the look on Tabitha's face that the girl didn't want to ask for anything, but when her mistress started to advance on her she hastily obeyed.

'P-please would you a-administer the candle punishment, m-ma'am,' she whispered.

'Speak up,' said Sir Edward sharply.

Tabitha repeated the request, and Judith produced a long white candle. 'Is this what you want?' she asked.

'Yes, ma'am,' muttered Tabitha, but her tone and demeanour said otherwise.

Judith and her brother advanced upon their whimpering servant girl. Marianne's eyes followed them. She wanted to know what was going to happen; needed to know, because it was going to happen to her as well. When Sir Edward shifted a little, Marianne realised that he also understood this and was making certain she had an unobstructed view.

He knelt on the floor, lifting one of Tabitha's feet and moving her legs apart. Then he ran his hand over her quivering belly before his fingers trailed down through her luxurious pubic hair. As Tabitha started to utter tiny mewing sounds of excitement, Marianne imagined what those fingers must be doing. But after a few minutes Tabitha's excitement clearly became tinged with discomfort. 'Please stop now,' she begged pitifully.

'It's the threads,' Judith explained, glancing over her shoulder to Marianne. 'As she becomes aroused so her breasts swell and the thread tightens. I hope you can subdue your wanton flesh better than she does hers, or I'm afraid you'll feel the same pain.'

Marianne was unable to answer, because she could imagine only too well what was happening. For the first time the threads of cotton made sense. Tabitha's breathing was heavier now and, despite the discomfort she was experiencing, it was obvious her pleasure was growing as her arms trembled so much the metal rings chinked softly.

'I think it's time to insert the candle,' said Sir Edward.

His sister knelt and Marianne watched in horrified disbelief as the tapered end was eased inside their hapless victim. It was inserted with wicked slowness, Judith's wrist twisting and turning. The long wax cylinder was pushed inexorably upwards until only a tiny portion was showing. Sir Edward checked it, tapping twice on the end in a gesture that made Tabitha groan. Then the couple left her and turned to Marianne.

'Now, Miss Marianne, it's time for us to do the same to you,' said Sir Edward. 'Once a candle is inserted in both of you, you are each to keep it inside until we give you permission to release it. Should you allow it to slip out, even a fraction, then you will have failed to convince me of your desire to learn obedience. Do you understand?'

Marianne nodded dumbly. She understood, but she couldn't yet imagine what it was going to be like. All she could do was wait in an agony of excited anticipation as Sir Edward bent over her and moved a hand across her belly, just as he had with Tabitha. Then his fingers moved lower, through the light blonde curls of her pubic hair, and she felt herself opening up to him, her flesh already damp with desire.

'See this, Judith. Feel how shamefully wet she is.'

Judith touched Marianne. 'I thought she'd been strictly brought up,' she remarked scornfully. 'It seems we may have as many problems with her as we do with Tabitha.'

'Indeed we will not,' said Sir Edward brusquely. 'Believe me, I shall subdue her flesh before many weeks are through.' Anger flared in his eyes, and then it was as quickly gone. 'But for now she's certainly ready to take the candle.'

Despite her excitement, Marianne was afraid, and when Judith began to insert the wax taper inside her she tried to close her thighs against the invasion. Sir Edward promptly slapped her belly with the backs of his fingers, the stinging pain only increasing her excitement. To her dismay, her nipples swelled. For the first time she felt the cotton thread bite into her tender flesh and couldn't suppress a cry.

'You see where this lascivious behaviour gets you?' said Sir Edward. 'Do not resist my sister further, or worse will follow.'

Marianne believed him. She felt the smooth candle being twisted, felt the delicious pressure as it filled her, but it was not as thick as she'd expected and when Judith released it she felt it start to slip out of her.

'You have to keep your muscles tightly clenched,' explained Judith. 'Surely you didn't think it stayed in place on its own. Tabitha's concentrating hard at this very moment, aren't you, Tabitha?'

'Yes, ma'am,' gasped the servant girl, and Marianne could tell the unfortunate Tabitha didn't really want to speak, because simply to do that would break her concentration.

'Tighten yourself,' insisted Sir Edward, and Marianne attempted to draw the candle back up inside her. She managed to stop it sliding out any further but, to her dismay, the result was an increase in pleasure. With sickening clarity she realised that should her pleasure spill, her muscles would first clench tighter around the candle and then relax, allowing it to slip out. It was only then that she understood what this punishment was going to involve. Sir Edward and his sister were going to pleasure both her and Tabitha, but neither of them could allow that pleasure to reach its pinnacle or they would fail the test.

She couldn't understand why it was that, in spite of her terror, she was still aroused. She wished she could control herself, could subdue her desire, because her nipples were aching terribly and simply fuelled her need.

'Since Miss Marianne is new to this I shall work on her and you can work on Tabitha,' said Sir Edward. Marianne was relieved. This was why she was here. This was what she'd wanted; to have Sir Edward using her in any way he wished; to be at his mercy and learn to understand his perverse desires.

'We must start together,' he said to his sister and, in unison, the pair began to work on their two victims.

Sir Edward's hands were clever. His fingers wandered lazily over Marianne's tautly rounded breasts, caressing lovingly one moment, and then pinching spitefully the next and drawing a wail of despair from her. She was trembling. Her strained position made every muscle ache, and yet, with his caresses her pleasure mounted. When he finally slid his fingers between her sex lips she experienced the same feelings she'd had when watching him beating Tabitha as she'd lain stretched over John.

She was so wet it was shaming, and then the tips of his fingers touched her swollen clitoris and she shuddered. 'You're anxious for your pleasure,' he smirked triumphantly. 'Do you not know your wantonness is unseemly?' He flicked casually at the centre of all her pleasure. The touch itself nearly made her come and she felt her internal muscles tighten around the candle.

Only a few feet away Tabitha was whimpering on an ascending series of notes that made it plain that her pleasure was mounting too.

Suddenly, Sir Edward moved his face close to Marianne's and he stroked her throat in a gesture that was almost tender. 'I know how you feel,' he whispered. 'I know what I'm doing to you, but it's for your own good that you learn how to behave like a lady. I have to train you to be a suitable companion for my sister. How can I allow her to have a woman of loose character around her?'

He was teasing, tormenting, and they both knew it. Marianne's entire body was struggling to prevent a convulsion of ecstasy, and every time her muscles tightened and she felt them contract around the candle, shards of pleasure pierced her being. Suddenly, with no warning, Sir Edward began to slap her full breasts one after the other. The slaps were slow and rhythmical. Her breasts swayed from side to side under the impact. The cotton bit harder into her flesh, the nerve-endings reached screaming point, and then he touched her once more on her swollen nub of pleasure and she could take no more. With a scream Marianne exploded in a muscle-tearing orgasm and she shuddered, helpless beneath the power of the muscular contractions, her arms still imprisoned behind her. As the delicious relief finally ended and her muscles went limp, she felt the candle begin to slip from her.

Sir Edward caught the end of it and pulled it from her. 'Is the candle still inside Tabitha?' he asked his sister.

'Yes,' said Judith. 'But not for much longer.'

'Leave her alone,' he instructed. 'I regret to say that Miss Marianne has already failed. Now we have to decide what's to be done with her.'

He thrust his fingers roughly inside Marianne and began to move them harshly in and out. 'Please stop...' she pleaded. 'Please leave me alone. I can't endure any more.' Then, to her dismay, everyone vanished and she was sitting alone on the floor of the outhouse.

Chapter Five

It took Marianne at least ten minutes to regain some semblance of self-control. Her body still felt as it had while Sir Edward and his sister were abusing her. Her legs ached and her breasts stung from the vicious blows he'd dealt her. Also, despite the fact that she'd orgasmed, she still felt incredibly needy. His thrusting fingers had thrilled her, and she was left with a hollow feeling inside, a terrible need for the brooding satisfaction only the past seemed able to bring.

It was almost impossible to believe what was happening. One minute she was naked, tethered to the rings that even now she could see fastened to the wall, and the next she was back in the present day, fully clothed. The tangible proof that she wasn't imagining things lay, as always, in her body. She felt very warm, and realised she was covered with a sheen of perspiration left over from the excitement of the past. When the aching in her legs eased a little she stumbled to the door and let herself out into the courtyard, anxious to get back inside the house. How she wished she hadn't protested when Sir Edward's fingers had started to violate her. If she'd kept silent she could still be there now, discovering greater pleasures. She wondered if he'd ever possess her, entering her properly, or if his status as master of the house had always prevented him from consummating his strange relationship with his sister's companion.

As she opened the front door she heard Sandra's voice

calling from the front gate. 'Marianne. Are you busy?'

Marianne sighed and turned. This was the last thing she needed, but she didn't dare turn Sandra away; Steve would be annoyed if he got to hear of it, and she had no real excuse to do so. 'No,' she replied, smiling as warmly as she could.

Sandra looked relieved, opened the squeaky gate and walked up the garden path. 'I was afraid you might be working, but I had to come this way and thought you might enjoy some company. Graham says Steve's away at the moment.'

'That's true, but that's when I do most of my writing.'

Sandra looked uncomfortable. 'I'm sorry. I hadn't thought of that. Are you writing now?'

Marianne shook her head. 'I've decided to take a break. In fact, I went for a walk on the moors.'

'I thought I saw you coming from the outhouse.'

'I went in there when I got back,' Marianne snapped defensively.

Sandra looked startled. 'I – I wasn't doubting you.'

Marianne made an effort to relax, knowing she was being unnecessarily touchy with her neighbour. 'I'm sorry,' she apologised. 'I'm afraid I was daydreaming in there, trying to picture the place the way it used to be. Steve gets very annoyed with me when I do that, so I'm a bit defensive about it.'

'I don't blame you at all,' said Sandra, following Marianne into the house and sitting herself down at the kitchen table. 'I love history.'

'I never used to,' Marianne admitted, filling the kettle. 'But since I moved here all that's changed. This place feels full of ghosts to me. Coffee?'

Sandra nodded. 'Really? Perhaps it's because your great-aunt lived here before you.'

Marianne shook her head. 'It's not her ghost I sense.'

Sandra looked intrigued. 'No? Whose then?'

Marianne wanted to confide in the girl. She desperately needed to talk to someone about Sir Edward, in the same way that when she'd first fallen for Steve she'd wanted to bring his name into every conversation. But it was somewhat more difficult when the man who obsessed you had lived over a hundred years earlier. 'It's the past owners who fascinate me,' she said at last. 'Particularly those you spoke about – they sound fascinating.'

'You mean Sir Edward Sharpe and his sister? Well, you're not the only person to be fascinated by them. Before your great-aunt lived here there was a woman called Judith Wells. According to my mother, she became utterly obsessed with the old days and even took to dressing in an old-fashioned way. Would you believe, she used to carry the keys of the house around her waist on a chain!'

Marianne could believe it only too well. She understood why, too. That woman's name had been Judith. Clearly Judith Fullick had come back to haunt and possibly possess her, just as Marianne Clifford had come back for Marianne herself. 'So what happened to the woman?'

Sandra looked uncomfortable. 'I think she went a bit weird.'

'How do you mean, weird?'

'She ended up in a psychiatric hospital somewhere. I never got told the details, but apparently that's why your great-aunt got the house so cheap.'

'I didn't know she did.'

Sandra nodded. 'Oh, yes. No one local wanted it, you see. There were rumours that Judith Wells used to roam the house late at night. And she started putting antique furniture in. I suppose she was trying to recreate the past as she imagined it. Quite sad, really.'

'She must have been unbalanced to begin with,' said Marianne.

'Absolutely. Somehow I don't think there's any fear of that happening to you.'

'No, the only thing that's likely to drive me mad is my book.'

'So what's it about, or aren't I allowed to ask?'

'I've changed it,' confessed Marianne. 'Because of the way I feel about this house I've changed it into an historical novel.'

'And that's difficult?'

'No, not difficult, but very different. My agent isn't keen on me doing it and neither is my publisher. That means it's got to be very special indeed.'

'But you're enjoying writing it?'

'More than anything I've ever written before,' said Marianne emphatically.

'Is it a romance?'

Marianne stirred the two cups of coffee thoughtfully. 'Not exactly,' she admitted, handing one steaming cup to Sandra. 'It's a tale of obsession.'

'Obsession?'

'Yes...' Marianne said carefully, unsure of how much she should confide in her new acquaintance, 'sexual obsession.'

'Hey, that sounds good. How explicit is it?'

'I haven't decided yet. Besides, you can't always tell. Often, once you get the right characters a book almost writes itself.'

'Does it? That must be fascinating for the author. You must feel you're not in control.' Sandra glanced at her watch. 'Well, your book might write itself but Graham's lunch doesn't cook itself. I'd better be going. We wondered whether you and Steve would like to come over next Saturday, say about eight?'

Marianne didn't want to go. She didn't want to leave Moorhead House in case she missed an opportunity to slip back into the past, but she managed a smile and accepted. Sandra finished her coffee and left, leaving Marianne alone in the house again.

After a quick lunch Marianne locked herself away in the study and began to work. It was two o'clock and she decided that at half-past three she'd stop, check her day's work and then decide what direction the story should take. Normally she was a good judge of time but when she finally stopped typing she was astonished to see that it was half-past four.

'I must have written pages,' she exclaimed, and her aching fingers testified to the truth of this. The extraordinary thing was she couldn't remember what she'd written. Leaving the computer to print the work off, she went to make a cup of tea.

When she returned she picked up the sheaf of papers with a feeling of excitement. Somehow she knew the work was good; it must have been to have flowed so easily, and she was anxious to read it. As her eyes travelled the pages she started to feel uneasy. What she was reading was an account of what had happened to her in the outhouse earlier, scarcely disguised at all, and she was shocked at the graphic way she'd described events. Her agent and publisher would be shocked when they read it too, but at the same time she was aroused by her own prose.

It was like nothing she'd written before. The highly charged eroticism she experienced every time she travelled back into the past was there in every word, and if it had the power to arouse her then she knew it would arouse other people. But this wasn't what she had intended to write. It wasn't the way the story had been meant to go, and the fact that she couldn't remember writing it frightened and disturbed her. It seemed as though past and present were merging more and more, the edges becoming less sharply defined. She wondered how this was possible. Clearly Sir Edward Sharpe's personality was very strong, but so too must Marianne Clifford's have been if she was able to reach out from beyond the grave and catch her.

'Perhaps it ended wrongly,' mused Marianne. 'Maybe they want to put things right, and they're trying to use me.' It seemed a distinct possibility but, if it were true, what would become of her, the Marianne of the present? She assumed that once Sir Edward got what he wanted she'd be released, free to live the rest of her life in peace. 'But that won't be enough for me,' she said. 'He's given me a taste for submission, for dangerous pleasure, and I'm always going to need it.'

She began to look forward to Steve's call that evening, hoping that by focusing on him she might be able to anchor herself in the present again. However, the moment he rang and she heard his voice, her desire to speak to him vanished. It was the wrong voice on the end of the phone, the wrong face she was picturing and the wrong words were being uttered. He wasn't Sir Edward Sharpe, and it seemed that no one else could satisfy her.

'Did you hear what I said?' asked Steve.

Marianne gave herself a mental shake. 'You're going to be home Friday?'

'That's right. Marianne, is there something wrong?'

'I'm exhausted,' she confessed. 'I've been working very hard on the book.'

'At least that's something. How about the house? Have you rung any kitchen people about having ours modernised?'

'No,' admitted Marianne. 'I'm beginning to think I'd like it kept in the old style.'

'But you always wanted a modern kitchen,' said Steve, sounding a little exasperated.

'I've been thinking about it, and I just don't think it will suit the house. We can discuss it when you get home.'

'Okay.' Now Steve sounded fed up. 'I don't suppose you've seen Sandra, either.'

'As a matter of fact I have,' she announced. 'I've accepted an invitation for us to go over there Saturday night. I hope that pleases you.'

'Yes, it does. But don't make it sound as though I'm being unreasonable. You're the one who's being difficult at the moment.'

'It'll be all right once I've got this book cleared with Angela,' said Marianne. 'The whole thing's getting me down.'

'Well, you shouldn't have changed it in the first place.'

It was unlike him to lose his temper, and Marianne suddenly felt guilty. 'Don't be late back on Friday,' she said, trying to change the subject and brighten up.

'Am I going to get a better welcome this time?'

'The best you've ever had.'

'Good – then I won't be late.'

In bed that night Marianne found it difficult to fall asleep. She was restless, constantly moving beneath the duvet. She wanted sex, needed to be aroused and satisfied. But not by Steve – by Sir Edward. For a moment she thought of trying to go back in time again, but quickly changed her mind. That way lay the danger of madness. Sandra's story about Judith Wells had frightened her. She must be careful not to make the same mistake as that woman and end up in a mental hospital. Her journeys back into the past must stop being such an obsession. She must try and enjoy the moment more, take pleasure from everyday things and stop her stupid fixation. The problem was, she didn't know how.

At some stage she must have fallen asleep, for she was woken by someone shaking her arm.

'Marianne! Marianne, wake up!' It was Judith Fullick.

Marianne rubbed at her eyes and looked up sleepily at Sir Edward's sister. It had happened again, she thought with a surge of triumph. She was back in the past. 'What's the matter?'

'Don't you remember? Edward's gone to London. Tonight's the night we're going to test John.'

'Test him?'

Judith looked angry. 'You can't have forgotten, Marianne? I told you what we'd do as soon as my brother had gone. John keeps protesting that he doesn't desire Tabitha, but both you and I know that isn't true. Tonight we're going to prove it, remember?'

Marianne nodded. 'Of course,' she said, although she had no idea what the woman was talking about. She climbed out of bed and was astonished to find herself wearing a long cotton night-dress, buttoned high to the neck, with frilled cuffs at her wrists.

'You'd better get dressed,' said Judith. 'It's cold in the drawing room, the fire's out. Come as quickly as you can. Tabitha's already there and John's waiting in the kitchen.

Naturally he wonders what I want of him at this late hour.' She laughed.

Hastily Marianne pulled on the familiar rust-coloured woollen dress and made her way to the drawing room. Tabitha, looking slightly more cheerful than usual, was standing in her maid's uniform next to her mistress' chair. She seemed surprised when Marianne entered the room.

'Tabitha's used to me pleasuring her from time to time,' Judith said casually to Marianne. 'Aren't you, Tabitha?' The girl nodded. 'Naturally, she doesn't know what's happening this time.'

Tabitha's eyes widened and for the first time she looked apprehensive.

'Don't worry,' Judith continued soothingly. 'You'll still have a wonderful time. Fetch John from the kitchen, Marianne.'

In the kitchen the young gardener was waiting, standing awkwardly by the sink, his cap scrunched up in his hands. 'Your mistress wants you in the drawing room,' said Marianne. The boy followed her without a word, although he looked bewildered. Marianne was bewildered, too. She couldn't imagine what was going to happen.

As they entered the drawing room Judith Fullick looked up and smiled. It was a smile totally without amusement or warmth, and Marianne shivered. She hadn't realised before quite how cruel the woman's face was.

'John,' said Judith, once Marianne had closed the door, 'I was discussing you with my brother before he left for London, and he told me that, according to you, you have no interest whatsoever in Tabitha. Is that correct?'

'Yes, ma'am,' the gardener mumbled, still wringing his cap.

'I'm afraid I don't believe you,' Judith continued.

'Many's the time Tabitha's been punished for going off to meet with you.'

'It's all over now, ma'am,' John assured her. 'The master's told me it must end, and it has. She means nothing to me. I've another young lady in the village.'

Marianne heard Tabitha give a tiny gasp of shock, a gasp that Judith Fullick couldn't possibly have missed. 'Indeed, and what's this fortunate girl's name?'

John hesitated. His brain was obviously not overly sharp. 'Abigail, ma'am,' he said at last.

'Does she have another name?' asked Judith, unable to conceal her amusement.

'I forget it,' confessed the boy.

'Do you indeed? Never mind. If tonight you can satisfy me that you no longer desire Tabitha, then I shall let the matter rest. However, should you fail, then I shall punish you for lying to my brother. In addition, everyone in this household will continue to be extremely vigilant where you and Tabitha are concerned. After all, the girl is our responsibility.'

As she spoke, Judith stood up and very slowly started to undress the motionless servant girl. She removed Tabitha's outer garments then unfastened the front of her bodice, but left her in her petticoats.

'Remove your clothes, John,' she ordered curtly.

'I beg your pardon, ma'am?'

'You heard me,' she snapped. 'Remove your clothes. Fold them tidily and put them on that chair.'

John glanced hastily from Judith to Marianne, and back to his mistress. 'It isn't right, ma'am,' he muttered.

'How dare you question me?' Judith hissed. 'Do you wish my brother to be told that you refuse to obey me?'

John shook his head. 'No, ma'am.'

'Then do as I say.'

Once the young gardener was naked, Marianne again noticed how compact and muscular his body was. His tanned upper torso positively rippled when he moved and his buttocks and thighs were tight. She licked her suddenly dry lips and then, realising John had seen her looking, glanced away from him.

'Now, Tabitha,' said Judith, her voice dangerously warm. 'Come and sit on my lap.'

Lightly, tenderly, she began to caress the girl's breasts, slowly parting the bodice and easing it back until both the full globes were fully exposed. Then, with one sideways glance at John, she bent her head and, using the tip of her tongue, drew a teasing circle around the servant girl's turgid nipple.

Marianne watched, fascinated, as the nipple leapt to life, growing immediately rigid while Tabitha squirmed with pleasure on her mistress' lap. When Judith drew the whole nipple into her mouth and started to suck, Tabitha moaned deep in her throat, her head lolling back until the sinews of her neck were clearly visible.

After a minute or so Judith released Tabitha's nipple and turned to look at John. 'I thought she didn't have an affect on you?' she said coldly.

Marianne looked at John. When he'd first undressed his cock had been hanging limply between his thighs, but now it was standing up sharply, the swollen helmet a dark shade of purple, a drop of pre-issue glistening at the tip.

'I suppose it's understandable,' Judith scoffed. 'Any man would be excited by her, but I think you have to be interested in a girl in order to gain such an erection simply by looking at her. Wouldn't you agree, Marianne?'

'I – um – yes, ma'am,' blurted Marianne, her head in a

spin.

'So now you understand the nature of this test,' Judith went on. 'You will watch while I pleasure the girl, and you will not allow your seed to spill. If it does, then in my opinion, you will have proved yourself a liar and I shall punish you this very evening.'

John said nothing, and Marianne realised she just didn't want this bizarre tableaux to end. She wanted to see how the game proceeded, to witness Tabitha's joy being coaxed from her and John's ultimate failure.

'Very well, Tabitha,' said Judith, turning back to the servant girl once more. 'I think it's time for us to proceed a little further.'

Judith was clearly fascinated by Tabitha's breasts. She played with them for several minutes more, her fingers squeezing and stroking them. Occasionally she would mould the two succulent globes together so her mouth could move easily from nipple to nipple, while the girl squirmed with restless delight against her thighs.

It was obvious to Marianne that whilst Tabitha was very aroused it would need more to bring her to orgasm, and she wondered how Judith intended to do that. John's erection looked painfully rigid. His testicles were drawn up tightly against the base of the shaft and the muscles of his stomach stood out as he attempted to control his breathing. Eventually, presumably knowing he would be unable to watch and remain in control, he looked away. But Judith noticed.

'I told you to watch, John,' she said sharply. Then she sniggered. 'So it seems Tabitha does hold some attraction for you, as we thought.'

The lad didn't answer and Marianne felt desperately sorry for him. It would have been impossible for any man to remain unmoved by what he was being forced to witness, but she knew this was the whole point of the scene. Judith was simply being cruel. She knew very well that the two young people were in love with each other and was simply using this diabolical exercise to make her point. The proof wasn't truly necessary, but she was clearly taking great pleasure from what she was doing.

Marianne knew she, too, was taking pleasure from the scene. She wondered how she could enjoy what was going on, why she didn't feel sorry for the victims and repulsed by Judith's actions, but the truth was that she was incredibly aroused. As usual, her journey back to the past was providing her with an incredible erotic charge.

Judith tired of Tabitha's breasts and, spreading her thighs wider apart, moved the girl into a reclining position on her before pulling up her petticoat. Tabitha's naked sex was revealed to both John and Marianne. Murmuring softly to the girl, Judith caressed Tabitha's belly and thighs before cupping her sex mound in her hand. Then, in a series of steady movements, she pressed and released the sensitive flesh and Marianne immediately began to imagine what that must feel like. She knew the moments of pressure would cause sparks of desire to run through the shaking, slender body and then, when the pressure was released, there would come the despairing ache of thwarted need.

Judith continued in this way for several minutes, until Tabitha began whimpering softly, her lower body writhing restlessly at this irregular stimulation that was arousing without ever becoming fulfilling. 'Wait a little longer,' Judith said quietly. 'Imagine how delicious it will be when I finally allow your pleasure to spill.'

Marianne glanced at John. His face was ruddy with

excitement. His spearing stem was visibly pulsing, and she wondered how much longer it would be before he lost control.

'Doesn't she look beautiful?' Judith purred, glancing up at the lad. As she spoke, she finally removed her hand from Tabitha's vulva and spread the girl's thighs wider apart. She was so open and ready that John instinctively took half a step forward, before suddenly realising his mistake and stopping abruptly.

'You want her, don't you?' Judith goaded. 'You want to thrust your manhood inside her, to fill her up and make her spend.'

John shook his head. 'No, ma'am,' he muttered, but his body was witness to the lie.

'No? Then I'll have to do it for you. Poor Tabitha's quite desperate, aren't you, my dear?' And with the tip of one finger she lightly probed inside the wet pink sex lips.

'Please, please,' cried Tabitha, her body twisting and turning at the touch.

'How prettily she begs,' continued Judith, her eyes still on John. 'I think she can wait a little longer, though. Don't you, Marianne?'

Marianne doubted it, but she knew she couldn't say so. 'You know best, ma'am,' she replied demurely.

Judith smiled with satisfaction. 'Indeed I do. Let's tickle this for a moment, it's such a pretty little thing.' She moved her finger delicately around Tabitha's protruding clitoris, causing the girl to gasp and moan even more. Tabitha was writhing all the time now, her breathing loud and uneven in the silent room. Her breasts seemed larger than normal, the nipples standing proud, the dark areolae a startling contrast to the surrounding alabaster flesh. As Judith tickled the mass of straining nerve-endings, Tabitha's body suddenly ceased its constant movement and she became very still. Marianne remembered this had been the prelude to a previous orgasm she'd seen the girl have but, unfortunately for Tabitha, Judith knew this as well and immediately removed her finger.

When the stimulation ceased Tabitha gave a wail of desperation and once more started to squirm on her mistress' lap, while Judith absentmindedly massaged the girl's lower stomach.

Marianne felt as needy as Tabitha looked. Beneath her woollen dress she could feel her own sex, moist and open. Her lower belly was cramping with desire while her breasts throbbed and the coarse material of the dress stimulated her nipples. This was the only stimulation she was receiving, but it sent messages of pleasure through her entire body.

'Marianne!' Judith's voice was sharp. 'What are you doing?'

Marianne jumped guiltily. 'Nothing, ma'am.'

'You look very warm.'

'The room's warm, ma'am.'

'I trust that is all it is,' said Judith coldly.

'Yes, ma'am,' said Marianne hastily. If anything, the fright had only increased her desire.

When Judith's hand moved again between Tabitha's thighs the girl, clearly deciding to throw caution to the wind, pressed herself down hard against the invading palm. Marianne wondered if she would be punished for being so forward, but Judith simply laughed.

'Have I kept you waiting too long?' she asked teasingly and then, apparently taking pity on the girl, she opened her with one hand and slowly inserted two fingers into the moist pinkness. Tabitha groaned with ecstasy.

Judith looked at John. 'Move nearer. Kneel between her feet.'

He obeyed, but reluctantly, clearly aware of what was going to happen.

'Now watch her spend,' said Judith, and she strummed Tabitha's clitoris until, with a shrill scream, the girl's pleasure finally spilled forth and, as the orgasm swept over her, her head rolled from side to side and her unintelligible cries proved her ecstasy.

Standing to one side, Marianne was witness both to Tabitha's moment of delight and John's downfall. As he watched the girl in the throes of delirious pleasure, his hips jerked a few times and he was spilling his seed on the drawing room floor, the sticky fluid discharging in uncontrollable spasms. Marianne heard him groaning in horror at what he'd done.

The moment Tabitha's pleasure had died away she scrambled off her mistress' lap, seemingly aware that Judith would not want her there any longer than was necessary. Her normally pale face was flushed and her breasts were still swollen. For a moment her eyes met Marianne's, and then she hastily looked down, but not before Marianne had seen an extraordinary mixture of excitement and shame in them, the same sensations as she herself was experiencing.

Judith stood up abruptly. 'How dare you?' she hissed at John. 'You're no better than an animal. Not only did you lie to my brother, but your animalistic behaviour is beyond belief. Such wickedness must be punished. Stand up immediately.'

John stumbled to his feet. His erection had vanished, his manhood hanging limply between his thighs again, and he looked terrified. 'Since you spent when I did not wish you to, I think it only appropriate that you should spend when I do wish you to,' said Judith.

John frowned. He glanced at Marianne, but she looked away, unable to offer any reassurance. She didn't fully understand what Judith meant, but she could hear the latent cruelty behind the words and guessed that, in some way, John was going to be made to suffer.

'You're young and strong,' Judith went on. 'How strong do you think you are, John?'

He shrugged.

'You seem very modest all of a sudden. Answer my question.'

'I don't understand it, ma'am,' he mumbled.

'It's perfectly simple. How quickly do you think you would be able to satisfy a woman again?'

'Do you mean now, ma'am?'

'Well I don't mean next week,' she said tartly.

'I couldn't say, ma'am,' he muttered, shifting restlessly from foot to foot. 'It's awkward, like, in front of you ladies...'

'Come now, you didn't find it difficult a few minutes ago. In fact, it was clearly impossible for you to restrain yourself. There's no one new here, so what possible excuse can you have for not being able to perform again?'

'It – it takes a man time.'

Marianne hated the way he was being humiliated so cruelly.

'How long?' Judith persisted.

Again he shrugged.

Walking over to him, Judith slapped him hard round the face, leaving the scarlet imprint of her palm on his cheek. 'Don't you take that attitude with me! Remember your place. Remember, too, what will happen to you if any of this reaches my brother's ears. Believe me, by the time I'd finished telling him what just happened in this room you'd be lucky to escape with your life!'

'I didn't do nothing,' he protested. 'Any man would have done the same.'

'That's a contradiction,' said Judith, with a warped smile. 'If you did nothing, how could any man have done the same?'

John shook his head, totally out of his depth. 'I reckon in a couple of hours I could do something,' he said at last.

'Two hours?' Judith mocked, shaking her head. 'I expected better than that from you, John. Tell me, Tabitha, do you have to wait two hours between your bouts of passion together?'

Tabitha, too, seemed to be having difficulty in following the conversation. 'John and me haven't done anything,' she protested.

'Oh, really,' said Judith, in exasperation. 'Very well, I'll tell you how long you've got, John. You have ten minutes in which to recover.'

'What happens then?' asked Marianne. Judith looked sharply at her companion. 'I don't remember asking you to speak.'

'Oh, I'm sorry,' Marianne apologised swiftly.

'Have you already forgotten what we planned?' Judith asked her.

Marianne didn't know what to say. How could she explain that she hadn't really been there when the plan was hatched, that she wasn't Marianne Clifford at all, but Marianne Kay?

'It seems I have to organise everything,' Judith muttered testily. 'John, sit there.' She pointed to a high-backed chair. Clearly very embarrassed and uncomfortable, John obeyed.

'You move only when given permission,' she ordered. 'Now, Marianne, start arousing him. It's my wish that he ejaculates again within ten minutes. You must do your best to help him.'

This was something totally unexpected and Marianne didn't quite know what to do. Hesitating briefly, she then stood in front of John and, after a moment's thought, sat across his thighs just as Tabitha had sat across Judith's.

'Lift your dress,' Judith commanded her. 'I trust you're naked beneath it?' Marianne nodded. 'Excellent. That should help him.'

Feeling extremely nervous, Marianne lifted the hem of her woollen dress and hitched it up, horribly aware that in doing so she was revealing herself to them. Then she sat down on the young man and felt his thighs tremble briefly as her naked buttocks touched them.

'Take hold of his shaft,' Judith instructed. 'Get some life back into the miserable specimen.'

Marianne didn't dare disobey. She took him in her fingers, but his flesh seemed to shrink at her touch.

'Seduce him,' Judith urged fervently. 'If you don't help him he's lost.'

'Please help him, miss,' cried Tabitha, then she squealed as her mistress spitefully slapped her naked breasts.

'Be silent, you wretched girl, or you'll go to your room,' Judith snapped.

Marianne writhed as sensuously as she could on John's lap. His muscled thighs felt delicious against her flesh and she rocked back and forth, stimulating herself with increasing abandon. For a few moments she forgot about John and concentrated solely on her own pleasure.

'Marianne, control yourself,' Judith cut in. 'It's John

whose pleasure I want to see spill, not yours. How dare you behave like this? It seems you've not yet learned to be a lady despite my brother's best efforts. Regretfully, I shall have to report you once more when he returns.'

Marianne didn't say anything. Instead, she lightly stroked John's testicles, and was relieved to feel them stirring. But still his cock refused to grow hard and, after a few minutes, Judith pulled Marianne off him.

'I shall have to do this myself,' she muttered brusquely. 'Stand up, John, part your legs, then bend over and touch your toes.'

'Please, mistress, not that,' the poor gardener gasped.

'But it always works, doesn't it?' Judith sneered.

'It always hurts,' he mumbled, sounding so desolate that Marianne's heart went out to him.

'Nonsense. Your pleasure comes every time. Tabitha, fetch the lard from the kitchen.' Tabitha scurried from the room, returning within seconds with a tub of lard. Judith inserted a finger into it, swirling it around until it was covered in grease, and then, while Marianne looked on aghast, she stabbed the greased digit abruptly into John's exposed rectum. It sank in until her palm cupped his buttock.

'There's a sensitive spot in here,' she explained to Marianne with bizarre detachment. 'Dr Francis Proctor, my brother's closest friend, taught me how to find it. It causes great excitement in members of the opposite sex. Isn't that true, John?'

John, his head bent down and his fingertips brushing his toes, could only gasp and groan as Judith continued to relentlessly massage his prostate gland. Eventually she withdrew her finger and wiped it with disdain on a piece of cloth that Tabitha had also brought with her. 'Stand up and turn around. Let's see if that's worked,' she ordered.

John straightened up and Marianne was astonished to see that he was rock hard, his erection as tight and angry-looking as it was when he'd been watching Tabitha.

Judith nodded with approval. 'It never fails,' she said to Marianne. 'Very good, John. Now let me see your pleasure spill once more.'

John shook his head. 'I'll do anything, ma'am, anything at all if you don't make me do this,' he cried.

'You silly boy, most men would be grateful,' Judith mocked. 'Tabitha, use your hand on him.'

'No, Tabby,' he said. 'Don't let her make you do it.' But Tabitha's fear of her mistress was greater than her regard for her lover and, falling to her knees, she gripped his penis hard and moved her hand briskly up and down, occasionally pausing to squeeze the engorged tip.

Marianne watched as John's body went rigid. She guessed how he must be feeling, knowing he was about to experience another spasm of ecstasy that would be followed by desolate humiliation. Glancing at Judith, she saw the woman was lost in contemplation of the scene, her eyes shining and her cheeks flushed.

'He's coming…' the sadistic woman stated with evident satisfaction, while Tabitha's dainty hand continued to work her lover's shaft.

'Stop Tabby, stop,' groaned John, but even as he pleaded she used her free hand to tease his swaying testicles, and this extra stimulation proved to be the final straw, drawing the climax from him as his fists clenched and his eyes closed. With a strangled cry of anguish his hips jerked, and Marianne watched as the lad's pleasure spilled forth again.

Judith clapped contemptuously, and Marianne wondered

what would happen next. Despite feeling sympathy for the humiliated young couple, she was aching for satisfaction, for some kind of release.

'Marianne, you may go now,' said Judith. 'Take John with you. Show the feeble specimen out through the kitchen door and lock it firmly behind him. He can sleep in the outhouse tonight. As for you, Tabitha, you can stay here and look after my needs. I'm sure you know what's expected of you.'

Tabitha nodded sadly.

Marianne hesitated. 'What's the matter?' asked Judith, and then she smiled knowingly. 'Ah, poor Marianne. I suppose you'd like someone to satisfy your simmering desires? Naturally, you'll understand that's impossible. You're a young unmarried woman in my care. I couldn't possibly allow such a thing to happen. Indeed, it's most unseemly that this whole affair has excited you. As I said before, I shall mention the fact to my brother.'

'I understand, ma'am,' said Marianne softly, wondering how it was that she knew the right thing to say, because Judith gave a nod of approval.

Even as she left the room, Marianne knew what she was going to do. The moment she got into her room she was going to peel off her woollen dress and satisfy herself. Her body simply couldn't wait, the urge was overwhelming, and once she'd ushered John out and locked up she hurried up the stairs with only the candle to show her the way, frantic to get to her bedroom. Opening the door, she was startled when the darkness was suddenly illuminated by a bright electric light-bulb.

Chapter Six

Marianne was determined that this time Steve's welcome home would be a better one, and she made a special trip into the nearest town on the morning he was due back. There, in a small back street, she was delighted to discover a sex shop tucked away between a pub and a newsagents. It took her a few minutes to pluck up the courage to go inside, but once there she was delighted she'd made the effort. It was full of exciting things she would have loved to try out. Even better, she thought to herself, would have been the opportunity to take them back with her into the past, to hand them to Sir Edward and see what he made of them. But she knew this would be impossible; she never even arrived back in the nineteenth century in her own clothes. Clearly, transporting any physical object apart from herself, anything which did not apply to Marianne Clifford, was out of the question. When she'd finally made her purchases she drove home to Moorhead House, feeling very excited. She hoped Steve would enter into the spirit of things.

He was later home than expected and full of apologies. 'The traffic was appalling,' he explained as he pulled her close and kissed her. 'I was in such a rush to get here it was really frustrating. God, I've missed you.'

'I've been on tenterhooks waiting,' said Marianne truthfully. 'Do you want to eat first?'

'First?' Steve looked a little surprised.

Marianne giggled. 'I'm sorry, it's just that I've been

waiting for you for so long, and...'

Understanding dawned in Steve's eyes. 'Hey, you're more important to me than food, you know that. Let's go upstairs.'

Once inside the bedroom, Marianne wondered how best to explain what she wanted. 'Steve...' she said hesitantly. 'I wondered if you'd mind doing something different?'

'Writing this new book's certainly spicing up our sex life,' he smirked. 'What do you want to do this time?'

'Play out a fantasy of mine.'

'I didn't know you had any fantasies.'

'Then you didn't know everything about me, did you?' she said teasingly.

'Apparently not.' He looked a little uncomfortable.

'It's nothing too way out,' she said hastily.

'If it turns you on, then it's fine by me,' he said, but his tone lacked conviction.

'I went shopping this morning. I've bought some special clothes.'

'Great, I've always wanted you to wear sexy nighties.'

She shook her head. 'Not those kind of clothes, Steve. Look...' She held up a set of leather cuffs.

Steve stared at them in total incomprehension. 'What on earth are those?'

'I want you to put them on me. I want to be helpless and at your mercy.'

Steve frowned anxiously. 'So, what do I do?'

Marianne sighed. The way things were going, all the eroticism would be lost before they'd even started. 'The larger leather loops go round the tops of my thighs,' she explained patiently. 'Then these smaller cuffs go round my wrists and they're attached with buckles to my thighs. That way I'm helpless. They make me your prisoner.'

'I'm not sure I'm going to be any good at this,' muttered Steve.

Marianne's heart sank. She could have screamed with frustration.

'What do I do with you then?' continued Steve.

'There's this as well,' she said, producing a leather cat o'nine tails. 'You can use it on me any way you like once I'm fastened with the cuffs.'

'You mean, hit you?' he asked incredulously.

'It's only a bit of fun,' she insisted desperately.

'I had no idea you were like this.' He sounded totally stunned. 'I can't hit you, Marianne. I want to give you pleasure, not pain.'

'But they can be the same thing,' she cried.

He snorted derisively. 'Don't be so ridiculous.'

'Steve, please, for my sake just give it a go,' Marianne begged, frantic to play out the game she'd been picturing all day. 'If you don't like it we won't ever do it again, but you might find you do.'

'Why can't we just make love as normal?' he asked.

'Because it gets boring,' she cried. 'I know what you're going to do and you know what I'm going to do. This will spice things up for us.'

'Charming,' he sulked. 'But...' he went on carefully, 'if it's really what you want...'

'I do, Steve. I really do.'

He removed his jeans and underpants, and Marianne's pulse quickened as she saw he was already becoming hard. Crossing the room, he gripped her round the waist, picked her up and set her on the bed. 'Don't move,' he said, but although he was trying to be authoritative his voice lacked the genuine harshness of Sir Edward's. Nevertheless, it was better than Marianne had expected, and she felt a thrill run through her.

'What are you going to do?' she asked tremulously.

At last he finally seemed to understand the game. 'You're to wear these,' he said, and she felt his hands parting her thighs, clipping on the strips of leather. Then, quite roughly, he pulled her wrists down, secured the cuffs around them and fastened the buckle to the thigh straps. Only once they were on did Marianne realise how totally helpless they rendered her. It was difficult to move her upper torso at all, because even the smallest movement meant she had to raise her thighs, which automatically parted her legs and revealed her sex. It felt delicious and she started to shiver with anticipation.

The room was dark and she could only just make out Steve's shadowy shape. He picked up the cat o'nine tails. She was beginning to feel almost as excited as she felt when in the presence of Sir Edward. Once more she was at a man's mercy, and although it was the wrong man, it was still the kind of arousal she now craved.

Suddenly, with no warning, Steve flicked the whip across her breasts. It didn't really hurt, but she gave a cry of surprise and felt her nipples harden in instant response. 'No, please,' she begged, desperately hoping he'd ignore her. Luckily he did.

Steve climbed on to the bed beside her and ran a hand over her breasts. 'God, you're excited already,' he said as his palm touched the hard peaks of her nipples. 'This really does turn you on, doesn't it?'

'Don't talk about it, just do it,' she gasped.

He drew the whip down over her belly and she clenched her stomach muscles, seconds before the second blow fell, catching the taut skin over her right hipbone. Once more she gave a cry, but this time there was more pain and it felt delicious.

Steve was breathing heavily. His hands explored her more urgently than she could remember, and when he touched her between her thighs and felt how wet she was he reacted by sliding two fingers inside her. She contracted her muscles around them, moaning with delight. Quickly he started to massage her and the heavy ache began. She wanted to thrust her hips up to get greater stimulation, but she was unable to move.

Just as she'd hoped she was at his mercy, and she tried to forget it was Steve who was in control. She began to imagine it was Sir Edward who had her lying spreadeagled and defenceless, displaying everything, her shameful response only too evident to him. As Steve's fingers continued to massage her, the delicious ache spread until finally it turned into a piercing moment of exquisite pleasure and her body shook in orgasm.

'Was that good?' asked Steve tenderly, and immediately the spell was broken. Marianne felt like screaming. She didn't want tenderness, didn't want his kind enquiries, she wanted him to continue as he had been and, above all, to keep silent.

'Mmm,' she murmured, hoping that if she didn't answer properly he'd stop talking.

'You were right about this,' he muttered. 'It is a turn on.'

'It's best if we don't talk much,' she whispered.

'I suppose it is,' he replied, and she gave a little sigh of relief. Now she could turn the scenario into anything she wanted. She was so lost in pleasurable sensations she didn't realise Steve was going to hit her again until the cat lashed down onto her breasts, catching her erect nipples and making her hiss. This time her skin burned and she whimpered with shock. Steve decided to lick the abused flesh and she felt his cool tongue moving across the rising weal. He drew a nipple into his mouth and his teeth grazed the sore bud, making her whimper with discomfort.

And her legs and arms ached. The muscles were cramping, but the feeling was exactly the same as when she'd been forced to crouch naked in the outhouse, and she was revelling in it.

Steve abruptly straddled her and, moulding her breasts between his hands, lowered himself so he could stimulate his throbbing cock between the soft globes. He'd never fucked her breasts before, and Marianne was excited both by the sensation and by the fact that he was entering into the game so wholeheartedly. She loved the way he ground his erection in her cosseting cleavage. It was obvious from his grunting that Steve was going to continue until he came, and Marianne knew she couldn't stimulate herself because her hands were trapped, her wrists fastened to her thighs. For the first time she understood the disadvantages of the contraption, and began to whimper with frustration.

Steve misread her reactions. 'Isn't this great...' he croaked urgently, thrusting his hips with increasing abandon. Because she didn't want to break the spell, because the whole point of this was to place herself in the position where she had no control, she didn't contradict him. With despair, she wondered why it was that she seemed doomed to spend most of her time stimulated beyond belief, her pleasure constantly ready to be released but with ultimate fulfilment never allowed.

She could tell Steve was fast approaching the point of no return. His fingers tightened convulsively around her breasts as he mauled the flesh even tighter around his erection. The ache between Marianne's thighs was now so intense it was almost unbearable. She could feel the moisture seeping from her sex, but there was nothing she could do to trigger her climax. Her fingers clawed helplessly at the night air.

Then, with shocking abruptness, strong hands gripped the tops of her thighs and she felt them wrenched apart so harshly that she uttered an astonished cry. Steve grunted his approval, clearly thinking she was urging him on to greater efforts.

She couldn't imagine what was happening to her. She knew the hands didn't belong to Steve because his were still busy working her breasts around his shaft... and then realisation dawned. Very faintly she was able to make out the figure of Sir Edward Sharpe looming over the bed. He was staring at her in his usual, penetrating way, his eyes glinting in the dark. Having parted her thighs so roughly, he waited a few seconds, then she saw him raise an arm, and tensed, because she knew he was about to strike her.

The first blow fell high up on her thighs. It felt like a whip, but the force behind it was far greater than anything Steve had used, and a dreadful burning followed instantly. Then, as it started to die away, he struck her again, a fraction higher. With increasing trepidation she realised he was moving nearer and nearer to her most vulnerable area.

She instinctively attempted to close her thighs, but Sir Edward was too determined and easily held her legs apart. She gave a tiny murmur of protest. Clearly this angered him, because the whip promptly cut down again and she squirmed, desperately trying to avoid the blows whilst trapped beneath Steve, who was lost in his own ecstasy.

It was a totally unbelievable situation – and she revelled in it. But all too soon it would be over. As another stinging blow caught her she knew her juices were flowing copiously. She'd never felt so wet or ready and the throbbing ache inside her was just about unbearable.

'I-I'm nearly there!' gasped Steve.

Marianne knew she was too. Sir Edward delivered two final sharp blows with the whip, both of them falling across her lower belly. The pain seared through her like an electric shock, and she wondered if she could stand any more. She wanted to cry out, to beg Sir Edward to do something to help her. Staring wild-eyed over Steve's shadowy shoulder, Marianne saw Sir Edward bend closer, examining her, and then she felt his fingers touching her juicy flesh. She gasped, and he rubbed expertly.

'Help me... help me...' she implored.

Through hazy vision she saw Sir Edward smile enigmatically, and then felt something smooth and sturdy penetrating her. She had no idea what it was, but her muscles tightened gratefully around it, clutching convulsively at this desperately needed object which was filling her so beautifully. Sir Edward moved it with careless force so that, even at this late stage, her pleasure was mixed with discomfort. But she welcomed it – embraced it. This was what she needed, this was what her increasingly debauched flesh desired – and suddenly she knew it was the handle of the whip that was skewering her.

Now she could picture the instrument of pleasure, now she knew what was being done to her, she was driven even more frantic. She heard herself gasping and moaning as he continued to thrust in and out of her greedy opening. Then, as the delicious pressure built to a climax, he pressed his thumb on her clitoris and, with a scream of ecstatic disbelief, Marianne finally climaxed.

As she writhed helplessly Steve withdrew from between her breasts and thrust between her gaping lips. 'Suck it!' he hissed aggressively, and her mouth immediately filled with his salty spending. She breathed through her nose and swallowed desperately, and Steve spasmed above her as her mouth filled again.

Gradually his hips stilled and his shoulders slumped, and for a few minutes the only sounds in the dark room were his heavy breathing and the suckling of Marianne.

'Bloody hell... that was bloody incredible,' he eventually gasped, ruining the moment with such an unnecessary and crass summing up, rolling off her and leaving her exposed to the chill of the night. He lay there, his chest heaving, while Marianne peered dreamily into the gloom through lowered eyelashes. But the man she was looking for was not there.

'You look stunning,' said Steve admiringly, slipping an arm round Marianne's waist. She stared thoughtfully at herself in the mirror. The sleeveless coral pink shift dress ended two inches above her knees and had a softly draped cowl neckline. The colour suited her. In it, she felt both confident and sexy, but surprisingly not as sexy as she felt on her journeys back into the past when she was wearing the complicated drawers, bodices and stockings that were the fashion of the time. She wondered what on earth Sandra and Graham would think if she turned up at their house dressed like that, and smiled to herself.

'What's the joke?' asked Steve, his hands lingering on her upper arms.

'Nothing,' she replied. 'We'd better go or we'll be late.'

'I keep remembering what you looked like in those

cuffs,' said Steve. 'Shall we have another game when we get back?'

'If we do it too often it'll lose its novelty,' she said, wanting to dampen his enthusiasm.

'You know, these days you seem to be two different girls,' Steve observed during the drive.

Marianne glanced sideways at him. 'How do you mean?' she asked carefully.

'Well, last night, although I admit I was a bit reluctant, you were incredible. You showed me a side of you I hadn't realised existed, and we both had a superb time. Then today you don't seem to want to talk about it. Your moods seem to keep changing. It's the same with your work.'

'My work?'

'Yes. First of all it's a modern romance, then it's a historical novel and now, despite the fact that you tell me you've started writing, I haven't seen a word of it. Why is that? You normally like me to read your manuscripts.'

'It's only a rough draft,' she countered defensively.

'But I always read the rough drafts.'

'This time I want to polish it more before I let you see it,' she said hastily, knowing that if he saw the explicit sex scenes with their bizarre erotic content he'd think he was living with three women, let alone two.

'You always used to be such a reliable person,' he went on. 'That was one of the things I loved about you. You didn't have moods and I always knew where I stood.'

'Are you trying to say I've changed and you don't like the new me?' she challenged.

'Of course I like the new you, I've already said that – or at least, I like some of you. I just wish you didn't keep having these mood swings. Take now, for instance. I feel

I'm irritating you, but you couldn't get enough of me last night.'

'I wish you'd stop harping on about the other night,' snapped Marianne. 'I haven't changed and you are irritating me. You've just never looked at me properly before.'

'That's not true,' he objected. 'You have changed and you know it. You just won't admit it.'

'Do you think we could stop arguing now we're here?' asked Marianne. 'You're the one who was so anxious for us to make friends with Sandra and Graham. The least you can do is be civil for the evening.'

'I'll be civil,' he said, climbing out of the car. 'You were the one who kept losing track of the conversation when they came to us.'

'Hello there,' called Sandra, opening the front door of the small cottage. 'What a lovely dress, Marianne.'

Marianne smiled. 'Thanks. I got it in London before we moved.'

'You can't get such lovely things round here,' said Sandra with a wistful sigh.

'What sort of lovely things?' asked Graham, appearing in the hall.

'Dresses like the one Marianne's wearing.'

Graham looked appreciatively at Marianne, his eyes crawling none too discreetly over her breasts. 'The dress is nice, but you set it off to perfection,' he said, with a suggestive smile.

'Thank you,' she responded politely, but the compliment seemed empty and she didn't like the undercurrent she detected in his smile.

The cottage had been thoroughly modernised inside and while Steve rhapsodised over everything, particularly the kitchen, giving Marianne meaningful glances as he did so, she wondered why on earth Sandra and Graham had done such a thing. If she'd inherited a quaint little cottage she'd have kept it the way it was. The whole atmosphere of the place had been ruined. If there had been any ghosts from the past here, they would have been banished by the indelicate changes.

'Graham forgot to get the beer in,' said Sandra apologetically. 'I wondered if you'd like to go with him to get some, Steve? Marianne and I can talk girls' talk while you're gone.'

'Sure,' said Steve agreeably.

'You don't like it, do you?' Sandra said to Marianne the moment their husbands had left.

'Like what?'

'The way we've done the cottage up.'

Marianne smiled. 'Of course I do. It's lovely. You must have spent a fortune on it.'

'It did cost quite a bit, but you don't have to pretend to like it.'

Marianne felt uncomfortable. 'Well, I suppose I'd prefer it if the interior was more in keeping with the exterior,' she admitted.

Sandra looked curiously at her. 'Steve was right, you really are obsessed with the past.'

'No, I'm not. I've just got different tastes from him.'

Sandra shook her head. 'Come on, admit it. Moving to Moorhead House has changed you, hasn't it?'

Marianne felt shocked. 'That's what Steve's just been telling me. But he's wrong, and so are you. Besides, you didn't know me in London so how can you tell whether I've changed or not?'

'I know how you were when we first met, and you've

changed, even in such a short time. You were so different from the people round here. Now you sound as though you've lived here all your life.'

'I—'

'And you look different. I can't explain how, but you do. It's as though you no longer want to be the person you were. Perhaps it's the change of pace, or maybe I'm just imagining it all.'

Marianne was worried. It was one thing for Steve to have noticed she'd changed and to be complaining about it. That was understandable. However, if even Sandra thought she was different, then that was dangerous. She knew she had to keep her two identities completely separate. Despite the fact the past now held more fascination for her than the present, she mustn't allow Marianne Clifford to take her over. She sensed the lurking danger of allowing such a thing to happen.

'Perhaps you're right,' she agreed, trying hard to smile. 'It's a bit of a culture shock, really, moving here so far away from everyone and everything. I've been surprised at how easily I've slipped into the new way of life, and I am beginning to forget the sort of person I was. But I don't think it's a drastic change.'

'Yet you say Steve's noticed?'

'Yes, but then he's still travelling all round the country. Nothing much has altered for him, he simply has a different base to come home to.'

'How about some wine?' asked Sandra, lightening the mood a little. 'We might as well start; the boys will be a while yet.'

After a couple of sips of wine Marianne decided to ask Sandra a question, one she wouldn't have dared ask if Steve had been there. 'Remember you told me about Judith

Wells, the woman who owned Moorhead House before my aunt?' Sandra nodded. 'Well, you haven't found out any more about her since then, have you?'

'I did mention it to my mum,' admitted Sandra. 'According to her, Judith Wells went totally mad after she was admitted to a mental hospital. Apparently she used to spend all her days waiting for a visit from her brother. She did have a brother – he was called Daniel, I think – and he went to see her several times, but she used to get terribly angry when he arrived, shouting that he was an impostor. In the end he stopped going. God knows who she was expecting. Whoever it was, he never came.'

'How dreadful,' said Marianne quietly, knowing very well who it was Judith Wells had been expecting every time the nurses told her her brother was visiting. She could imagine how terrible it would be to look across the room, hoping to see those dark, unfathomable eyes, to feel that erotic pull – a pull she was certain existed between the brother and sister even though it was forbidden – only to have her hopes dashed.

'How's your book coming along?' asked Sandra, trying hard to generate some brighter conversation.

'Very well.' At last Marianne was able to be genuinely enthusiastic about something. 'I can't stop writing. To be honest, I wouldn't have minded if Steve hadn't come home this weekend because I was in full flow, but naturally I'd never tell him that.'

Thereafter the atmosphere and chat eased, and when the boys returned the rest of the evening passed quite pleasantly. Marianne was relieved there were no distractions from the past. Clearly she'd been right in assuming that her connection with Sir Edward and his household only existed when she was at Moorhead and the surrounding moorland, places where Marianne Clifford had been. Though this was a comfort because it meant she could concentrate properly on the evening's socialising, she also suffered a sense of loss at being separated from the house.

'That was a good evening,' said Steve, as they drove home. 'They're nice, aren't they?'

'They're okay.'

'I think we're lucky to have them in a place like this. If it weren't for them it would be like being buried alive here at weekends.'

'I'd no idea you disliked it that much,' said Marianne. 'You'd better not come home if that's how you feel.'

'Don't be silly,' said Steve, his voice softening. 'How could I possibly stay away from the new, exciting you?'

'So I'm exciting now, am I? I thought I was a confusing schizophrenic earlier in the evening.'

Steve rested his left hand lightly on her knee and squeezed. 'Not now,' he said. 'I don't want to argue. I just can't wait to get into bed.'

Marianne's heart sank.

To her relief, once they were in bed Steve seemed to sense her reluctance. 'Are you tired?' he asked sympathetically.

'A little,' she lied.

'Okay, let's just go to sleep then.'

Marianne felt guilty, because he was being so considerate. She wondered if it was really possible to be unfaithful to someone with a man who'd died over a hundred years previously. If anyone had suggested such an outrageous thing could happen before they'd moved to Yorkshire, she'd have had them carted off to the nearest loony bin! But now she was here, and it was happening!

Steve quickly fell asleep and started snoring quietly, but for Marianne it was different. What Sandra had told her about Judith Wells preyed on her mind. She was terrified of losing control of her sanity. In some ways she had an advantage over her aunt's predecessor. With Steve around most weekends and Sandra and Graham as friends she wasn't alone all the time. If she had been, then, like Judith, she assumed she would in all probability spend more time in the past until the present became not just boring and irritating but of total insignificance. Clearly, for the second Judith there had come a time when the modern world ceased to exist, and it was this Marianne feared the most. She didn't always want to come back, but when she did she wanted to be herself and not Marianne Clifford.

She was afraid that when she did finally fall asleep she'd have nightmares but, when she dropped off she slept soundly and didn't wake until the rays of the sun shone through the gap in their bedroom curtains and she saw from the bedside clock it was half-past eight.

'I've been watching you sleep,' said Steve, running his hands up inside the long T-shirt she wore to bed, caressing her urgently. 'I don't think I tell you often enough how beautiful you are.'

'You never tell me,' said Marianne.

'I'm sure I did when I first met you.'

'Perhaps then,' she conceded. 'But not since.'

'Well, I'm telling you now.' With that he began to kiss her, and soon the T-shirt had been thrown to the floor. 'Shall we use the cuffs again?' he whispered.

She shook her head. 'I've already told you, we should indulge sparingly.'

'Is there anything else you'd like to do?' he asked.

She would have liked to say that all she really wanted was get up, have breakfast and go for a walk on the moors, but as Steve was leaving that afternoon she felt it would be too unkind. 'Let's just do what we usually do,' she said softly.

'You're sure that's enough for you?'

'Absolutely sure,' she lied.

Unfortunately her body was not so willing to lie and Steve, with his new-found awareness of her capabilities, was quick to spot this. He tried everything he could think of, but still her stubborn flesh refused to respond until she started to wish that he'd just get on with it.

'I know,' he said suddenly. 'I'll give you a massage. Sit on the end of the bed and watch in the mirror.'

Marianne did as he suggested and sat gazing into the mirror on the wardrobe door, while Steve knelt behind her, his hands working on her shoulders and back, occasionally gliding round to caress her breasts and nipples. The sensation was very agreeable and she felt herself start to relax. Her eyes closed a little and her reflection became blurred. Then the mirror images changed, and instead of her own reflection she was suddenly watching a scene from the past.

The room was Tabitha's, and she was once more standing on the stool where Marianne had first seen her, but this time there were two men with her. One was Sir Edward, but the other was a stranger. He was a little shorter than Sir Edward. The two of them were examining Tabitha closely and she was trembling from head to toe, obviously trying to suppress her fear.

'She's deliciously tempting,' the new man said, after he'd studied her for a few moments. 'You're a lucky devil, Edward.'

'You just wait until you examine Miss Marianne, my dear doctor,' replied the master of the house.

Watching and listening to this scene, Marianne felt her excitement rising. The implication was that at some time Marianne Clifford would be examined by the doctor friend of Sir Edward's, and the thought both aroused and unsettled her. She longed to be there, to become the original Marianne when that happened, and wondered if it would ever come about.

'This seems to be working,' said Steve, his voice threatening to break the spell.

'Don't stop, it's gorgeous,' murmured Marianne, her gaze still fixed on the mirror.

Suddenly Sir Edward picked up a flexible cane and handed it to his friend. 'Why don't you use this on her?' he suggested. 'She loves it.'

'No, I don't,' cried Tabitha. 'Please, doctor, don't hit me again.'

'But it was so wonderful last time,' the doctor stated firmly, tapping her breasts with the end of the cane. 'I don't think I can resist. Besides, they're such a wonderful target, aren't they, Edward?'

'Indeed they are,' Sir Edward concurred.

Then the doctor raised the cane and it swept viciously down across the upper slopes of her breasts, leaving a thin red line in its wake. Tabitha jerked, but was unable to avoid the second stinging blow of the supple cane, a blow that fell precisely below the first to leave two vivid stripes upon her flesh.

Then the doctor set about his task with increased gusto, striking her belly and buttocks, but to Marianne's frustration, as tears rolled down Tabitha's flushed cheeks, the hypnotic image began to fade. Suddenly, all Marianne could see was her own reflection once again.

'Oh no…'

'Shouldn't I have stopped?' asked Steve.

Marianne was desperate. She'd been incredibly excited by what she'd seen and she needed to know more, but she sensed that for now it wasn't to be. So she lay back on the bed, pulling Steve on top of her. 'Take me,' she begged him. 'Quickly… *quickly*!'

Steve eagerly covered her and she pulled his hands over her breasts. Her skin was burning. It was as though it was she and not Tabitha who'd been caned, and she pressed hard on Steve's fingers so that delicious pleasure-pain swamped her swelling tissue. 'I want you inside me,' she gasped.

Her urgency spurred Steve on and he began to rut against her. Within a few seconds she convulsed in an ecstasy of release as the dreadful sexual tension caused by the scene she'd witnessed in the mirror was relieved.

'There, I read that a massage was a good prelude to sex,' gasped Steve once he'd come too. 'All you needed was a little time.'

Time, thought Marianne dreamily. Yes, time was giving her pleasure – though not a little of it, but a hundred and seventy years…

Chapter Seven

Marianne glanced at her watch. It was nearly four o'clock and Steve had said earlier that he had to be away by then. She wondered what on earth he could be doing upstairs. Because he travelled so much he was used to packing, and normally it didn't take him more than ten minutes. She'd spent most of the day in a dream, her mind constantly recalling the sensations she'd experienced when she and Steve had been joined by Sir Edward.

There were, she realised, very few occasions now when the man didn't manage to make his presence felt in some way or another. Certainly over this weekend he'd hardly left her and Steve alone. She sensed he was jealous, not wanting her and Steve to have pleasure. Yet that was strange, because she couldn't imagine him being a jealous man. Perhaps, she thought, it was more a question of control.

Marianne Clifford had been his employee, paid by him to keep his sister company, and it appeared that since she had no living relatives there was never any danger of her having a life outside Moorhead House. If this had been what he'd liked, if he'd grown used to total possession of the girl, then her own life with Steve must present itself as a threat to him.

She wondered whether he had ever felt any genuine affection for his sister's companion, whether his desire was for the young woman herself or simply lust for any attractive female who was helpless. Perhaps the real

Marianne hadn't known either, she thought, and then stopped abruptly.

Why was she thinking of Marianne Clifford as real and herself, by extension, as unreal? She was just as real as the first Marianne, she simply lived in a different time, but already her own life seemed lacking in substance. 'Be careful,' she whispered to herself. 'That way lies madness. Remember Judith Wells.'

At that moment Steve burst into the room. Marianne had never seen him look so angry. He was clutching a sheaf of paper in his fist. 'I've been looking at your manuscript,' he shouted. 'It's disgusting. I can't believe you've written it.'

Marianne stood up. 'You've no right to go snooping around in my study,' she said angrily. 'I told you I didn't want you reading it yet.'

'And I'm not surprised. It's nothing but filth, absolute filth. It's not a novel, it's pure pornography. You must be sick to think of things like that.'

Marianne glared at him. 'You don't know anything about writing,' she shouted back. 'It's all different these days. Anything goes, you've only got to visit a book shop to see that.'

'I do visit book shops,' he snapped, 'and you might be surprised to learn that I've never seen anything like this in my whole life.'

'Then all I can say is you must lead a very narrow life.'

'You know that's not true. What's Angela going to think when she sees this? Besides, no one's going to publish such filth.'

'This wasn't quite your attitude to the new, sexually liberated me on Friday night, or this morning,' Marianne reminded him scornfully.

'We didn't do anything like this.' He waved the manuscript at her. 'All this business with candles. And you were thinking of our outhouse when you wrote it, weren't you? There's no point in denying it, the description's too good.'

'I've no intention of denying it,' said Marianne, trying to keep her voice calm. 'I've always used places I know in my books.'

Steve shook his head. 'I don't want you doing this any more. There's something nasty about it. Get rid of it. You're sick. If you want my opinion you should see a doctor.' With that, he stormed out of the house.

When the sounds of his car had died away Marianne sank back in her chair and closed her eyes. She'd meant to hide the manuscript, but had forgotten to. Despite her show of bravado, his words worried her: 'You should see a doctor' had an ominous and strangely familiar ring to it.

Even as she was turning the words over in her mind the by now familiar darkness started to creep into the room. The furniture began to fade, its edges blurring, and it seemed as though a mist was filling the room. Then the mist cleared and Marianne found herself sitting in the dining room as it had been in the nineteenth century. Seated at the table with her was Judith Fullick.

The meal in front of Marianne looked distinctly unappetising. The meat was probably boiled beef and the vegetables just potatoes and turnips. Although not hungry she felt strangely compelled to eat, but the meat was tough and she found herself chewing and chewing, not daring to put it back on the plate.

'Are you not hungry?' asked Judith.

'Indeed yes, ma'am,' Marianne said politely between chews. 'The meat seems a little tough today, that's all.'

'I trust you're not going to have trouble with your teeth,' said Judith. 'It's tiresome and expensive.'

'My teeth are in excellent condition,' Marianne assured her.

Judith sighed. 'I suppose it's of no importance. My brother keeps saying that you should eat less since you're gaining weight. Perhaps once you've eaten a little more of Tabitha's food the weight will fall off you anyway. Poor Tabitha is not the most accomplished cook I've ever had the good fortune to employ, but she's been with me a long time and she understands our ways, don't you, Tabitha?'

'Yes, ma'am,' said Tabitha, bobbing a swift curtsy.

'You do look a little pale,' Judith continued, looking closely at her companion. 'I really think you should see the doctor, Marianne.'

So that had been the trigger, Marianne thought, remembering Steve's angry parting words. Then she remembered Dr Francis Proctor and suddenly she was very afraid. 'I have no need of a doctor,' she said hastily. 'I feel very well.'

'Nonsense. It's my duty to make sure that nothing ails you. He will be here tonight and is due to see Tabitha. I think he should examine you at the same time. Once you've eaten it would be best if you and Tabitha rested quietly until tonight. Anxiety can cause fluctuations in the blood and confuse Dr Proctor.'

'I don't need the doctor, ma'am,' said Tabitha hastily, and Marianne could see the girl was terrified at the prospect. 'He only saw me the other day. I feel very well.'

'The choice is not yours to make, Tabitha,' Judith said coldly.

'Might I not at least take a little air before retiring to my room, ma'am?' Marianne asked, not wanting to be cooped up for any length of time.

Judith shook her head. 'I can tell you've been hearing stories about Dr Proctor, Marianne. You look anxious, but there's no need to be. He's an excellent physician.'

When the meal was over, Marianne and her employer drank tea and then, much to Marianne's surprise, John was summoned from the garden. 'John,' said Judith briskly. 'Take Tabitha and Miss Marianne to Tabitha's room. Move the extra truckle-bed in there and lock the door after you. Neither of them is to leave the room until my brother and his visitor arrive tonight. Do you understand?'

John nodded.

Marianne couldn't understand why his presence was necessary and she wondered, too, why she had to go to Tabitha's room rather than her own. But her thoughts were interrupted as Tabitha gave a little wail and ran from the room.

'Search all the usual places,' Judith told John, showing little surprise at the girl's flight. 'If you don't find her you'll take her place tonight.'

'I'll find her,' the young man said, hastily following Tabitha's exit.

'Why is Tabitha so afraid?' Marianne asked, not sure that she wanted to know.

Judith's smile only increased her nervousness. 'Some of the things Dr Proctor has had to do to Tabitha in order to keep her well seem to cause her some distress,' she explained calmly. 'In any case, the wretched girl is far too highly-strung and forever running off. Sometimes I think it would have been better for us if we'd left her in the workhouse.'

Marianne felt her palms dampen. 'I trust he won't hurt

me,' she said hesitantly.

'I'm afraid I've no idea what he'll need to do to you,' replied Judith. 'However, whatever he does it will be for your own good. Now, please, go to Tabitha's room and wait there.'

'Why can't I use my own room?'

'Because there is no lock on the door,' explained Judith, her tone brooking no argument.

Although Marianne went straight to Tabitha's room, it was nearly half an hour before John finally dragged the sobbing servant girl in to join her, pushing her roughly over the threshold and then slamming the door as she fell to the floor, wiping her eyes with the backs of her hands.

She looked up at Marianne despairingly. 'Oh, miss, I never thought he'd examine me again so quickly. I don't think I can bear it a second time.'

'Bear what?' asked Marianne. Although the scene she'd witnessed had plainly made Tabitha uncomfortable it scarcely seemed to warrant this kind of distress.

'I can't say,' muttered Tabitha. 'I'm too ashamed.'

'I think you must be exaggerating,' responded Marianne, hoping against hope that she was right but already filled with a terrible sense of foreboding.

'You don't know nothing,' cried the servant girl, before flinging herself on her bed, where she lay face down and weeping, the sound driving Marianne to distraction.

Time passed very slowly. Marianne walked restlessly around the tiny room, wondering what it must be like for Tabitha to have nowhere else that she could count as her own. Even here, the girl had no true privacy, for Sir Edward and his sister could enter at any time.

A little later and Marianne was starting to feel annoyed. 'I don't see why we have to stay here,' she said to Tabitha, who'd thankfully ceased her crying. 'Why can't we carry on with our normal duties until we see the doctor?'

'Mrs Fullick knows I'd run off,' explained Tabitha.

'I wouldn't,' Marianne retorted indignantly.

'It's not just that,' Tabitha said slowly.

'What is it then?'

Tabitha looked around anxiously, as though checking to see if anyone was listening. 'You'll find out,' she eventually said.

'Why are you so afraid?' Marianne asked. 'Does Dr Proctor hurt you more than Sir Edward?'

Tabitha pushed her hair back off her face. 'They won't leave me alone,' she whined pitifully. 'It's my breasts, you see; they fascinate them. The doctor's given me exercises so they don't sag, but I don't think that's the truth. I think they just like tormenting me. It's not my fault I'm so big; I grew a lot when I got to fifteen.'

'You've been beaten before. Why is it worse when the doctor does it?'

Tabitha shook her head. 'It's not the beatings I mind, it's the other things the doctor does.'

'Like what?' Marianne's heart was beginning to race.

'He says I'm full of germs or something, things that have to be got rid of if I'm to be clean for him. It's that I don't like.'

'I still don't understand,' said Marianne.

'You'll find out,' muttered Tabitha. 'It won't be no different for you just because you're a sort of lady.'

Another hour passed and Marianne realised she was becoming uncomfortable. 'Do you have a chamber-pot under your bed?' she asked Tabitha, deciding that she couldn't stand it any longer.

Tabitha shook her head. 'They take it away before the

doctor comes.'

'What on earth for?' asked Marianne in astonishment.

'It's all part of it,' said Tabitha slowly. 'The doctor says it makes his examination easier.'

'That's utter nonsense,' said Marianne, wondering if the girl had got hold of the wrong end of the stick. 'What are we expected to do, then?'

'We mustn't do nothing,' said the girl hastily. 'If you have an accident you'll be punished.'

Marianne began to think Tabitha's fears might not be as ridiculous as they seemed. She was already uncomfortable, her bladder full and aching. If she wasn't allowed to relieve the pressure before the evening then she'd be in acute discomfort; in fact, she doubted if it would be possible for her to hold on that long.

'I really do need the chamber-pot,' she said, beginning to panic. 'Surely if I knock on the door...?'

'It won't make no difference,' said Tabitha. 'No one will come. That's why you've been locked in here with me.'

Marianne started pacing around the room again, trying to distract herself from the discomfort, but it was impossible. She had no idea what time of day it was but, judging by the light, she thought it must be approaching seven o'clock. She sat on the edge of the bed with her thighs clenched tightly together, desperately trying to ease the terrible sensation.

Yet another half-hour passed before the door was finally unlocked, and two men stood framed in the doorway. One was Sir Edward, and the other his doctor friend. As they stood tall and silent in the doorway, with Sir Edward holding a candle aloft so that it cast strange flickering shadows in the room, Marianne felt terrified. And

Tabitha's whimpers did nothing to ease the tension.

'Here you are, Francis,' said Edward, his sonorous voice seeming like a caress, despite the dangerous expression on his face. 'The two patients we discussed over dinner.'

'Excellent,' said his friend, advancing into the room. 'I'll begin with Tabitha. Take off your clothes, young lady. I need to see if the exercises are working.'

Marianne hastily climbed on to the other truckle-bed, shrinking back against the wall. She was anxious to stay out of the way of the two men, frightened that should she attract their attention the doctor might decide to attend to her first. Tabitha was pulling off her clothes, and when the girl was naked Sir Edward pulled her to her feet.

'What do you think?' he asked, cupping each of her breasts. 'Has the muscle tone improved?'

'I'll measure her,' replied the doctor, and Marianne became a genuine witness to the scene as he threaded the leather straps around Tabitha's breasts. 'Have you exercised every day, my girl?' he enquired.

'Yes, sir,' whispered Tabitha.

The doctor fingered her breasts thoughtfully, squeezing and pinching the nipples, which grew rigid beneath his touch. 'I can see very little difference as yet,' he remarked. 'Extend the exercise time each evening.'

'But it makes me ache so,' cried Tabitha. 'My arms hurt and my breasts get sore.'

'It's for your own good,' said the doctor, leaving her breasts ringed by the leather straps. 'Now, let me examine you properly. Lie back on the bed, if you please.'

Marianne was astonished when Tabitha suddenly rushed across the room and flung herself down beside her. 'I don't want to be examined, miss,' she cried. 'Don't let them. Please, tell the master I'm well.'

'Get up at once!' Sir Edward roared furiously, striking Tabitha across her buttocks. 'How dare you make such an exhibition of yourself? You should be grateful that we take such good care of you. Dr Proctor is an excellent physician and you are fortunate indeed to have his services.'

Marianne felt she should do something to help Tabitha, who was so obviously distressed. But instead she watched in silence as the two men laid Tabitha on her back on the bed. Then Sir Edward pressed down on her slight shoulders, securing her upper torso firmly, while the doctor, seating himself on the edge of the bed, began to run his hands over Tabitha's belly.

As his fingers started to prod and probe the flesh, so Tabitha started to utter despairing cries, and suddenly Marianne knew why. The girl's bladder must be as full as her own and the probing fingers would be almost unendurable. At the same time she realised this might well be what lay in store for her. She couldn't bear the thought, because she knew she'd lose control. Already the ache was so terrible and her need so intense that she felt like crying. If the doctor began to touch her in that way, the consequences would be so humiliating.

'The girl doesn't keep still when I'm examining her,' the doctor remarked as Tabitha squirmed helplessly beneath his fingers. 'I think there must be something wrong.'

'Please stop, sir, please stop,' Tabitha sobbed. 'You're hurting me.'

'Hurting you? Does she have some stomach complaint?' enquired Dr Proctor.

Sir Edward laughed. 'I think not. The only problem Tabitha has is lack of self-control in all areas.'

Marianne continued to watch in dread, until suddenly Tabitha uttered a wail of despair and the doctor tutted his disapproval.

'You were right about her self-control, Edward. The wretched girl has wet herself.'

'That's the second time in the past three months,' said Sir Edward.

'I know, it's in my notebook,' replied his friend. 'It seems she's still unable to control herself, no matter how much treatment she receives. I shall continue treating her as I did last time. Eventually it will work.' The doctor sounded confident.

'It isn't my fault!' cried Tabitha, drawing her legs up to her stomach. 'We've been shut up here all the afternoon. It's because you kept poking me like that.'

'I'm quite sure Miss Marianne has better self-control,' said Sir Edward, and the two men turned to look at her.

Marianne couldn't help herself; she moaned and tried to scramble to the head of her bed. 'Don't touch me,' she said, her voice strained. 'Tabitha's quite right, it isn't fair.'

'My goodness, she's rather spirited for a companion, isn't she?' said the doctor.

'Extremely spirited.' Sir Edward nodded sagely. 'Both her flesh and her spirit need subduing.'

'You're fortunate to have such a considerate employer,' the doctor said to Marianne. 'Not many men are so concerned about their servants. Now, take off your clothes and I'll examine you. Mrs Fullick has already explained your various problems to me.'

'I don't have any problems,' Marianne protested indignantly.

'Stop arguing and remove your clothes,' snapped Sir Edward. 'Dr Proctor's a busy man. We don't have all night and there's a lot to be done.'

Marianne hesitated, and suddenly Sir Edward sat down on her bed and pulled her roughly over his knees. 'You will obey me,' he said through gritted teeth. 'However long it takes for you to learn that lesson.'

She started to struggle, but in vain, and soon his hand was rising and falling rhythmically against her bottom. Despite the protection of her dress and undergarments, it hurt. Even worse was the fact that because she was lying face down over his thighs the pressure on her bladder was intensified. She was terrified she was going to have an accident there and then while he was spanking her, and knew she had to stop the punishment before she lost control.

'I'm sorry… I'm sorry…' she gasped. 'I'll do as you say, I promise.'

It was clear Sir Edward was in no hurry to stop punishing her, for his hand continued to rise and fall rhythmically. 'You mean you won't cause any more problems during the whole evening?' he demanded.

'No… none,' she promised, mortified by the terrible indignities she was being made to endure. But despite everything she could feel her clitoris swelling, clamouring for a touch, however light, to trigger relief from the torment of trapped sexual arousal.

Sir Edward delivered one final blow that shook her shapely frame, then pushed her to the floor. 'Very well, I believe you. Remove your clothes immediately.'

Trembling from head to foot, Marianne obeyed while the two men watched, strangely silent. The room was heavy with a sense of forbidden eroticism.

Finally, after taking as long as she dared to undress, Marianne stood naked before them. Sir Edward murmured his approval, while Dr Francis Proctor gazed at her with an expression that was distinctly lascivious and totally unprofessional.

'I see what you mean about her form,' he remarked. 'She's certainly well rounded and looks as though she should eat less. However, until I've examined her thoroughly it's impossible to say whether this is caused by over-indulgence on your sister's part.'

Marianne couldn't believe they had the audacity to criticise her shapely figure, a figure she was very proud of and which always turned heads. Her heckles rose. 'How dare—'

'You speak only when given permission,' Sir Edward silenced her. 'Sometimes, Marianne, you seem to forget your place. Now, lie on the bed. The doctor wishes to examine you.'

'There's no need, I'm perfectly well,' she insisted.

'You'll do as you're told,' he said threateningly. 'You see, Francis,' he added in a lighter tone, 'I told you she'd presented me with problems.'

'I'm sure that with my assistance both body and spirit can be subdued,' replied his friend, and the two men exchanged surreptitious glances.

The doctor's hands slid slowly over Marianne's body. He began by examining her breasts, cupping them in the palms of his hands, his fingers moving smoothly over them and pulling lightly on each nipple until they started to swell. 'Her responses are quick for a woman of her class. Unmarried women of this age should not take such pleasure from a man's touch.'

'I regret to say Marianne's lascivious flesh is always quick to respond to a man's touch,' said Sir Edward.

'And her waist is interesting. I think the leather belt I

mentioned to you earlier must be worn each night. I'll measure her for it before I go and suggest the right notch for you to use. That, combined with the attachments that come with it, should help solve many of your problems, particularly since you fear self-abuse at night.'

Now his hands were moving over Marianne's stomach, lightly caressing the slight curve of her flesh. Marianne tensed. Already tormented by her full bladder, she didn't want to be touched. Yet despite this, she was becoming increasingly aroused as he examined her. Her traitorous body was more than ready to respond to the slightest touch.

Only when the doctor's fingers started to probe into the tender flesh above her pubic bone did she gasp with discomfort, because he was deliberately using a massaging movement, causing the dull aching in her bladder to spread. Incredibly, at the same time, this made her sex lips swell and she could feel she was growing damp between her thighs. Her body craved an orgasm but she was terrified of giving in to her need, because to climax during a medical examination would clearly be considered a punishable offence.

Also, she wasn't certain that if she came she would be able to control her bladder, and she dreaded shaming herself in the same way as Tabitha had. She attempted to twist away from the probing fingers and Sir Edward slapped her sharply across the breasts.

'Keep still,' he ordered. 'This is a medical examination. I expect intransigence from Tabitha, but not from you.'

'But he's hurting me,' she protested.

Sir Edward tweaked one of her rigid nipples. 'Hurting you, you say?' he mocked. 'But your body says otherwise.'

'I can't bear it,' she cried. 'May I not use the water-closet before the examination continues?'

'I need her like this for the examination,' replied Dr Proctor blandly, and she saw him exchange a smile with Sir Edward. Clearly the two of them were used to playing this game and her heart sank as she realised that, no matter how hard she tried, they were determined to make her do something which would allow them to punish her.

'Are you in discomfort?' asked Sir Edward, with apparent kindness.

Marianne didn't bother to answer him. She knew he was well aware how she felt. The brute was rejoicing in seeing her struggle against the paradoxical sensations he and his doctor friend were causing her.

The doctor took a notepad and quill pen from his leather medical bag, but instead of writing he started to tease her inner thighs with the feather, drawing it lightly over her damp flesh, then stopping just short of her throbbing nub of pleasure. She knew if he touched it she'd be lost. She longed for relief, but was terrified of the consequences. This dreadful mixture of need and fear seemed to act as an aphrodisiac; the greater her trepidation, the more her body responded to the cruel stimulation the two men were inflicting upon her. She held her breath, and then the tormenting feather flitted across her engorged clitoris.

'Oh no...' she whimpered. 'Please stop... I'm coming...'

'Such wanton behaviour,' Sir Edward said with disdain.

With a scream, she finally gave herself over to the contractions and heard herself crying out, begging for forgiveness even as her body was torn apart by savage spasms of bittersweet pleasure.

When her orgasm finally died away she was sure that at any moment she was going to disgrace herself and, to the obvious astonishment of both men, she struggled free and got up. 'I have to use the water-closet,' she announced, her head held high.

'Very well,' Sir Edward conceded, with admiration in his eyes. 'But then you are to return here instantly. Such lewd behaviour as you've exhibited calls for punishment. You and Tabitha have both transgressed during your examinations and the punishments will take place in the kitchen.'

Marianne sat on the water-closet and sobbed with a mixture of relief, shame and terror. She wasn't sure she could endure whatever lay in wait for her in the kitchen, but on the other hand, neither did she want to return to the safety of the modern day.

That decision made, it was easier for her to return to Tabitha's room and allow herself to be led, together with the distraught servant girl, down the stairs to the kitchen where Judith Fullick was waiting for them.

'The kitchen table's been scrubbed and prepared, Francis,' she said with a smile. The tone of her voice was so unusually gentile that Marianne looked sharply at her, and knew at once that Judith Fullick was infatuated with Dr Francis Proctor.

'I'm afraid both Tabitha and Marianne disgraced themselves during their examinations,' explained her brother. 'I wish Marianne to be punished first. I think a beating followed by a cleansing would be best.'

'Why does she need to be cleansed?' asked Judith.

'Because I want to take her,' said Sir Edward, his eyes locking on to Marianne's. 'I want to test this far too willing flesh, to take from her what she offers so wantonly.'

'I'm not offering myself to you,' Marianne said quietly. 'I can't help what my body does, it's the result of what you all do to me.'

'How dare you argue with my brother?' hissed Judith,

her usual spiteful persona returning instantly. 'Sometimes you seem to forget your place entirely.'

Marianne bit her lip. It was difficult to remember her place when she wasn't used to a subservient position in life.

She was manhandled into a corner of the kitchen. There, to her surprise and dismay, her arms were secured in the air by a hanging rope. Almost immediately her arms and her shoulders started to ache. A leather belt was tied tightly around her waist, the doctor tugging on it until she felt she could scarcely breathe.

'This is the belt she'll wear at night in future,' he explained to Sir Edward. 'It will also have a strap that will run between her thighs, fastening back and front. Either you or your sister will have to put it on each night and remove it each morning. That way self-abuse will be avoided.' With the belt in place, a cord was attached to it at the back and she was fastened to a metal ring set in the wall.

Naked apart from the belt, her hands above her head, Marianne watched, her body quivering, as Sir Edward busied himself at the sink. When he turned and faced her she saw he was holding a tightly rolled strip of damp towelling, and she shook her head. 'Please don't hit me with that,' she cried, knowing how much it would hurt.

'This is your punishment,' he said coldly. 'You should have behaved better during your examination.' As he advanced on her she could see Tabitha, Judith and Dr Francis Proctor were watching closely, Judith clutching the doctor's arm.

Sir Edward stood in front of Marianne with his back to the others in the room, and smiled at her. It was a genuine smile and her legs felt weak with shameful desire for him.

Then, as he continued to smile, he flicked his wrist sharply and the damp tip of the towel struck her just above the leather belt and below her breast. The pain was indescribable, and she screamed, only to scream again as he struck once more, this time below the other breast.

Relentlessly he continued to flick at her shrinking flesh until her breasts, shoulders and the area over her ribcage were red with raised weals. She couldn't stop herself from begging him to stop, but her distress only increased the savagery of the blows. When he did suddenly cease hitting her she could scarcely believe it. She slumped in her bonds and cried softly. 'Why do you like hurting me so much?' she sobbed.

'Because it excites you,' he said softly, 'and it excites me, too. In any case, you're never punished unless you deserve it. Sometimes I think you disobey deliberately because you enjoy the punishments.'

'I don't, I don't,' she protested, but even as she spoke the pain began to change into something else. Tingling warmth suffused her breasts and she knew her nipples were hardening.

'That's enough of a rest,' said Sir Edward, and Marianne yelped with renewed anguish as the brutal towel lashed across her lower belly and upper thighs. She was sobbing continually now, hating herself for crying out but unable to stop.

At last the beating ended. Sir Edward unrolled the towel and pressed the damp material to her burning flesh, gently moulding it to her. When he pressed the coolness against her belly, to her horror and total disbelief, she trembled from head to toe as a tiny climax rippled through her.

'You see,' whispered Sir Edward, his mouth close to her ear. 'You too like dark pleasures.'

Marianne wanted to tell him she didn't, that this had been too much, but it would have been a lie. No matter how much she denied it, her body had taken pleasure from the beating, although she was still unable to understand why.

She was removed from the bonds and the two men lifted her on to the kitchen table, which had been covered with more towels. Judith sat at the end where Marianne's head was and pressed down on her shoulders, while the doctor parted her legs and opened his bag. 'I'll make her clean for you,' he promised Sir Edward, who was standing looking down at Marianne. She looked back up at him, wondering what lay in store for her yet knowing that, whatever it might be, he was ultimately going to possess her.

She still wasn't prepared for what the doctor did next. Opening her up, he inserted a length of rubber tubing inside her vagina. It felt thick and strange, and as soon as it was in place she felt warm liquid gurgling out of the tube to flood her. She gasped, more in shock than discomfort.

'It's only a douche,' said Judith. 'My brother is naturally anxious about disease.'

Marianne knew this wasn't true. Sir Edward didn't really believe there was anything unclean about her, he simply wanted to savour her humiliation.

She began to cry, feeling trapped and shamed in front of them, but they ignored her. A few minutes later the doctor removed the rubber piping.

'I think that's enough,' he announced.

'Excellent,' said Sir Edward. 'I shall now take Marianne to my room. While we are gone I wish Tabitha to be totally cleansed and then the pair of you may punish her in any way you choose.' His fingers tightened around Marianne's wrists. As he dragged her from the room she glanced back over her shoulder.

Judith was placing fresh towels on the table and a timid Tabitha was being positioned on her side with her knees pressed up to her chest while the doctor was taking a particularly evil-looking contraption out of his bag, a contraption Marianne devoutly hoped would never be used on her. Then the door was slammed shut, cutting off Tabitha's cries, and she was hustled up the stairs and along the corridor to Sir Edward's bedroom.

Once inside she stared about her. It was beautifully furnished, with heavy gold and green drapes at the window. In the centre stood a large canopy bed with silk hangings. There were lit candles around the room, and a rocking chair in one corner.

'Now we're finally alone,' said Sir Edward. 'It will be interesting to see if we suit each other as well as I anticipate.' Marianne remained silent, having no idea whether she should speak or not. 'Have you nothing to say?' he asked.

'I – I'm afraid,' she whispered, knowing that, although the moment she had longed for was finally here, she spoke the truth.

'How wise of you,' he said dryly, and led her over to the waiting bed.

Chapter Eight

Marianne's eyes searched Sir Edward Sharpe's face as she tried desperately to read his emotions, but it was impossible. As usual, his eyes were bright with excitement but his expression was impassive. She longed to see a softening in his features, some indication that he desired her because she was special rather than because she was helpless and his to do with as he wished.

'Why are you looking at me like that?' he asked.

Hastily Marianne lowered her eyes. 'I'm sorry,' she murmured.

He gave a harsh laugh. 'Not as sorry as you'll be by the time I've finished with you.'

She wanted to ask him why, needing to discover why he felt this need to hurt her, but she didn't dare frame the question. Instead she waited, quivering from head to toe. Despite his words, she felt her body tighten with desire.

'I don't think I want you wearing the leather belt,' he remarked, reaching for the buckle. For a second, as he pulled it tighter in order to release it, Marianne found herself unable to breathe. She gave a gasp of relief when she was released from its confining stricture. As he ran a finger round the deep red indentation left behind she felt the sensitive flesh leap beneath his touch.

'How delicious,' he said to himself, before picking her up and depositing her in the centre of the canopied bed. The mattress was soft and deep, her head was resting on a mass of pillows and the silken fabric of the bedding was highly sensual against her bare skin. She watched as Sir Edward removed his clothes before pulling on a brocade dressing gown, then sat on the bed next to her supine form.

For a moment he simply stared down at her, and everywhere his eyes travelled her flesh began to glow, as though his gaze radiated a strange warmth. Then, when he'd seen all he wanted, he gave a guttural groan of desire and buried his head between her soft breasts.

'Such glorious, wanton curves,' he mumbled, his teeth gently grazing the yielding flesh. Marianne sighed with delight. This was what she'd longed for; to feel him touching her in a normal way, to have him making love to her as though concerned about her pleasure. His mouth covered hers and she felt his lips urgent against her own. His tongue probed her mouth, searching until it met hers.

The kiss went on for a long time, and as they kissed his hands were on her breasts, caressing them, lightly teasing the nipples to hardness. Soon she was murmuring sensually as she responded to his skilful lovemaking.

When his mouth left hers she wanted to pull his head back down. Remembering she was meant to be Marianne Clifford, who would never have done any such thing, she kept her arms by her sides, and when his tongue began to lick lightly down the slender column of her throat she swooned. He moved his mouth and tongue up and down the delicate flesh, and all the time he was caressing her breasts. Soon her breathing grew rapid and she could feel her sex opening for him, already anticipating the moment when he'd plunge into her, filling the aching void his touch was creating.

Gradually, with deliberate slowness, he kissed lower down her body. Occasionally he nipped her flesh between his teeth, but the tiny flashes of discomfort only heightened her excitement and she moved restlessly as the pleasure seemed to swamp her. She felt as though she was melting, liquid already seeping from her entrance. At last, to her delight, his head was between her thighs and he was licking away the evidence of her excitement, his tongue briefly moving inside her, swirling around for one bliss-inducing moment that almost brought her to orgasm. At last she felt his tongue travelling towards her yearning clitoris and, despite her best intentions, she gave a cry of excitement.

'Oh yes... *yes*!' she gasped.

Immediately he lifted his head, shifting his body until his face was once more level with hers, and then he kissed her hard again, forcing her to taste her own juices. 'How dare you!' he hissed threateningly, while his fingers tightened cruelly around her breasts. 'Have you no sense of decency at all? Do you think I don't know what you want?'

'I just want you,' she sobbed with frustration. 'Is that so wrong?'

'You're trying to trap me,' he accused furiously. 'You with your ripe curves, your lush charms and your air of false innocence. Do you think I'm a complete fool? Do you really believe I'd let a girl like you become important to me?'

Marianne didn't know how to reply, but she was beginning to understand what motivated Sir Edward. Clearly this cruel, sexually perverse man was obsessed with his sister's companion, but he hated himself for it. She sensed that whilst he claimed to be attempting to subdue her flesh, he was actually trying to subdue his own by destroying the hapless Marianne.

'Look at you,' he continued, flicking contemptuously

at her breasts with a series of rapid blows that had her squealing at the injustice. 'No decent young lady would behave the way you are. No decent young lady should take pleasure in any of this.'

'Then why are you doing it to me?' she wailed.

'You want me, do you?' he continued, ignoring her question. 'Very well then, you shall have me.'

Tearing off his robe, he caught hold of Marianne and turned her roughly over before pushing a bolster, folded double, beneath her hips so her buttocks were raised high into the air. 'Don't move,' he ordered as he left the bed.

Marianne turned her head and saw him take a small cut-glass bottle from a mahogany table. He removed the stopper and poured some sort of fragrant oil over his fingers, before returning to the bed and placing the bottle beside it. She felt him parting her buttocks with one hand and then, even as she realised what he was about to do and tried to twist away, he gripped her tightly and thrust two oiled fingers inside the puckered opening, invading her where she'd never been invaded before.

It hurt. Marianne screamed but he merely pushed her face into the bed, muffling the sound, before continuing to move his fingers in and out while she sobbed.

Despite everything, despite the humiliation and discomfort, she wanted to stay with Sir Edward in his time, to find out what else he had planned for her. She curled her fists into the bedspread, determined to keep back her cries of protest, and gradually realised that the pain was changing to a different sensation. As his educated fingers moved waves of pleasure rolled through her. Soon she could feel the heavy pulse of rising desire throbbing within her.

She was no longer aware of any pain, only a perverse

excitement, and she groaned at the realisation of how much Sir Edward was changing her.

As she relaxed and embraced the sensations, Sir Edward withdrew his fingers. He gripped her hips with both hands, and she felt the tip of his erection nudging insistently at the opening where his fingers had so recently been. She was uncertain, fearful that this intrusion would be much worse. Yet she had to know, had to discover whether this, too, would give her pleasure. He moved against her, sliding inside her just a fraction, but even that was enough to make her hold her breath anxiously.

Seeming to sense her reticence, Sir Edward reached lower and caressed her sex lips, which had swollen and parted in their shameful excitement. He massaged around her clitoris, although never touching the tiny swollen nub directly, and soon she was writhing in ecstasy as her enjoyment increased again and her muscles grew taut with desire.

She was very close to coming now, totally open and vulnerable, her flesh desperate for ultimate satisfaction. For a moment he allowed two fingers to enter her but, as she tightened herself greedily around him, he withdrew those fingers and sank his erection into her bottom with one smooth thrust of his hips.

For a moment Marianne froze. The pain returned, temporarily blotting out all pleasure, and her body, confused by the conflicting signals, halted its inexorable rise to orgasm, leaving her stranded.

'Relax,' he whispered gruffly. 'Don't fight me. You feel so tight and delicious. Don't you want to give me pleasure too?'

'Yes, I do…' she wept softly. 'I do…'

'Then stop resisting me.'

Marianne tried to obey him, breathing slowly and deeply to relax, and slowly the discomfort ebbed again. Now as he moved inside her there was only pleasure, and she gave herself over to his control totally.

He seemed to recognise the moment when her resistance vanished because his hips moved more insistently while, at the same time, his fingers began to caress her sex again. She could feel her climax approaching once more and when he coaxed her clitoris she screamed with delight. A red mist seemed to settle in her brain and all she wanted was to be further debased and humiliated. She longed for this terrible form of pleasuring to continue so that her body would finally be free of its incredible tension.

Sir Edward's breathing rasped harshly, and through her own swirling orgasm Marianne knew he too was on the point of no return. She heard herself wantonly encouraging him, and Sir Edward finally spent inside her previously virginal and most private of places.

After a few minutes she felt him slip free, and waited for him to pull her from the bed. But to her surprise he lay down beside her exhausted form, catching her face between his hands and staring intently into her eyes.

'Well, well. You're full of surprises, aren't you, little Marianne. Who could have pictured a scene like this on the day I interviewed you?'

She didn't want to look at him, didn't want to admit how much pleasure she was getting from the dreadful things he was doing to her, but his hands kept her face imprisoned and his eyes held hers with arrogant ease. He smiled at her obvious discomfort.

'You're ashamed, aren't you? And so you should be. I hate to think what Dr Proctor will have to say when he hears of this.'

Marianne was mortified. 'Please – please don't tell him,' she begged.

'But he's your physician and he's trying to subdue your flesh. Should he not know everything about your lascivious nature?'

Marianne felt tears welling in her eyes. 'I know it's wrong,' she sobbed. 'But I can't help it. The things you do are terrible, and yet...'

'And yet they please you,' he said confidently.

'Yes,' she whispered shamefully.

'Then Francis and I must continue to work on you until you become a respectable woman again.'

'But that's not what you really want,' she said without thinking. 'You like me like this.'

His expression darkened. 'I trust you're not arguing with me, Marianne?'

'Oh, no, of course not,' she hastily corrected herself.

'Good... good.' His possessive hands released her face and she turned sulkily onto her back, staring up at the canopy above her. Her lover, because that was how she now thought of him, reached down to the floor and picked up the glass bottle from which he'd taken the oil earlier. He poured some more into the palm of one hand before beginning to massage it into her breasts and belly. It felt wonderful; his touch was once more gentle and attentive, the movements gliding, quietening her over-stimulated flesh until she felt her eyelids begin to droop.

'It seems you have an infinite capacity for pleasure,' he remarked, his fingers moving insistently over the soft flesh of her thighs.

'Please stop,' she murmured, but her voice carried no conviction.

'Your body does not say that,' he replied curtly. 'Subdue

your flesh and I will stop.'

Marianne groaned. It was impossible to resist these astonishingly delicious caresses. Her nipples were erect, showing clearly that his touch was arousing her once more.

Marianne heard Sir Edward chuckle quietly when he parted her sex lips, and she instinctively flinched, pressing herself down into the bed to try and escape the falling drops of oil she knew would only heighten her desire even more. Escape, however, was impossible. She was moaning, her head rolling restlessly on the pillows while he remorselessly massaged the oil around her sex lips, into the incredibly sensitive channel and around the clitoris, still recovering from her previous orgasm.

'How swollen with lust you are,' he murmured thoughtfully, his hand cupping her sex. 'I wish you could see yourself.'

Marianne didn't need to. She could tell precisely what was happening to her.

'You like this?' he asked, lightly gliding an oiled fingertip over the head of her clitoris.

'Yes,' she gasped, 'I love it.'

'And this?' His fingers moved inside her, stimulating, teasing. She groaned, her pleasure threatening to peak again.

'Oh, yes,' she murmured.

'I don't want your pleasure to spill until I permit it.'

The very fact that she was forbidden to come whilst so near the edge was almost enough to precipitate her pleasure, and she moaned despairingly as his knowing fingers continued their mischievous duties. She held her breath, closed her eyes, and concentrated as best she could – but the inevitable happened. With a violent shuddered she groaned and climaxed as the oiled fingers drew every last drop of ecstasy from her drained body.

'You are a wanton little hussy,' he accused icily. 'I find it difficult to imagine how Francis and I are ever going to control you. There's no doubt in my mind that you will need a great deal of discipline.'

Clearly the prospect delighted him. In a strange way it delighted Marianne, too, but it also made her fearful. 'Why do you do this to me?' she asked weakly. 'I don't understand you.'

'It isn't your place to understand me,' he said, getting off the bed and pulling his robe on once more.

Marianne sat up. 'Do you wish me to go now?'

Sir Edward shook his head. 'Position yourself over the bolster again, face down.'

She glanced at him and saw, through the opening in his brocade dressing gown, that he was once more erect. With no resistance left, she obeyed without another word.

'Keep your face in the bedspread and your eyes closed,' he ordered. When she seemed to be positioned exactly as he wanted, she was astonished to hear him open the bedroom door and start talking. Because of what he'd said she didn't dare lift her head to see what was happening. Instead she waited, every muscle tight with fearful anticipation. Then the door closed and she heard two sets of footsteps moving to the bed.

'There she is,' she heard Sir Edward say. 'You know what you have to do, John. I trust you won't disappoint me.'

'Of course not, sir,' she heard the lad gabble, and only then did she summon the courage to lift her head. Glancing back she saw the young gardener tugging at his breeches, clearly unable to believe his good fortune.

'What are you doing?' she implored, as Sir Edward

looked down at her. 'I don't want him in here.'

'You're living under my roof and this is my bedroom,' he replied. 'You're in no position to question what I do.'

'But this is all wrong,' she persisted desperately. 'Why do you want him to have me?'

'Because it amuses me.'

'Well, it doesn't amuse me,' she shouted, suddenly losing her temper. 'I don't want him. Do you understand? I don't want him and I won't have him!'

Immediately the sound of her voice began to die away, the room started to fade and Sir Edward's features grew dim. For once Marianne didn't mind. To be violated in that way by him was one thing, but to allow him to watch while another man did it to her was entirely different and she knew she couldn't have borne the humiliation.

'Why do you always spoil things?' she heard Sir Edward saying softly. 'You must learn to want what I want, Marianne. That way lies your happiness and your salvation.'

His words were still ringing in her head when she opened her eyes and found she was lying in the king-sized bed she and Steve had brought to Moorhead House. In a moment of terrible clarity, she wondered if his words were true.

For the first time Marianne was in a different room to the one she'd been in when she left the modern day. And, since sunlight was clearly visible through the window, time had moved on. Did this mean the past and the present were becoming more closely entwined? An icy finger slithered down her spine as she wondered what effect this might have on her in the future. Until now she'd been able to witness scenes from the past even when people were with her, and without them knowing. But if she were to start moving physically into the room she was seeing, then it would be obvious that something incredible was happening. Perhaps, she thought, this was what had happened to Judith Wells. Total isolation from outsiders would have to become a necessity if she was to keep her secret.

As she climbed off the bed she realised she was aching. She was sore between the cheeks of her bottom, as though her recent violation was still affecting her, and her flesh felt sore from the beating she'd received with the cold towel. Suddenly anxious to see if there were any visible signs of her torment she hurried into her great-aunt's old bedroom where there was a free-standing full-length mirror. There she took off her clothes in order to study herself carefully.

At first glance there didn't seem to be anything wrong with her. She ran her hands down over the sides of her body, lingering at her waist and hips, remembering the way the doctor's hands had pressed inwards there. She had an excellent figure, she thought indignantly, gently voluptuous without being in the least fat. In the nineteenth century women's waists had been tiny, fiercely laced in order to keep an hourglass figure, and she could tell that by those unnatural standards she would perhaps appear overweight. As she recalled the way she'd felt when the doctor had touched her she saw her nipples harden and stepped nearer to the mirror, cupping her breasts together, pushing them close so they jutted forward proudly.

It was then, as she stared at her naked body, that she noticed the tiny red marks beneath her breasts, marks where the stinging corner of the towel had caught her tender flesh. Startled, she ran a finger over her skin and felt the slightly raised welt. This was worrying. If she was now bringing back visible proof of what had happened to her then how much longer would it be before she started to change in other ways?

With a frown she started to dress, and a feeling of melancholy crept over her like a heavy blanket. Now she was back in the safety of her normal life she was beginning to wish she'd remained behind. She'd missed the opportunity to see how Edward would have responded to watching her being buggered by the young gardener, and suddenly that was important to her. And how would she have responded? Would she have submitted without a fight?

'I'll never know,' she said miserably. 'Why did I choose to come back?'

The answer was that she'd been afraid, and rightly so, but she knew the more trips she took back to join Sir Edward the more lost she'd become in that world until, eventually, it was possible that all prudence would vanish. 'I must be careful,' she muttered. 'He's dangerous.' But even saying the words excited her. Yes, he was dangerous. But that was why she was falling in love with him. Realising there was little chance of seeing him again in the immediate future, she decided to use the experience in her book.

The newspaper lying on the hall mat confirmed that it was now Monday morning, and thirty minutes later her fingers were flying over the computer keys as the words poured in a torrent of erotic description. Although she'd changed the names of the characters and slightly altered the situation, she was describing in minute detail the erotic torments she was suffering at Sir Edward's hands. By writing them down she was able to relive her experiences, bringing them vividly to life again and she knew that, despite Steve's criticism, her writing was more powerful than it had ever been.

When the phone rang she was immensely irritated. Certain it was Steve she snatched at the receiver. 'Yes?' she said curtly.

'Is that you, Marianne?' asked her agent, Angela.

Marianne quickly changed her tone. 'Angela, it's you. I'm sorry, I thought you were someone who lives nearby. She keeps trying to come over when I'm working and it's infuriating.'

'So you're working, are you? That's good news. How much have you done now?'

'I've no idea,' said Marianne. 'Quite a lot.'

'You must know how many pages.'

Marianne glanced at her computer screen. 'Um, a hundred and fifty,' she confirmed.

'Excellent,' said Angela. 'You normally take months to write a book. At this rate you'll be finished in a few weeks.'

'It is going well,' admitted Marianne.

'And is it an erotic historical novel or the one you originally promised to deliver?'

'It's an erotic book, the one I told you about.'

Angela sighed. 'I really don't think that's your kind of thing, Marianne. You've never done anything like it before and when you've had to put small sex scenes into your books they haven't been particularly convincing.'

'Well, they're certainly convincing now.' Marianne smiled to herself.

'Do you think you could fax me a sex scene?' asked her agent. 'Send the pages through now and I'll have a quick look at them. Then I'll call you back and let you know what I think.'

Marianne hesitated. 'I don't want anyone to see this until it's finished,' she said at last.

'What's got into you, Marianne?' Angela asked, her tone suggesting she was losing patience with her author. 'You've always been so easy to deal with. You know perfectly well that I've got to look at it. It isn't as though you're writing the book you're meant to be writing. How can I go to your editor and tell her you're writing an incredibly steamy novel if I haven't seen any of it? I've got to sell this thing, you know. In fact, you've put me in a very difficult position. The least you can do now is let me have a look at it, and quickly.'

Marianne knew Angela was right. The problem was the book felt private, like a diary. She didn't want other people snooping around looking at it, reading about the things she and Edward had done or the things she'd seen him do to Tabitha.

'Well?' demanded Angela.

Marianne sighed. 'All right, I'll fax you some of the work I've done today. It'll take me a few minutes to run them off the computer so I hope you don't mind waiting that long.' She couldn't keep a note of sarcasm out of her voice.

'I think I can accept that,' said Angela. 'I'll be in the office for the rest of the day.'

After exchanging a few strained pleasantries the conversation ended and Marianne was left to run off her most recent work. When she read it through her cheeks turned pink. By anyone's standards it was an extraordinarily explicit piece of writing and she knew it would be difficult for Angela to believe that she, Marianne Kay, had really written it. Nevertheless, she eventually faxed six pages through to her agent's office and then went to make herself a coffee while she waited for the phone to ring.

She had to wait for over an hour and was just wondering whether or not she could go for a walk on the moors when the call came.

'I've read the pages you faxed me,' said Angela, her voice carefully controlled.

'What do you think?' asked Marianne eagerly.

'If you want to know the truth, I'm shocked. This isn't acceptable, Marianne. Robertson and Hall don't publish this sort of filth.'

'It isn't filth,' protested Marianne. 'It's erotica.'

'Really? And how would you know?'

'I—'

'Look, I think I can guess what's happened,' said Angela briskly. 'You've moved house, for all I know you've got yourself a new lover, and you want a change. Fine, but wait until you've delivered the original book. After that you can write what you like if it makes you happy. Not that I'm going to be able to place this anywhere, but if it's what you want to do—'

'What do you mean, you won't be able to place it anywhere?' Marianne interrupted. 'This is an incredibly arousing story.'

'Marianne, it's horrible,' said Angela. 'We're not living in Victorian times. Women are emancipated, in control of everything – including their sex lives. They don't want to read this sort of thing.'

'How do you know that?' demanded Marianne. 'I thought erotic novels were all the rage now.'

'Even if this is the sort of thing that's selling in that particular area, it's not something I want to deal with,' said Angela firmly. 'It may be something you need to get out of your system, and that's fine by me, but I'm not sending it around a series of publishers. I do have a reputation to consider and so do you, Marianne. You're a very well respected romantic novelist. You'll shock your readers.'

'I'll use a pseudonym.'

'You can't use a pseudonym for this contract. They want a Marianne Kay book, and that's what you've got to deliver.'

'Are you saying you're not going to take this book?' asked Marianne.

There was a long pause. 'I don't think I can. Do you want to cancel your contract with Robertson and Hall?'

'God, no!' exclaimed Marianne. 'I need the money.'

'In that case I need the book. Write your new one when you've finished it.'

'When have I got to deliver this romantic novel by?' asked Marianne.

'You've still got four months.'

'But, I don't know if I can write it now.'

'You told me your new house and the surroundings were perfect for writing a rollercoaster of a romantic novel. That's how we got such a large advance. Has the house changed or something?'

A chill ran through Marianne. Without realising, it Angela had put her finger on the real problem. The house *had* changed: it was no longer a cosy retreat from the world, the ideal place for a writer to work. The house was possessed, and so too, was she.

'Marianne, are you still there?'

'Yes, sorry, I was miles away. No, it's not the house that's changed, it's me.'

'You've found someone, haven't you?' asked Angela,

with a knowing laugh.

Marianne hesitated. 'In a way,' she said slowly.

'Goodness! Well, have we got an agreement then?'

'I suppose so.'

'Excellent. Fax me the first chapter as soon as it's done and then I can tell Elaine that you're well on with it. A slight exaggeration, but what else are agents for?'

'I suppose I ought to thank you,' said Marianne.

'Not if you don't mean it,' said Angela crisply. 'Oh, Marianne, I'm beginning to wish you'd never moved out of London.'

'Sometimes, I wish the same,' said Marianne slowly. 'I must go now, there's someone at the door,' she lied, before hanging up.

Would it have been better if she hadn't left London? It would have been safer, certainly, but then she'd never have known the incredible pleasure, the wonderful, frightening sensuality of Sir Edward Sharpe, nor witnessed the incredible scenes of punishment and humiliation that Tabitha and John were forced to endure at the hands of their employers. No, it wouldn't have been better because she knew that this was a world that excited her. But it was a world that no longer existed and, in order to satisfy her craving for it, she had to keep letting Edward possess her by taking her back in time.

'I wonder what he really wants of me,' she mused. 'Are we just replaying scenes from the past or is he looking for some kind of ending?' There were no answers. She could make educated guesses but, in the end, only by going further along the path that Judith Wells had trodden before her would she find the truth.

After lunch, Marianne tried to concentrate on the commissioned book. She read through her first attempt and threw it aside in disgust. It seemed feeble, so lacking in truth and depth. The characters were simply playing at romantic love with no understanding of what obsession meant. Before she'd moved to Moorhead House, Marianne would have thought the book well up to standard, but now she was different and less easily satisfied.

Deciding that the best thing to do was start again she gritted her teeth and once more began her modern equivalent of *Wuthering Heights*. She worked away for the entire afternoon, only now she wished someone would ring her to give her a break. As was always the way at times like this, no one did. However, just before tea Steve finally called.

'I thought you'd like to know I'm in London,' he said cheerily. 'I'm going to take in a film at Leicester Square tonight. I wish you were here, Marianne.'

'Well, I don't,' she snapped.

'Come on, you must miss the bright lights a little bit,' he teased.

'I don't,' she said truthfully. 'I wouldn't go back there if you paid me.'

'You're still angry about what I said before I left, aren't you?'

'No, I'm not angry, I just think your reaction was rather pathetic.'

'I didn't know you had that sort of imagination, that's all,' he said, defending himself. 'Does that kind of thing really turn you on?'

'You know what turns me on.'

'I thought I did, but lately you've been showing me a whole new side of yourself. I admit I'm enjoying it, but that stuff you've written is nothing like what we're doing. It's so extreme. Your hero's an absolute sadist. No woman would want a man like that.'

Marianne wanted to scream 'I do!' down the phone at him, but she bit her tongue. 'It's a fantasy.'

'If you want the truth, I don't like it because it's too realistic.'

'What do you mean, realistic?'

'I get the feeling you've really done those things, Marianne. Your descriptions of the way the heroine responds to everything that happens to her – you couldn't write that if you hadn't felt it.'

'Now you're being utterly ridiculous,' she said, wishing he hadn't been so perceptive. 'When have I ever mixed with those sort of people?'

'I don't know…'

Marianne laughed dismissively, but without conviction. 'Surely you can't think I've got a lover, Steve?'

'I don't know what to think,' he muttered. 'How do I know what you do when I'm away? You're always wandering off on the moors. Perhaps you've met some stranger there and you and he indulge in weird games together.'

'You've no idea how ridiculous you sound.'

'Has Angela seen any of the book yet?' he asked.

'Yes, she has.'

'And what did she think?'

'The same as you,' she admitted.

'Then what are you going to do?'

'I'm trying to write the book I was meant to write in the first place, and I'm loathing every minute of it,' she said with feeling.

'If you have got someone else, Marianne, if you're

messing around when I'm away, I'll find out and believe me I'll make him sorry,' he said calmly, but she could detect his simmering rage.

'There isn't anyone,' she said. 'If there was I'd tell you. We're not married, I don't have to stay with you. I stay with you because I want to.'

'Is that true?'

'Yes,' she assured him, and in a way it was true. There wasn't any other flesh and blood male she wanted to be with; she'd been seduced away from him by a spirit, and for obvious reasons that was something she could never talk about – not even to him.

'I don't know what to say,' he admitted. 'Perhaps it's not such a good idea, me travelling around so much and leaving you alone. Maybe I don't give you enough attention.'

'I need solitude for my work, I always have done. You travelled when we were in London.'

'I know, but we had more friends down here. Now everything's changed.'

'Nothing would have changed if you hadn't read the manuscript. Perhaps that'll teach you not to go poking and prying into my work.'

'I never shall again,' he said contritely.

Marianne wished she could tell him the truth, but she couldn't change things. Sir Edward Sharpe and his household were steadily staking their claim on her, taking her away from Steve, her work and reality. This possession seemed inevitable, utterly beyond her control, but she felt that if she could only get to the end of her journey of discovery, learn what it was Sir Edward wanted of her and experience the full extent of his desires, then perhaps she'd be set free. Maybe, after that, real life would seem more attractive again.

'I've got to go or I won't have time to eat before the film starts,' said Steve. 'Good luck with the book.'

'When are you coming home?' she asked.

'I don't know,' he said evasively. 'You'll see me when you see me. Love you, Marianne.'

She didn't reply. It was obvious what he was doing. He intended to come home unexpectedly, hoping to catch her with the lover his fevered imagination had conjured up. She could understand it. Her behaviour must seem extraordinary, totally out of character, but the truth was even more bizarre.

'What am I going to do?' she said aloud. 'What's going to happen to me, Edward?' She half wondered if he'd answer her, if he'd still manage to hear her voice through the many years between them, but nothing happened, and she felt stupid. She was completely alone. Alone to contemplate past and present and try to work out where she truly belonged.

Chapter Nine

The following afternoon Marianne was still struggling with her romance novel. She needed to get it to a standard where she felt able to send a sample to Angela, but it was proving difficult. By three o'clock she felt she was beginning to get somewhere, but the atmosphere wasn't right. Having set the story on the Yorkshire moors, it was important that every detail added to the description, but she felt she was repeating herself and decided to take a notebook and pencil out to the moors to jot down the many sights and sounds she experienced.

It was another windy day, chill despite the sun, and a few threatening clouds were scudding across the sky. For a moment Marianne wondered if she was being wise or whether it would be better to wait a little longer, as the weather could be so changeable. No, she had to get the book in order before teatime.

She set off along the footpath, but after about ten minutes decided to branch out in a different direction. This part of the moor was far more hilly than her usual route, and as she pushed on she grew slightly breathless. The scenery was incredibly beautiful, wild and rugged, and the glorious colours of the heather made her wish she was a good artist and able to capture it all in a painting.

She walked on, deciding she'd go as far as the top of the first hill where she could see a large boulder. The sky was growing darker and it seemed foolish to attempt to go further than that. As it was, it would take her a good twenty-five minutes to get back home.

Suddenly, out of nowhere, Edward Sharpe appeared in front of her, as though conjured up by her imaginings. He was wearing dark knee breeches and shiny black boots, while his shirt was white with a ruffle down the front of it. A grey waistcoat completed his outfit. The wind buffeted him, ruffling his shirtsleeves and making his hair dance. His powerful presence filled Marianne with such intense joy that she wanted to fling her arms around him. Only the realisation that she was now Marianne Clifford stopped her.

'You came, then?' he said, his brooding eyes fixed on hers. 'What did you tell my sister?'

'That I had a letter for the mail coach.'

'Did she not ask to whom you had written?' Marianne shook her head. 'I see. Come along, we haven't much time.' Taking her hand, he pulled her up to the top of the hill, as far as the boulder where she'd been intending to go anyway. 'You should have worn a cape,' he admonished paternally. 'The wind is fresh.'

Marianne looked down at herself and saw that this time she was wearing a coarse green linen gown, less warm than her usual woollen one. 'I was in such a hurry I forgot,' she explained.

'You have still to learn patience,' he said, and then his arms entrapped her and he began to kiss her harshly. She responded instantly, melting into his embrace. She felt him lifting her off the ground, moving her around to the other side of the boulder and out of the teeth of the wind. Then, without warning, he pushed her away and she staggered back against the boulder. 'Here's your companion, Judith,' he said with a laugh. 'As you rightly guessed, there was no letter.'

Marianne gave a gasp of horror. Clearly Edward had lured her here deliberately, but he must also have alerted his sister to what was happening. She was trapped, betrayed by her own desire for the man.

'I told you that she lies constantly to me,' said Judith.

'But Sir Edward said he wanted to see me,' stammered Marianne.

'Why didn't you tell me that, instead of lying?'

'Because...' Her voice trailed off hopelessly.

'Because she knew she had no right to meet me,' sneered Edward.

'You tricked me,' cried Marianne.

'I tested you,' he corrected her. 'That's an entirely different thing. What are we going to do with her?' he asked, turning to his sister.

Judith glanced at Marianne, who had pressed back against the boulder in a desperate attempt to get away from them, knowing all the while that it was hopeless. 'Punish her, of course,' she said casually.

'Fortunately, I've come prepared for that,' replied her brother. At that moment the sun came out briefly. 'Take off your gown,' he instructed Marianne. She hesitated, but when he took a step towards her she changed her mind. Within seconds she was stepping out of her dress to leave her standing on the moors clad only in a bodice with ribbons down the front, long cotton drawers and silk stockings.

Without a word Sir Edward started to undo the ribbons, tugging gently, peeling the bodice back from her skin, and she felt the warmth of the sun coupled with the faintest of breezes on her exposed flesh.

He didn't expose her breasts entirely; instead, he bent his head and began to suck and lick at her nipples through the material. The sensation was exquisite, far more subtle than normal, and despite her situation, Marianne felt her body respond as her nipples hardened and her breasts swelled. His hands were also fondling her through her underwear and, after a few moments of this, she realised that she wanted to feel his touch on her bare flesh, but there was nothing she could do except wait and see what lay in store for her.

While he contented himself with her breasts, Judith slowly pulled down her drawers. She was forced to lift first one leg and then the other as her shoes were removed, enabling Judith to pull off the cotton drawers and discard them. Now the woman was able to slide her hands up the silk stockings until she reached the soft flesh at the top of Marianne's thighs.

Sir Edward suckled Marianne's nipples, drawing both flesh and material into his mouth, and her belly began to tremble.

'She's starting to get damp,' Judith noted, her fingers exploring between Marianne's sex lips.

'Is she opening up yet?' enquired her brother.

Marianne gasped as Judith's fingers intruded yet further, pressing against the entrance to her vagina. 'Not really.'

'Perhaps she isn't receiving enough stimulation,' he murmured, lifting his mouth from Marianne's breasts for a moment. 'The leather belt is in my back pocket, Judith.'

'I don't want to be hit,' cried Marianne, but her protest was in vain. While her brother kept Marianne pinned against the boulder Judith stepped slightly to the side, drew back her arm and then, with practised aim, cracked the belt across Marianne's stomach, the end just catching her on the hip.

Marianne gave a cry of protest as pain seared through

her, but she could feel her nipples tighten even more. 'It seems I was right,' Sir Edward observed. 'Feel her again, Judith.'

Judith's fingers once more explored the folds of Marianne's sex, and this time they slid into her more easily.

'Your pleasure's very near now, isn't it?' Edward asked her.

Marianne knew there was no point in lying to him. 'Yes,' she whispered.

'Excellent,' he said briskly, and promptly stepped away from her. 'I think it's time we removed all her clothes, Judith. Although you used the belt well, it would have been more efficient if it had fallen on naked flesh.'

Marianne was horrified. Despite the protection of material the pain had been severe. The prospect of being beaten without anything between the belt and her skin filled her with dread, yet this dread was tinged with a desire she still didn't understand. 'Please don't do this to me,' she sobbed. 'I really don't like the pain.'

'If that were true your body would tell us so,' said Sir Edward coldly, and then he did expose her breasts to the moorland air, stripping all garments from her, including her stockings.

The sun had gone in. Marianne's teeth started to chatter, but whether from cold, fear, or a mixture of both, she couldn't tell. All she knew was that, despite everything, she was once more filled with a terrible desire to be brought to a climax by this sadistic stranger who gave pleasure with one hand and took it away with the other, leaving her in a perpetual state of bewilderment and need.

'Face the rock,' he said as she stood shivering before him and his sister. She turned, and then he pushed her hard between the shoulder blades until her tender breasts made contact with the harsh surface of the ancient rock. It hurt and she tried to draw away, but he merely pressed harder, squashing her yet more.

Then he parted her legs before pressing her lower back forward so the entire front of her body was touching the rough stone. She realised that when the first blow fell her body would rub against it even harder, adding to the pain of the blow. She started to whimper, tears rolling down her face.

'Why are you crying?' asked Judith. 'This is what you enjoy. This is why you came out here. You wanted to meet my brother and be treated like this.'

'I didn't want to be treated like this,' cried Marianne. 'I just wanted him to make love to me.'

'My brother's never made love to anyone in his life,' retorted Judith. 'You enjoy the way he gives you pleasure. Why is it different when I'm the one administering the punishment?'

'It seems to me she's insulting you, Judith,' remarked Edward. 'You must make sure the blows are strong ones.'

Marianne stared at the boulder only inches from her face and tensed in readiness of the first blow. She was expecting it to be on her buttocks or thighs but, when it fell, it was high up on her back, and this time the tip of the leather belt curled round beneath her breast so that a flickering tongue of fire exploded across her ribcage. Throwing back her head she screamed, but a gust of wind carried her protests away.

'Shout as much as you like,' said Sir Edward. 'There's no one to hear you.'

Marianne knew he was right. Just the same, when the second blow fell she screamed again, the burning intensifying, and after the blow had fallen the pain continued to increase until it threatened to consume her. It was soon apparent that Judith intended to work her way systematically down Marianne's back, and by the time Judith was striking the lower half of her buttocks Marianne was crying in earnest, her fingernails desperately scrabbling at the unyielding stone.

The pain from the blows would have been terrible enough on its own but, in addition, she was forced to endure torment from the boulder as her skin was grazed by its roughness. Every time her body jerked under the impact of the leather belt the rock agitated her poor flesh.

'Please, please make her stop,' she begged of Sir Edward as his sister paused for breath.

'Are you sorry?' he asked.

'Yes, yes I am,' sobbed Marianne, who'd entirely forgotten what she was being punished for.

'I'm not certain my sister's ready to forgive you yet,' he said in mock regret. 'Perhaps one more blow.'

'Please, no,' cried Marianne.

'Your skin looks wonderful like this,' he said, running his fingers delicately over her blazing flesh. 'So warm and arousing.' He licked his fingers and she felt a cool, damp sensation on the burning weals as he began to trace their outline down her body. At this dreadful moment, as she awaited the final blow, the agony turned to ecstasy and the liquid warmth began within her once again.

'Just one more, Judith,' Edward said, and as Marianne tensed she felt desire knotting her lower belly. Then, as the blow fell and she was forced against the face of the boulder, she felt a throbbing in her clitoris and suddenly she was coming, her muscles pulsating in harsh contractions that took her abused and burning body by surprise.

Whilst Marianne was enduring her orgasm, Judith fell to her knees and thrust two fingers inside her sex. She touched the inner walls with a steady pressure that caused an ache deep within Marianne, an ache that mingled with the final contractions. It seemed to extend her climax so she continued shuddering and gasping as she felt the weathered rock against her cheek.

'You see,' said Judith triumphantly. 'Even I can make your pleasure spill. No doubt it helped that my brother was watching but, far from your wanton behaviour improving, you seem to be even more depraved now than when you first joined us.'

'I agree,' said her brother. 'But we mustn't give up on her, Judith. It's our duty to continue to chastise her until she learns how to behave like the lady she's supposed to be.'

Marianne didn't dare look at either of them. She remained with her face against the rock and waited for her temporarily satisfied senses to come down from their pinnacle of pleasure.

'Leave us now,' said Edward to his sister. 'I'll bring her back to the house shortly.'

'You think she needs further punishment?' asked Judith.

'Yes, but not punishment that you should witness,' he said shortly.

Turning her head a little, Marianne saw a look of annoyance cross Judith's face, but clearly the woman was also unable to disobey her brother because, with a shrug of her shoulders, she set off down the hill, leaving Marianne alone with him.

For several minutes Edward Sharpe stared silently at Marianne. She felt the flesh on her back prickling where the belt had struck, but the sensation was arousing and she longed, more than anything, to have this man possess her, here on the wild moors; filling her, thrusting so deep. She couldn't ask him, couldn't beg to be satisfied; all she could do was wait and hope.

'Alone at last,' he said thickly. 'Now you can find out why I sent for you.' He began tearing off his waistcoat and shirt, reaching greedily for Marianne. His hands grasped her upper body as he flicked his tongue around her breasts, groaning with need. He was breathing heavily and, without thinking, Marianne was fumbling at his breeches, tugging them down with desperate urgency.

Freed from restraint, his erection sprang up, rock-hard, pressing against her lower belly, and his hands gripped her buttocks tightly, raising her up to meet him. Instinctively she lifted her legs, wrapping them around his waist, and suddenly he was pushing her back against the rough surface of the boulder. The raised weals began to sting afresh, but she didn't care because she wanted this animalistic coupling where, for once, Edward's need was as great as her own.

They were both totally lost in the moment. He thrust into her fiercely, his hips grinding against her, and she cried out with ecstasy, because she'd never had a man fill her so completely before. At last, after all the waiting, she was able to trap him deep inside her while he continued to groan with frantic desire.

He thrust in and out of her regardless of her sore back against the boulder, intent solely on his own pleasure. Marianne was almost weeping with gratitude. Their primitive rutting dragged a guttural exclamation from his throat. He bit her throat and his hands mauled her breasts ferociously.

'What is it about you?' he grunted through clenched

teeth. 'Why do I want you so much? You should mean nothing to me, nothing at all.'

Marianne heard the words vaguely through her swirling passion, and elation increased her desire as she realised that, behind all the torments and punishments, Edward was indeed concealing an insatiable lust for her.

She felt the first snaking tendrils of her orgasm and knew that soon she'd come. No longer was she aware of her abused flesh being rubbed against the rock; all that mattered was the hard fullness of him inside her, the way her breasts were being possessively moulded in his hands and the glorious tightness beginning to pervade her entire body. 'I'm coming,' she screamed as the sensations intensified and, when she began to shudder violently, her muscles grasping him in their rhythmic contractions, he finally came as well. His rigid body ground her fiercely against the boulder as his buttocks jerked and his top lip drew back in a snarl of climatic release.

By the time it was over their bodies were drenched with sweat. Edward immediately pushed her legs down to the ground, turning away from her as though anxious to pretend that nothing special had happened. 'Put your clothes on,' he said sharply as he began to dress.

Marianne obeyed. She was trembling so much from the incredibly exciting violence of their lovemaking that it was difficult for her, and she fumbled with all the fastenings. At last, when she was decent, she turned to walk back down the hill. She thought Edward was going to remain where he was, gazing silently out over the windswept moors, but at the last moment he caught hold of her hair and jerked her head back, causing her to squeal with shock and pain.

'Tell no one of this,' he snarled. 'If my sister asks what

happened say I beat you again. Is that clear?'

'Y-yes,' Marianne gasped, his sudden animosity hurting her almost as much as the fist entwined in her hair. 'Please... you're hurting me.'

With a grunt of apparent contempt that made her heart sink, he released her, pushing her away. She stumbled as she set off down the track, but all the way back to the house she kept thinking about what had happened before his mood changed for the worse, and how wonderful it had been.

When Marianne got back to the house Judith took absolutely no notice of her. It was as though her companion had ceased to exist. Uncertain as to how she should behave, Marianne went to the kitchen, but Tabitha was too busy to talk and eventually Marianne took refuge in her room until it was time for the evening meal. When she went down to dine she found Edward was eating with them, and her stomach tightened at the memories the sight of him brought back.

'Is Dr Proctor coming to visit you this evening?' Judith asked her brother.

Edward shook his head. 'Unfortunately not. However, he hopes to be with us within the next couple of days. He will take the opportunity to see how Tabitha and Marianne are progressing.'

'After today I scarcely think that Marianne can be said to have progressed at all,' Judith observed icily. 'Did she repent after I left you on the moors?'

Edward glanced at Marianne, who shifted uneasily in her chair, recalling the way it had felt as he'd thrust his rigid member in and out of her, biting and scratching so savagely in his haste to slake his lust.

'I fear not,' he replied with a sigh. 'Tonight we'll take her to the outhouse.'

'An excellent idea,' replied his sister. 'I didn't like to mention it to you when you first returned, but Tabitha has become increasingly clumsy of late. She claims it's because her arms are aching due to the exercises Francis prescribed for her. However, I believe it's her way of showing her annoyance that she is not allowed to meet with John.'

'You mean she needs disciplining, too?' asked Edward.

'In my opinion, yes. But of course the final decision must rest with you,' Judith gushed demurely.

Marianne knew this wasn't true. Edward and Judith never contradicted each other because they both took pleasure from the same things. The prospect of the outhouse was a fearful one, but this time she was determined that, no matter what, she would endure whatever punishment they had planned for her right through to its conclusion, and not spoil it all by escaping back to the modern day.

Despite her brave intentions she found her appetite had evaporated, and pushed the rather greasy stew aimlessly around her plate.

'At least Marianne is eating less,' remarked Edward. 'That, coupled with the belt she wears at night, has presumably improved her shape.'

'You'll see for yourself in the outhouse,' said Judith. 'In my opinion the difference is very slight. Perhaps the belt should be worn tighter.'

Marianne fully expected to be led to the outhouse as soon as the meal was over, but her employers kept her waiting, plainly delighted by her increasing tension as the hours ticked by and darkness fell on the house.

'Is this the normal time you retire, Marianne?' Edward asked her.

'Yes, sir.'

'Then come with us. You will spend tonight in the outhouse with Tabitha.'

'Tabitha's already retired,' Judith told him.

'I'll fetch her from her room,' said her brother. 'Marianne, go with my sister. I'm sure you realise there's no point in resisting?'

Marianne did realise, but her heart was thumping heavily behind her ribs and she could feel tension in her neck and shoulders. Any fear she felt was coupled with arousal, but once inside the gloomy outhouse, as she watched Judith light two tapering candles and place them in brackets on the walls, fear became the dominant emotion. Driven by an instinct for survival, Marianne inched back towards the door, but Judith saw and slammed it shut.

'Where would you go?' she asked her companion contemptuously. 'There is no one near here to take you in. You belong to us, just as Tabitha belongs to us.'

At that moment the heavy wooden door creaked open again and Edward dragged in a sobbing Tabitha, still wearing her nightshift. 'She was a little reluctant,' he said, with a mirthless smile at his sister. 'As you said, she claims her clumsiness is due to aching arms. After tonight I think she'll have learned her lesson.'

He flung the serving girl into a corner and then turned his attention to Marianne, pulling off her dress and her undergarments so she was forced to stand naked, shivering with cold, as he produced the thick leather belt with which Judith had beaten her on the moors.

'Since it's night time you must wear this,' he remarked, laying it around her waist. He tugged it tight, his efforts making him grunt, until she could scarcely breathe, before finally fastening the buckle.

'There, that improves your shape immediately,' he said, his hands roaming possessively over her hips. 'And now for the other strap.' Marianne parted her legs a little as he pulled a strap up between her thighs, fastening it at the front and back of the leather belt. Watching her closely, he pulled tighter and tighter until she felt the belt biting into her sensitive sex lips, causing an insidious pressure, a form of stimulation that both hurt and aroused. 'Now you're protected from yourself,' he said with evident satisfaction, before pushing her up against the wall and fastening her arms into two metal rings placed higher than those she'd seen the first time.

She felt shamed and humiliated to be standing there, naked apart from the two strips of leather, her hands fastened securely to the wall, forcing her breasts forward and emphasising her curves. The brick wall irritated her sore flesh and she tried to ease herself away from it, but Edward saw her slight movement and pressed against her shoulders, urging her back and making her whimper at the discomfort.

'Don't move from that position,' he ordered her. 'Simply watch what happens to Tabitha. Watch, and remember that after we've finished with her you will be dealt with similarly.'

As he dragged Tabitha to her feet the poor maid began to sob. 'Don't hurt me, please don't hurt me,' she blabbered. 'I never meant to break nothing. It's the exercises I have to do, they've made the muscles in my arms hurt.'

Ignoring the pitiful pleas, Judith pushed the sobbing girl to her knees and lifted her skirt. Beneath it she was naked, apart from her stockings. 'Stop crying and pleasure me,' she ordered Tabitha. As she spoke, she turned to face the fettered Marianne. Marianne glanced at Edward, who was watching with interest, his gaze travelling from his sister to Marianne and then back to his sister.

'I want her to watch me spend,' said Judith calmly, nodding towards Marianne. 'It will do her good to learn that others may have pleasure whilst she may not.'

Already Marianne was thoroughly aroused. She could feel her juices damp against the leather strap that was now working its way between her sex lips as she blossomed with mounting excitement. She yearned for more stimulation, however light, to help satisfy her needy flesh.

Tabitha's head and shoulders disappeared beneath her mistress' skirt, and Judith kept her eyes fixed on Marianne's as the girl worked in secret beneath the concealing fabric. Marianne could hear suckling sounds and was able to picture vividly how Tabitha's tongue and lips must be tantalising her mistress' flesh. She watched as Judith's eyes opened wider and her body started to grow rigid. Obviously Tabitha was doing her work well, because soon Judith was flushed and shaking, her entire body trembling with her impending climax.

Marianne's breasts ached. Her nipples grew tight and she felt her insides knot with excitement. The constant pressure of the belt against her now erect clitoris was almost unendurable. It kept her at a high level of excitement without ever allowing her pleasure to spill, and she could have cried with thwarted need.

Sir Edward was now watching his sister intently, but when she finally uttered a suppressed whimper and shook from head to toe he switched his gaze back to Marianne. 'I expect you wish that was you,' he said quietly. 'Tell me how you feel.'

Marianne lowered her head in shame. She couldn't tell him. If she spoke the truth she'd be punished, but she sensed he already knew the answer. He knew how much she was yearning for release, how her body was pulsing with desperate desire. He must have understood only too well that the strap, intended to act as a restraint, was in reality constantly titillating her, driving her into a frenzy of frustration so intense that she had difficulty in remaining silent.

Once Judith's orgasm had died away she lifted her skirt a little, turning to one side to reveal Tabitha crouching on the floor with her back to Marianne. The servant girl remained on the floor waiting to see what would happen to her next – and she did not have long to wait.

'Do you realise what you've done?' Sir Edward asked the frightened girl, pulling her to her feet and staring down at her. 'You have tried to influence my sister with your wanton ways. I can scarcely believe what I have witnessed.'

'But she told me to,' Tabitha wailed at the injustice of his words.

'I didn't hear her,' said her master.

Tabitha looked at Judith appealingly. 'You did tell me, didn't you, ma'am? You wanted me to pleasure you, you said so.'

'I did no such thing,' said Judith coldly. 'I'm a respectable widow and consider you a dangerous influence on me.'

Tabitha turned frantically towards the tethered Marianne. 'They're always doing this to me,' she cried. 'It isn't fair. If I disobey I'm punished and if I obey it's even worse for me. Can't you help me?'

Marianne didn't dare respond. She was in no position to help Tabitha, and besides, it was obvious that the girl, like herself, did gain pleasure from these sessions of intense punishment mingled with moments of sweet sexual release.

Edward pulled a mounting block forward from one corner, sat himself down on it and then pulled the struggling Tabitha over his knees before immediately beginning to spank her with the flat of his hand. At first the blows were light, scarcely marking the pale flesh, but gradually they increased in strength until Tabitha was squirming frantically against him, trying to evade the blows. He continued remorselessly, striking again and again, his hand rising and falling while Marianne watched, hypnotised by what was happening.

Eventually, when Tabitha's buttocks and upper thighs were glowing bright red, she was turned over and, despite her protests, her master started to slap her belly until that too glowed with heat.

By now Tabitha was weeping, the tears streaming down her face as she implored him to stop hurting her. Then, as Marianne wondered how much more the girl could endure, her crying changed to a moan, which she realised was one of pleasure. Marianne was almost beside herself with frustration. She'd already watched Judith climax and now she was having to watch while Tabitha writhed in ever increasing ecstasy as the stinging heat spread through her body until she was shuddering violently, uttering despairing cries of forbidden pleasure.

When her body was at last still, Sir Edward pushed her upright. Marianne yearned to feel Edward's mouth on her breasts, to feel his tongue tracing the outline of her nipples and his fingers tightening around them, but still she was ignored. She was left fettered to the wall, poised on the edge of a shattering climax that refused to come.

'Did you see her pleasure spill?' Sir Edward asked his sister, with studied indifference.

'Yes, all too clearly.'

'It didn't…' protested Tabitha, but Judith slid a hand between the poor girl's thighs and drew some of the moisture that had seeped there over her flat stomach.

'On the contrary,' she said coldly, lifting her glistening fingers. 'I think this betrays you.'

Sir Edward eyed the serving girl thoughtfully. 'You become even more debauched as the years pass, Tabitha,' he said slowly. 'I thought Dr Proctor had taught you better control.'

'I don't know why it excites me so,' she sobbed. 'It isn't my fault.'

'That's what Marianne says,' retorted Edward, glancing over at her. 'Isn't that true, Marianne?'

Marianne looked at him despairingly. 'I may have said that,' she confessed.

His lips curved in a half smile. 'You'd like to spend now, wouldn't you? How fortunate that we've tied you in the way we have. It means you can do nothing to satisfy yourself. At least you may learn some self-control tonight. As for Tabitha, we'll see how she copes with this punishment, since the last one resulted only in giving her pleasure.'

He held out a hand and Marianne heard a strange clicking sound. Tabitha heard it, too; with a scream, she hurled herself into a pile of straw in the corner of the room. 'No, I can't bear those,' she cried.

'The doctor gave them to us,' said Judith. 'He knows what's best for you, Tabitha.'

Tabitha was arched backwards over the mounting block, her legs splayed apart with her sex totally exposed to the watching Marianne. Judith pushed her back a little until her hips were on the top, and the back of her head was resting flat against the floor out of Marianne's sight. Edward advanced on her, as she whimpered quietly.

Marianne's mouth went dry. Suspended from Edward's hand were what looked like several rounded pebbles joined together by a piece of cord, and he carefully parted Tabitha's sex lips with one hand whilst slowly feeding the first of the pebbles inside her vagina. Tabitha tried to move her hips, attempting to make it impossible for her master to insert the pebbles, but Judith simply laid herself over the girl's lower body so she was unable to move a muscle and then, very lightly, she tickled Tabitha's clitoris. This caused her to open up even more and her muscles spasmed involuntarily, drawing the pebbles in.

Marianne tried to imagine how it must feel for Tabitha to have them inside her, to feel their round smoothness against the sensitive walls of her vagina. When she was abruptly pulled upright, standing with only a tiny piece of cord hanging between her thighs to show that the stones were inside her, Marianne watched in fascination. She almost envied the wretched girl because Edward was palpating the flesh above her pubic bone, first pressing and releasing it and then rocking his hand from side to side in a movement that Marianne remembered so well from when the doctor had examined her.

'You're to keep walking around the room,' said Edward. 'Your muscles must be tightly clenched all the time in order to prevent a single pebble from escaping, but at no time must you spend. You are to walk for five minutes. After that time they will be removed.'

'I can't,' cried Tabitha. 'I'll spend, you know I will.'

'I know no such thing. The doctor tells me that if his treatment is working you'll be able to accomplish this.'

'But I can't,' she sobbed. 'No girl could.'

'Indeed?' Sir Edward turned to Marianne. 'I'm sure you'll manage it when your turn comes,' he said with a smile.

All at once Marianne remembered that when they'd finished with Tabitha this was going to happen to her, and the realisation nearly triggered her orgasm. For a moment her head rocked back and, as her breasts moved forward slightly, Edward watched her keenly, stepping closer and placing a hand over her belly to test for the contractions of a climax. But he applied no stimulation and finally, to Marianne's relief, the moment of danger passed. Despite her frustration she was grateful because she knew she would have been punished even more if she had come.

'Start walking,' Edward repeated, looking at his fob watch, and Tabitha began to move slowly around the room. Marianne could see from the frown of concentration on Tabitha's face how difficult it was for her to walk, keep her internal muscles clenched and at the same time not take pleasure from what must have been the most intense torment.

After a few minutes Tabitha's breathing had become shallow. Her breasts were tight and the nipples scarlet peaks of desire, and at one point Sir Edward reached out as though to touch them, before withdrawing his hand. 'No,' he murmured, 'it would be unfair. The pebbles alone are enough for her to contend with.'

Marianne watched as Tabitha tried to walk more slowly. 'She's making it easier for herself by going at that pace,' said Judith and, picking up a riding crop, she struck Tabitha sharply across the buttocks. With a squeal Tabitha began to walk more quickly round and round the gloomy room.

Marianne could tell Tabitha wasn't going to last the full five minutes. Clearly Tabitha knew it too. Abruptly she stopped and stood with her legs apart, then suddenly, in front of all of them, she started to tremble. The trembling turned into a violent shaking as her pleasure was finally forced from her, and she came with a scream of despair.

Reaching down, Sir Edward tugged on the cord, pulling the whole string of pebbles out of the girl in one movement that made her gasp. 'You've learned nothing,' he snarled. 'I shall tell Dr Proctor when he comes. I'm sure he'll be as disappointed as I am.'

Tabitha crept into a corner, trying to cover her naked body with her arms as though desperate to protect herself from yet more forbidden pleasures, but she needn't have worried because both Judith and Sir Edward were now turning their attention to Marianne. Sir Edward unfastened Marianne's hands from the rings and she moaned as the blood surged back into the numb areas. Before she had time to recover from that, she was thrown roughly over Edward's knees and felt his hand rising and falling against her flesh, just as it had fallen against Tabitha's, until her buttocks and thighs were burning. Next, just as he had with the servant girl, he turned her over and when he struck at her softly rounded belly she screamed at the erotic pain suffusing her. She could feel the blood coursing through her veins, feel her flesh swelling as the deliciously forbidden tightness mounted.

'Put her over the mounting block,' snapped Sir Edward.

Astonished by the speed with which it was all happening, Marianne struggled violently, but was helpless against the combined strength of brother and sister. Within seconds her head was on the floor of the outhouse, her legs lifted high on the mounting block and her thighs parted as Sir Edward began to separate her sex lips in readiness to fill her with the string of pebbles.

'No,' she complained frantically. 'I won't let you do that to me. I don't want it. Let me go. I want to go home.'

As soon as the words were out, a mist began to fill the outhouse and she realised she was leaving them. To her surprise Edward suddenly knelt beside her, and although his body was blurred his voice remained clear.

'Stay with me,' he whispered urgently. 'Don't go. I need you here. Please stay, we're meant to be together.' Suddenly she wanted to change her mind but it was too late. His voice was fading and a few seconds later she was back in the cold outhouse of Moorhead House in her own century.

Chapter Ten

Hastily Marianne checked her clothes but, to her relief, she was wearing the same ones she'd had on when she had left the house for her original walk on the moors. Stumbling to her feet, her arms still aching from the way she'd been tethered in the outhouse by Edward, she made her way to the courtyard and saw it was now dark.

Running indoors, she checked the grandfather clock she'd inherited with the house and saw it was eight o'clock. Five hours had passed since she'd set off for the moors, five hours in which she'd been trapped in a bygone era. What she didn't know was where she'd actually been. She wondered what would have happened had Sandra called at the house. Would she have seen her in the outhouse, possibly over Edward's knee being beaten and fondled? Or would she have simply thought that Marianne was out? There was no way of knowing.

She knew for certain that mentally she was in the past, but if she was now physically there as well then that was more dangerous. Things were changing; the past was reaching out and claiming her. At the moment she was still able to come back whenever she wished, but she wondered how long that would last – and, if it stopped, what would become of her?

Exhausted by all that had happened, she put a frozen meal in the microwave and tried to push Edward to the back of her mind. Somehow she had to fight her overriding obsession with him and spend time in the real world, otherwise she wasn't going to be able to finish her book.

No sooner had she eaten than the phone rang. 'Hi, it's Sandra. Graham's out with his mates tonight. I wondered if you'd like me to come over? Or you could come here if you preferred.'

Marianne simply couldn't be bothered with the girl. 'I'm sorry, I'm working,' she said abruptly.

'Oh.' It was obvious that Sandra was offended.

'Some other time,' said Marianne quickly. 'Right now the words are flowing and I've got to get them down.'

'I rang earlier,' said Sandra. 'Were you out?'

'I don't answer the phone when I'm working.'

'Then you should use an answerphone.'

'I do sometimes, but I forgot to put it on,' she said impatiently. 'Are there any other instructions you've got for me?'

'There's no need to be like that,' exclaimed Sandra. 'I thought it would be nice if we had a girls' evening together, that's all.'

'Thanks, but no thanks,' said Marianne.

With a sigh she replaced the phone. She knew she'd handled the whole thing badly but Sandra, Graham, and even Steve had no relevance to her now. They were an unnecessary intrusion, people she had to put up with, rather than people she wanted to be with. 'That's terrible,' she murmured. 'They're the ones who are real, not Edward.'

Eventually, knowing she'd already let Angela down, Marianne returned to the study and recommenced work on her book. She was at last pleased with her hero and heroine, feeling that although the setting was modern, the obsession the girl had for her boyfriend in many ways reflected the obsession she felt for Edward. She was delighted with the way she was putting this across, and knew her readers would understand exactly what she was saying, but the plot had reached the stage where this obsession needed a physical outlet. She decided to do the first modern sex scene she'd written since coming to Moorhead House.

As her hero worked as a farm labourer she set the scene in a barn, albeit one which bore a strong resemblance to the outhouse where she'd just been tormented by Edward and his sister. As a result the scene sprang instantly to life, and soon she was lost as the words poured out, just as she'd told Sandra they would.

Nearly an hour later she stopped typing and printed the pages off. When she read them they shocked her; not because they were particularly explicit, but because the feelings she'd attributed to the heroine were so exactly those she was experiencing every time Edward touched her. Also, since her heroine was well-bred, her confusion at enjoying the things her lover was doing to her reflected exactly her confusion at enjoying the forbidden perversions of Sir Edward's household.

After she'd finished reading she felt unbearably aroused. She longed to have Edward in the room with her, touching her, beating her, and then slowly but surely coaxing forth her orgasm while her flesh struggled to subdue itself. Unable to bear the sexual tension any longer, she turned out all the lights and went upstairs. She took a quick shower before taking her vibrator from the bedside drawer. Then she put a pillow in the middle of the bed, lay on her stomach so that her hips were raised, and reaching beneath her, began to masturbate with the deliciously vibrating plastic.

She always preferred to lie on her stomach when she was masturbating. Somehow her climaxes were more intense that way, but for the first time ever her rising pleasure was tinged with guilt. She knew how Edward would disapprove of what she was doing and remembered the belt so cunningly designed to stop her playing with herself. How she wished she could be with him, because even though it would undoubtedly mean she would be forced to wait for her pleasure, she would have the excitement and sexual confusion her body now seemed to crave.

Despite her best efforts, she couldn't turn herself on. 'Oh, I wish you were here,' she whispered. 'It would be so much better then.'

'What are you doing?' asked a deep voice and, with a cry of alarm, Marianne twisted on to her back. Edward Sharpe was standing there – there in her modern bedroom at Moorhead House. Despite his dated clothing he didn't look out of place, because she was the one he was there for and the surroundings didn't matter.

Marianne realised she was just as afraid of him here and now as when she met him in his own time. The aura of authority surrounding him and the way his pitiless gaze penetrated her soul was enough to have her trembling before he'd even touched her.

'What's that?' he asked, taking the vibrator from her.

'It's for my pleasure,' she murmured, too embarrassed to say more. He inquisitively touched the little switch, and as the tip started to vibrate he examined it thoughtfully, running it over his wrist and then nodding in understanding.

'You realise I have to punish you for possessing such an obscenity,' he stated softly, looming nearer the bed.

'Yes,' she said, her voice shaking.

'Fetch me rags with which to bind you.'

Marianne's mind went blank for a moment, and then she scrabbled through one of her drawers and brought out some of her silk scarves. Immediately he tied her hands to the bedhead, stretching them up and out to the sides.

He eyed her nakedness thoughtfully. 'You're not wearing the belt,' he eventually said.

She didn't know what to say. It seemed he wasn't aware he was in a different century, one where the belt did not exist. 'I – I forgot,' she blurted lamely.

'No wonder the results of your training are so disappointing. I'm surprised my sister didn't check on you.' He glanced around the room and his eyes fell on the belt on her jeans. 'That will do,' he decided.

Marianne lifted her hips to help him slip the belt around her waist, but saw him raise it in the air instead and lash it down in a diagonal stroke that travelled from breast to hip.

'Ouch!' she protested. 'That hurts!'

He frowned. 'It's meant to hurt,' he said, his voice tight with rage. 'What do you expect when you constantly disobey us?'

'No!' she screamed again as he raised his arm, but despite her protestations the belt swept down, hissing through the still air and cutting with a loud splat into her vulnerable flesh. Both blows were vicious, and she squirmed helplessly, trying hopelessly to get out of his range.

She felt a moment's relief when he tossed the belt to the floor before coming to kneel on the bed next to her, the vibrator gripped in his hand. 'This was what you wanted, wasn't it?'

'Yes,' she admitted meekly, surprised at how easy it was to become Marianne Clifford, despite her modern surroundings.

'I've never seen anything like this before,' Edward muttered, again studying the buzzing head. 'Where did you get it?'

'It was a present,' she said truthfully.

He didn't pursue the point, but instead circled each of her breasts in turn with the vibrator and then, as pleasure spread through her soft globes, he moved the vibrator gradually to her nipples.

He was clever, using the sex aid with cunning dexterity until she was urging her breasts up to him, straining against the silk bonds, yearning, her moist lips slightly parted in mute appeal.

'How wanton you are,' he muttered, his voice thick with desire as he drew the vibrator down between her breasts, and then lower to circle her navel.

Edward watched her pulling on the silk scarves as she instinctively tried to free herself, in order to give herself sexual relief, but the scarves only tightened around her wrists and she moaned her frustration.

'Don't you understand that it's wrong to do this to yourself?' he asked quietly.

'But why is it wrong for me to do it to myself, but right for you to do it to me?'

He raised his eyebrows. 'When I touch you I'm simply trying to discipline your flesh. It's your own wanton behaviour that causes my touch to make your pleasure boil over.'

'You know that's not true,' she objected. 'You know exactly how to make a girl orgasm and you enjoy doing it. You like making me suffer, pretending it's my fault when it's really yours.'

'You're very argumentative tonight,' he remarked,

reached between her parted thighs, slid his fingers into her moist sex and pinched her swollen clitoris between finger and thumb. She gasped, feeling the first faint fluttering of her climax. Her muscles were tightening, and at last everything was gathering itself together.

Edward pushed down his breeches and lay on top of her, his hands gripping her shoulders, the tips of his fingers digging savagely into her as he moved himself up and down over her. She could feel his rigid shaft grinding over her lower belly. He was gasping and groaning, the tendons on his neck tight, the veins standing out. She squirmed desperately beneath him, loving the feeling of his body against hers, but no matter how hard she tried she was unable to get sufficient stimulation to trigger her climax.

'It's all your fault,' she heard him mutter through clenched teeth as he pressed himself down against her, trapping the tip of his erection between her thighs. Then he continued to move until suddenly he was shuddering violently, spilling his seed all over her flesh, and she felt it oozing stickily between them as he gasped in ecstasy.

Raising himself, he stared deep into her eyes. 'Such delight,' he whispered quietly. 'Such sweet release. Don't you understand that's what it's really about? You give me so much pleasure and that's why I employed you, to please me, not to please yourself.'

She was almost out of her mind with need, and to hear him talking about his pleasure, the release he'd achieved, was more than she could bear. Once more he was leaving her unsatisfied, and he didn't care.

'Make me come,' she pleaded. 'You've had your fun, now let me have mine. Touch me the way you were earlier, that's all I need. I want to come, don't you understand, I want to come!'

Even as she was begging she heard the sound of footsteps on the stairs and the door was flung violently open. Startled, she stared across the room to where Steve stood framed in the doorway.

'Where is he?' he demanded. 'I heard you begging him to touch you. I'll kill him, I swear I will.'

'There's no one here,' blurted Marianne as Edward slowly faded from sight.

'What do you mean there's no one here? You weren't talking to yourself,' shouted Steve. He began rampaging round the room, pulling open wardrobe doors, going down on his knees and peering under the bed and even flinging open the windows, as though imagining her lover had escaped that way despite the fifteen foot drop to the cobbled courtyard below.

'I told you there wasn't anyone,' said Marianne.

Steve stared at her as she lay on the bed. 'Why are you hanging on to the headboard like that?' he demanded.

Marianne realised her wrists were no longer bound. The scarves – like Edward – had disappeared. 'I was afraid,' she said defensively. 'I heard footsteps on the stairs and didn't know who it was.'

Steve stared at her suspiciously. 'Have you any idea what you look like?'

She had a pretty good idea. She was naked, trembling, and visibly aroused.

'If there's no one here, what were you doing?' he asked accusingly. 'I heard you begging. Have you gone totally mad?'

Marianne didn't know what to say. Things had got well out of hand. Having Edward in the room with her had seemed wonderful, but now she was left to explain the inexplicable, and it was obvious Steve was in no mood to be fobbed off with stupid answers. 'It's for my book,' she said feebly. 'I was acting out a sex scene.'

'I thought you said you'd given up that erotic writing lark.'

'This is for the one that's been commissioned,' she assured him.

'Don't tell me you've turned that into a kinky one, too?'

'Of course not, but my heroine's obsessed with this farm labourer who she's known since childhood. She wants him desperately but the first time they're together he does these extraordinary things to her, only he won't actually make love to her because he knows how much trouble it could cause.'

'You don't need to tell me the whole plot,' snapped Steve. 'I've never known you act out scenes from your novels before.'

'I was trying to get the emotion right,' she explained. 'You know how in *Wuthering Heights*—'

'I've never read *Wuthering Heights*,' he snapped. 'Quite honestly, Marianne, I think you should see a doctor or something.'

'There's nothing wrong with me,' she snapped back. 'How was I to know you were going to come bursting home like this without so much as a phone call?'

'What do you expect after our last conversation?'

'What do you mean?'

'You made me feel I was intruding, that you had something – or someone – more important on your mind.'

'I did – my book.'

'I still think there was someone here.'

'Now you're the one who needs to see a doctor. You're getting paranoid. If there was someone here, where do you think they've gone?'

'Perhaps there's a secret hiding place,' he said, clutching at straws. 'The house is old enough. A priest hole, perhaps.'

Marianne sighed. She was beginning to pull herself together, to feel more in command of the situation, although she realised how dangerous the situation was. No wonder Judith Wells had ended up being taken to a mental hospital. If Steve had arrived quietly, creeping up the stairs and peering round the door, then presumably he would have seen Marianne begging Sir Edward to touch her without being able to see the man. If that had happened she couldn't possibly have explained it away because her body's responses would have shown that her flesh believed the fiction to be fact.

'Come on, now you're being ridiculous,' she said gently, getting up and pulling on her jeans and a sweatshirt. 'How long are you home for?'

'Only one night.'

'I'd better get you something to eat,' she said, suddenly feeling sympathy for Steve, and a degree of guilt for what she was putting him through.

Suddenly he grabbed her arm. 'You haven't got a lover, have you?'

Marianne shook her head. 'No, Steve, there is no other man here and there never has been.'

He let her go, but she had the feeling he didn't believe her, and she couldn't really blame him. Things were becoming too complicated now. She knew it would be better if Steve were to stay away, but at the same time he represented a safe anchor, an anchor she was beginning to think was necessary for her own survival.

'Was that all right?' Marianne asked Steve as he pushed away his empty plate, having eaten his cheese omelette and salad in absolute silence.

'Fine, thanks.'

'You're not going to sulk all night, are you? I dread to think how you'd have behaved if you had caught me with a lover.'

'I don't know where I am with you any more,' he said glumly. 'I'm beginning to think your books are more real to you than I am.'

'That's ridiculous.'

'Well, perhaps not the books, then. Let's say the characters in them.'

Marianne stared at him. 'What do you mean by that?'

'I think your fantasy lovers give you more satisfaction than I do.'

Hearing him say it, hearing the truth spoken, was shattering. Marianne knew she should laugh, make it clear to Steve that he was being totally ridiculous, but she couldn't because he was right. Only Edward wasn't a fantasy lover, he was a ghost. He really had lived, breathed and done the things he was doing to Marianne to other women as well. She wished she could confide in Steve, explain to him what had happened to her, because none of it was his fault. But how could she admit she no longer needed Steve; all she needed was Moorhead House and her journeys back into the past.

'I think I'll ignore that,' she said. 'It really isn't worthy of an answer.'

'You mean it isn't true?'

'Of course it's not true,' she snapped, and immediately heard a whispered chuckle. Hastily she turned her head in the direction from which the sound had come, fully expecting to see Edward standing in the kitchen with them, but he wasn't there. Or at least, he wasn't visible to her, but he was there just the same. She could sense it.

As she removed Steve's dirty plate and took a tub of vanilla ice cream out of the freezer for him, she knew Edward was watching her. She could feel his eyes watching every movement and she felt on edge, constantly terrified that he was suddenly going to materialise.

When Steve had eaten his desert he pushed back his chair and gave a small sigh. 'Where do we go from here?' he asked her.

'Go? Why should we go anywhere? Nothing's changed, Steve. We'll carry on as we are.'

'But do you still feel the same about me?' he asked.

She knew she had to reassure him. If he started to believe his imaginings were the truth then he might confide in Sandra and Graham. Once that happened they'd probably tell him about Judith Wells and then all of them would be watching her closely, waiting for her to give some sign that she, too, was losing her grip on reality. She couldn't allow that to happen. 'I'll show you what I think of you,' she whispered, catching hold of his hand and leading him into the front room.

As soon as he'd settled himself in his favourite armchair she sat on the floor between his legs, letting him stroke her hair, and soon he was bending forward, kissing her passionately. She knew Edward was watching them, she could almost hear his breathing, but there was still no sign of him. A sense of bravado filled her. Not only was she going to make Steve happy, she was also going to show Edward that she did have a life away from him.

Reaching up she unfastened Steve's jeans and pulled them slowly down his legs, caressing his thighs. Reaching inside the leg of his boxer shorts, she lightly tickled his testicles and within seconds his erection was pushing its way through the opening of the material, swelling rapidly. Marianne knelt up so she could draw him into her mouth.

With a murmur of contentment Steve closed his eyes, allowing the pleasure caused by her lapping tongue to wash over him. Only then did Edward Sharpe make himself visible to Marianne. He was standing behind Steve's chair, glaring at her, his eyes dark with fury. Marianne removed her mouth from Steve's erection and smiled sweetly at her ghostly lover, before turning her attention back to Steve.

She did all the things she knew Steve liked best. Her tongue caressed the sensitive ridge of flesh beneath the glans, occasionally swirling around the tip and dipping into the tiny eye. Every time she did this Steve would jerk and his hands, which were resting on her shoulders, tightened convulsively. After a time she used her mouth to suck him, and as she sucked she gripped the shaft with one hand, then slowly pumped it up and down, providing a different kind of stimulation from the soft caress of her mouth.

'God, that's good,' moaned Steve, opening his eyes for a second and looking down at her. 'You've no idea how great it feels.'

'I can imagine,' she said, and she could because the memory of how she'd felt when Edward's tongue had licked her clitoris was still clear in her mind. 'I love doing it for you,' she murmured, raising her eyes to see how Edward would take this. He was pale, and she was suddenly alarmed because he looked down at Steve as though he'd like to kill him.

Releasing Steve's erection, she moved her fingers lower,

lightly caressing his tightening testicles instead, but all the time she continued to lick and suck on the head of his penis until he was groaning helplessly, close to coming.

Marianne started to suck harder but then Steve gently pushed on her shoulders. 'I want to come inside you,' he said huskily.

She saw Edward watching them both. He was still very pale but he also looked excited, aroused by what he was seeing, and for the first time since she'd met him Marianne felt a surge of power. Now he was the one experiencing the frustration, now he would know what it was like to suffer, and she stripped off her clothes and lay on the carpet, holding her arms up to Steve. 'Quickly,' she said throatily. 'I want to feel you inside me.'

Steve needed no second invitation. Within seconds he was lying on top of her, sliding into her moist, welcoming warmth and she deliberately gave a loud cry of ecstasy, knowing it would infuriate Edward. 'Oh yes... *yes*!' And because she knew they were being watched, her excitement really did soar.

Steve was moving spasmodically in and out of her. 'I can't wait much longer,' he grunted.

Marianne wrapped her legs around him, drawing him deeper inside her. 'It doesn't matter,' she assured him. 'I'm nearly there, too.' It wasn't true but she was very close. As Steve gave three final thrusts before spasming above her, her body teetered on the brink of release, but it was over just seconds too soon and he left her stranded.

Edward Sharpe was standing over them, glaring down in much the same way as he used to glare at Tabitha and John. Marianne decided to pretend she'd come. Letting out a cry of satisfaction, she clutched at Steve. 'That was bliss,' she gasped. Steve rolled off her and lay on the carpet with one arm over her breasts and his eyes closed. He was obviously exhausted.

To Marianne's disappointment Edward had vanished, but she was certain she'd managed to make him jealous. It was only fair, she thought, because Steve, without realising it, was jealous of Edward. Then, to her shock, she felt hands on her ankles and her legs were pushed apart as the familiar fingers began to snake up her inner thighs. 'No!' she hissed.

'Is my arm too heavy?' Steve asked sleepily.

'No... you just relax,' she said gently, hoping he might doze off after his exertions.

'So what's the matter?'

'Nothing. I had a twinge of cramp.'

'Well, that's okay then,' he muttered.

He was almost asleep, but not quite, and Marianne didn't dare utter another sound. Edward's fingers were moving incredibly lightly now, stroking her sex lips with insidious gentleness until she felt them parting, opening to allow him easier access.

She was horrified. She wanted to move, to jump to her feet and leave the room, but that would have upset Steve and she was anxious not to give him further reason to doubt her. Instead she lay in rigid anticipation, waiting for Edward to do as he wanted with her.

He played with her for several minutes, massaging the succulent flesh, occasionally sliding a finger inside her, but never for quite long enough to trigger her release. Then, clearly tiring of the game, he began to circle her clitoris with two fingers. The pressure was firm, the movement exactly what she needed until, with shocking abruptness, all the pent-up desire waiting to be released spilled out. Despite her determination to keep silent, she heard herself groaning in ecstasy as her body trembled and quaked when she finally climaxed.

Steve's eyes flew open and he propped himself up on one elbow. 'What happened to you then?' he asked.

'I shivered,' she said lamely. 'It's cold in here.'

'You were playing with yourself, weren't you?'

She grasped the excuse gratefully. 'Yes,' she admitted, pretending to be ashamed.

'Bloody hell, you're insatiable. Soon it'll take more than one man to keep you happy.'

She nearly laughed at this, and just before he disappeared, she saw Edward smile.

As he'd obviously intended, his actions had spoilt the moment and when Steve got to his feet, grumpily pulling on his jeans, Marianne hastily got dressed too. 'I think it's time we went to bed, especially if you have to be off early in the morning,' she said.

'I need to find my old briefcase,' said Steve. 'It's got some papers I want for tomorrow's meeting. Have you any idea where it is?'

'It must be in one of the cases I haven't unpacked yet. They're all in the attic.'

'Right, I'll have a look before we go to bed.'

Marianne decided to go into the attic with Steve. She was drawn to it, associating it with the past and forbidden pleasures. As Steve started going through the packing cases she opened her great-aunt's old trunk and took out the book on Moorhead House. All she wanted to do was read the piece about Edward again. Now she knew him better it would be even more intriguing.

When she opened the book a square of old paper fell out from between two pages and floated to the floor. The paper was yellow with age, the edges curled, and Marianne stared at it in astonishment because she knew perfectly well it hadn't been there the first time she'd opened the book. Someone had placed it there since, and it wasn't difficult to guess who.

'What's that?' Steve asked absentmindedly.

'I don't know, probably an old recipe.'

He turned his attention back to the packing cases and Marianne lifted the paper so the light fell on it. It was a drawing of Edward and his sister, and the artist had captured the essence of them with incredible accuracy. Despite the fact that they were both dressed in their best clothes and Judith was smiling, they were still intimidating.

'I can't find the bloody thing,' muttered Steve. 'Are you sure you haven't unpacked it?'

'Of course I'm sure,' snapped Marianne.

'What's the recipe for?' he asked, pausing in his search for a moment. 'Don't tell me you're going to try it out on me?'

'It isn't a recipe.'

'What is it then?'

'A drawing.'

'A drawing of the house?'

'No,' she said, and without thinking, she clutched the paper to her breast.

'Hey, let me have a look,' said Steve. 'Come on, it can't be a secret.'

'It's just a drawing of two people, that's all.'

'Then let me see,' he insisted, making a grab for the paper.

'Careful, you might tear it,' she admonished.

'So what?'

'So, it could be valuable.'

'I doubt it, it can't be that old.'

'But it is,' she whispered.

'What d'you say?'

'I said, it is old.'

Steve frowned. 'How do you know?'

She didn't know what to say. She could hardly tell him she'd met these people, they'd lived in this very same house a hundred and seventy years earlier and the drawing must have been done around that time. 'You can tell by the clothes they're wearing,' she muttered.

'That doesn't mean it's an old drawing, stupid,' he scoffed. 'Any artist can draw people in old-fashioned clothes. Come on, let me see it.'

Marianne didn't want him to touch it. She didn't want him anywhere near it, but she knew she couldn't refuse. Grudgingly, she handed it over. 'There you are. I told you it was nothing special.'

Steve looked at it carefully. 'That man looks familiar,' he said pensively.

'Familiar...? What do you mean, familiar?'

Now it was Steve's turn to seem uncomfortable. 'When I came home earlier and burst into our bedroom, thinking there was someone there, just for a brief moment I did see someone, a man, and he looked just like this man.'

'And I thought I was the one going mad,' said Marianne, trying to lighten the suddenly oppressive atmosphere.

Steve shook his head. 'I don't understand it. I could have sworn...'

'Sworn what?'

'Nothing, I'm being utterly ridiculous. He doesn't look very nice though, does he?'

'I think he's quite attractive.'

'Look at the lines round his mouth and eyes,' said Steve, pointing at the paper. 'He looks like someone who lived a life of excess and debauchery.'

'That sounds delicious,' laughed Marianne, still trying to lighten the mood. Then she peered more closely at the drawing. 'There's another figure in the background,' she exclaimed.

'I didn't see one,' said Steve.

'Well, there is, sitting down behind them… look.'

'I think you're right,' agreed Steve, squinting as he peered closer. 'It looks like a young woman, but her features are very vague. I suppose she's of no importance.'

Marianne felt as though he'd slapped her. 'How can you say that?' she asked angrily.

'Say what?'

'That I'm of no importance.'

'That *you're* of no importance?' he said incredulously. 'I never mentioned you. I was talking about the young woman in the picture.'

Marianne felt the blood rush to her cheeks. She couldn't believe she'd said what she had. 'I – I didn't mean me… I…'

'What are you getting so worked up about?' asked Steve.

'I'm not getting worked up.'

'Yes, you are. You've gone all red and you sound really flustered.'

'Oh, for God's sake, just find your briefcase and let's get to bed,' she snapped.

'Are these people in fancy dress?' asked Steve. 'Is this someone you know? Someone who lives round here?'

'It's an old drawing,' Marianne repeated. 'Look at the paper. You don't get paper like that any more.'

Steve tested it between finger and thumb. 'Artists still use paper like this.'

'Steve, don't you think you're being just a little bit

paranoid?' said Marianne. 'If you're trying to say that this man's my lover, why on earth would I keep a picture of him hidden in a book in a trunk in the attic?'

'To look at when I'm not here.'

'But I'm looking at it now, when you are here,' she pointed out.

'He excites you, doesn't he?' Steve said perceptively, watching her reactions closely. 'Even the sight of him is enough to arouse you.' He ran a hand over the front of her sweatshirt. Marianne tried to push him off but she wasn't quick enough and she knew he'd felt how hard her nipples were beneath the fabric.

'Listen,' said Steve slowly. 'I'm not stupid, Marianne. There's something going on here and I want to know what it is. I've always thought of you as being absolutely honest and I want an honest answer to this question. Have you got a lover?'

'No,' she said firmly.

'But you're falling in love with someone else, aren't you?'

She shook her head. 'I'm not, Steve. There isn't anyone else. If I'd wanted to have an affair I'd have had one in London. Let's face it, I had plenty of offers. Think about this logically. Our nearest neighbours are Sandra and Graham and you don't think it's Graham, do you?' Steve shook his head. 'Okay then, apart from him, who do I meet?'

'The postman,' Steve suggested, without conviction.

'He's nearly sixty.'

'The milkman, then?'

'He delivers around four in the morning. Anyway, I wouldn't know him if I met him. Believe me, Steve, I haven't met anyone who lives near here apart from Sandra and Graham, and that's the honest truth.'

'So why are you so fascinated by this drawing then?'

'Well, it's an extraordinary coincidence, but he looks like the hero of my book,' she explained, not untruthfully. 'He's exactly how I'd pictured him and it was a bit of a shock seeing him like this.'

'Maybe you'd seen the picture before and he'd stayed in your subconscious,' suggested Steve.

'Maybe,' agreed Marianne. 'Mind you, that doesn't explain why you thought you knew him.'

'No, and I haven't even read your book.'

'Maybe he's a ghost,' said Marianne, knowing she was beginning to tread on thin ice.

'A ghost?' Steve stared at her. 'Are you saying this is a drawing of someone who used to live here?'

'Well it could be, couldn't it?'

'I suppose so,' Steve conceded.

'If it is, then perhaps in a way we've both seen him. Maybe that's why I've used his face in my book, and why you thought you saw him in the bedroom. Perhaps his presence has remained behind for over a hundred and fifty years.'

'Why do you say a hundred and fifty years?' he asked. 'You don't know that's when he lived here, if indeed he did.'

Marianne could have bitten off her tongue. 'I, um, I'm only guessing because of the clothes.'

'I see.' Steve stared at the drawing once more. 'Well, if he is still around, I think we ought to have someone in to exorcise him. He looks a very unhealthy influence to me. Maybe that's why you started writing all those lurid sex scenes. Perhaps you were picking up perverted vibes from him.'

Marianne was furious. Suddenly she wanted to blurt everything out, to tell Steve what was happening and what incredible pleasure Edward had brought her. She was so angry she actually opened her mouth but then, at the last moment, self-protection took over and she turned away without uttering a word. 'I think this is all getting rather silly,' she murmured.

'I don't know, you might have a point. You do hear about things like that.'

'Well, I think I'd know if I'd seen him,' she said.

'I'm not suggesting for one moment he's a ghost who materialises,' Steve argued. 'All I'm saying is that your idea about his presence lingering on might be true. I'm not a total sceptic where these things are concerned.'

'But you wouldn't be jealous of a ghost, would you?'

Steve laughed. 'Of course not! A ghost wouldn't be any competition. Besides, if he really did live over a hundred and fifty years ago I don't suppose he did anything interesting. I rather think modern man could see him off any day.'

Marianne knew different, but decided against telling him so. 'And what about all that "life of excess and debauchery" you were talking about?'

'That would be drinking and prostitutes,' said Steve casually.

Suddenly Marianne wanted to change the conversation. The more Steve dismissed Edward the more she was tempted to hurt him with the truth. 'I don't think we're going to find your briefcase,' she said, deflecting the subject and pretending to yawn. 'Let's go to bed.'

'It's damned inconvenient,' said Steve, but he switched out the light and followed her down to the bedroom.

As usual, Steve was soon asleep but Marianne lay wide

awake. She lay staring into the darkness, thinking about the picture and how it had also featured Marianne Clifford. And then, to her delight, she heard the whisper of familiar voices.

'And how's Miss Marianne today?' asked Dr Francis Proctor.

Chapter Eleven

Marianne stared around her. She was standing in the middle of Edward's bedroom, clad only in a thin shift. A fire was burning in the grate and the room was hot. Seated in the rocking chair was Tabitha. The girl was naked and looked more frail than ever. Her arms were resting on the sides of the chair, her hands clenched tightly around the ends until her knuckles showed white. Although she could only touch the floor with the tips of her toes she constantly kept the chair rocking back and forth, but the terrified expression on her face told Marianne this wasn't what the servant girl wanted.

Judith was standing slightly to the side of the chair and in front of Tabitha. She was watching her serving maid carefully, and Marianne could tell from Tabitha's swollen nipples that she was very aroused. Then, as Marianne watched, Tabitha uttered a whimpering cry and trembled violently. Immediately Judith began to beat her breasts with birch twigs while tears rolled down Tabitha's face and she cried out beseechingly.

'I can't help it. I can't help it, ma'am,' she whimpered.

'Keep rocking,' said Judith, her voice harsh.

'But the pebbles make me so excited,' Tabitha cried. 'The more I rock the worse it gets.'

Suddenly Francis Proctor, who'd been standing in the shadows watching Marianne, stepped forward. 'Your mistress is quite right,' he said, his voice calm and measured. 'You may think we're being unkind, Tabitha, but we're trying to help you. It is my experience that if you continue with the treatment you'll eventually learn to control yourself.'

'It doesn't work that way,' Tabitha wailed.

'Then you must keep doing what the doctor says until it does,' said Judith crisply, and she pushed the back of the rocking chair to start it moving again.

Marianne realised the pebbles she'd seen inserted into Tabitha once before must be inside the girl again. 'Ask them to let me go, miss,' Tabitha cried, looking imploringly at Marianne. 'I'm so tired.'

Marianne kept silent. There was nothing she could say, and in any case, she knew the doctor was about to examine her. The last thing she wanted to do was antagonise him or Edward before the examination began. Despite her apprehension, her skin was prickling with excitement. She started to imagine how it would feel when their hands touched her once more.

'Perhaps her waist is a little smaller,' said the doctor, squeezing his hands tightly around Marianne's waist. 'You could tighten the belt another notch, I think.'

Remembering how tight it had felt the last time she'd worn it Marianne couldn't suppress a tiny sigh of protest.

'What's the matter?' asked Edward.

'I won't be able to breathe,' she whispered.

'I think the doctor's the best judge of that,' he replied. 'But we can always test his theory.' As he spoke he produced the wide leather belt, pulling it swiftly round Marianne's waist and jerking hard until he found the hole he wanted. Once the belt was fastened Marianne's worst fears were proved right. She could scarcely breathe, and yet she remembered from what she'd read in books that women had always been tightly laced at this time, in order to keep an unnatural hourglass figure. No wonder they'd fainted so often, she thought to herself.

'It emphasises your other curves,' murmured Edward, running his hands thoughtfully over her muslin chemise, and she felt her flesh leap beneath his touch. 'You see,' he added with a smile. 'You're still alive so I assume you're breathing. You were right, Francis. From now on the belt will be tightened.'

'Tighten the strap between her thighs also,' said his friend. 'If nothing else it will make her nights more interesting.' The doctor laughed.

At that moment Tabitha gave a muffled gasp of ecstasy. Marianne turned her head and saw the birch twigs rising and falling even while Tabitha's body was still shaking from the contractions of her climax. Her cries of joy turned to cries of pain and she cowered back in the chair.

'Perhaps you should have a little ointment on your breasts to soothe the discomfort,' said Judith.

Tabitha shook her head. 'I don't need the ointment, ma'am,' she said hastily.

'I think you do,' said Judith. 'Do you have some with you, Francis?' The doctor handed her a small jar and she quickly spread the cream over the raised marks on the servant girl's breasts. Tabitha sat very still, as though waiting for something dreadful, and Marianne guessed that whilst the ointment might heal, it also hurt.

Sure enough, a few seconds later Tabitha was writhing in discomfort, moaning and weeping. 'It's burning me,' she cried. 'Take it off, please, take it off.'

But Judith spread the cream over a larger area of Tabitha's breasts and, just as Marianne felt she must do something to stop Judith tormenting the helpless girl, Tabitha's eyes widened. 'Oh no!' she cried, and then shuddered violently as yet another climax, triggered by the strange properties of the ointment, was wrenched from her.

'Have you ever seen such wanton behaviour?' Edward asked Francis Proctor.

The doctor shook his head. 'It's a very sad case,' he declared. 'She needs a lot of discipline and attention if we are to cure her.'

As the birch twigs began to fall on Tabitha's belly and the rocking chair was set in motion once more, Marianne turned her head away. She couldn't bear to watch any longer because, despite her sympathy for Tabitha, she was becoming excited.

The leather belt was now discarded and the doctor looked thoughtfully at Marianne. 'Please remove your chemise,' he said gently. 'I need to do a full examination.'

Marianne crossed her arms protectively over her body. 'I don't want to be naked,' she murmured, well aware that a young lady of that time would never have stripped, even for a doctor.

'Don't tell me you're going coy on us, Marianne,' laughed Edward. He waited a few seconds and then, when she still made no move to remove the garment, he hooked two fingers in the neckline and, with a savage downward movement, split it from neck to hem. 'Will that do, Francis?' he asked.

Marianne felt worse standing in a garment whose ragged edges had opened to partially expose her body than she would have done if she'd stripped herself, and she hastily eased the rags off and then waited passively for the doctor's instructions.

'Lie on the bed,' he said.

This time she was lying full length on a bolster, just

slightly elevated. The doctor sat on the bed next to her, moving his hands over her body, poking and prodding, palpating the flesh of her breasts and belly and constantly murmuring to himself.

His touch was gentle and skilfully arousing. Marianne felt her body relaxing beneath his fingers, her muscles softening. Then, as he continued to touch her, her desire began to grow.

The doctor's hands parted her legs and instinctively she tried to close them, but Edward caught hold of her ankles and spread them apart, giving his friend free access. The doctor laid the middle finger of each hand against the join at the tops of her thighs and pressed, lightly at first but then more heavily. At the same time he rolled his fingers slightly inwards. It felt delicious, and she struggled to remain still because the sensation was so exciting.

Eventually he stopped, then he parted her sex lips and swirled a finger lazily around her entrance. 'She's already very wet,' he said, his voice clinical and detached. 'It's surprising how little it takes. Are you quite sure she's a lady of good breeding?'

'Quite sure,' Edward confirmed. 'However, there must be bad blood in her somewhere.'

Marianne was determined to keep silent. In the background she could hear Tabitha climaxing at regular intervals, gasping with delight and then whimpering pitifully as she was punished by Judith's birch twigs. Even that sometimes caused a renewed gasp of ecstasy, and the constant reminder that someone was having countless orgasms was an added aphrodisiac for Marianne.

'She's very quiet,' said the doctor, when Marianne remained silent. 'I really need to hear her responses in order to assess whether or not we've made progress.'

'I'd have said we haven't,' remarked Edward. His fingers joined his friend's between her thighs.

'She still hasn't uttered a sound,' said his friend. 'Admittedly, her flesh appears to indicate her behaviour is wanton, but perhaps I'm wrong.'

'Do you think we should test her further?' There was no mistaking the eagerness in Edward's voice.

'Yes,' said his friend, and at that moment Tabitha gave a loud moan.

'Please can I stop now?' she cried, her voice breaking with distress.

'The intention is that eventually you'll tire of constant stimulation and release, then your disgraceful lasciviousness will cease,' said the doctor.

'But I want them to stop now,' cried Tabitha.

'Oh do stop whining,' said Edward irritably. 'Keep her quiet, Judith.'

There was the sound of birch twigs against naked flesh and after a few shrieks Tabitha fell silent, obviously realising she was only making things worse for herself.

Sir Edward lay down on the bed next to Marianne and turned her on her side, still on the bolster, so she was facing him. 'Wouldn't you like to be stimulated constantly?' he whispered. 'Tell me, don't you envy Tabitha?'

'No,' she said uncertainly. 'I couldn't bear it.'

'Nonsense, your capacity for pleasure is unlimited. We both know that.' His voice was still quiet, intimate, and he was staring at her hungrily.

'Why do you keep tormenting me?' she asked.

'Why do you keep coming back for more?' he asked, and she had no answer for him.

She didn't hear or feel Francis Proctor climb on the bed

behind her. It was only when she felt his manhood pressing against her lower back that she realised he was there and jumped with shock. 'What are you going to do to me?' she asked in a panic.

'Nothing so very terrible,' said Edward, but the look in his eyes belied his words.

She waited, trembling and helpless, as the two men fed a long piece of silken cloth between her thighs, pulling the ends up on either side of her. Then, with her body sandwiched between them, they tugged the ends, pulling upwards against her vulva. Immediately her clitoris began to swell, blood suffusing the area as she became engorged with excitement, and she trembled on the edge of a climax. Then the pair loosened their grip and the pressure eased.

She was left in a state of hopeless frustration, longing for fulfilment, unable to control the situation at all and aware that her every response was being monitored by the doctor. He was judging her, listening for any sound she might make, and although she knew she should stay silent she also knew another tightening of the cloth would make it impossible.

After a few seconds, during which her body calmed a little, they pulled on the silken cloth once more, and this time, as she'd feared, she gasped with delight.

'Did you hear that?' asked Edward.

'She's responding.' Francis nodded, and there was a note of disapproval in his voice. 'I'm afraid she hasn't made as much progress as I'd hoped.'

The cloth was loosened for a moment, and to her shame Marianne couldn't prevent a cry of frustration.

'What's the matter?' asked Edward.

'Nothing,' she gasped.

He caught hold of her chin. 'Don't lie to us.'

'It's just that...'

'You're enjoying it, aren't you?' he said. 'You wanted us to continue then, admit it.'

'No, no, I didn't,' she lied.

Immediately the two men tightened the cloth again. They continued to tighten and release in a steady rhythm so she was constantly brought to the peak of desire and then left there, silently begging for a chance to explode in orgasmic release. They were very clever, and soon she was sobbing with frustration, no longer caring what they thought of her.

'I think this might help,' said Edward, leaving the bed for a moment. When he returned he was carrying the glass bottle of oil he'd used on her once before. He poured a few drops over his fingers and, as he continued to manipulate the length of silk between her thighs, he pinched her flesh.

He chose the most sensitive places, and every time he pinched he would hold the flesh for a few seconds until she cried out, and only then would he release it. Each time the pressure eased a strange glow would spread.

'Her responses are very audible now,' remarked the doctor.

'Indeed,' said Edward. 'I think perhaps we should satisfy her wanton flesh.'

'Oh yes, please do,' she cried, abandoning all pretence at ladylike behaviour.

The two men removed the silk and she felt their hands gripping her. Edward drew her nearest nipple into his mouth, swirling his tongue around it before closing his teeth over the tip, biting so hard she screamed in protest, but as soon as his mouth was removed she felt her body begin to arch upwards in a spasm of pleasure.

'Quickly, take her now,' Edward urged his friend.

To her horror, Marianne felt the doctor's fingers parting her buttocks and then he was pouring some of Edward's oil around the sensitive opening. His excitement was such that he could hardly wait and he thrust inside her before she was really ready for him. She groaned in protest at this cruel invasion.

His turgid penis seemed to stretch the walls of her violated bottom and his staccato movements were rough. As a result the pain almost outweighed the pleasure and she moaned despairingly, but he ignored her. Wrapping his arms around her waist he pulled her back firmly against his groin.

'Now it's my turn,' said Edward, staring into her eyes. She felt the tip of him sliding up and down her inner channel, moving in teasing circles around her aching entrance. All the time he was doing this his friend was moving inside her, sending wave after wave of forbidden pleasure-pain through her. She was shocked to realise she wanted to be filled by the pair of them; at that moment, it was the most exciting thing she could imagine happening to her.

'Beg me,' Edward goaded harshly.

Marianne shook her head. She knew she couldn't; she didn't dare, because if she did such incredibly wanton behaviour would only be punished.

'You know you want me,' he went on. 'Beg. Do as I say. Beg for it.'

Almost delirious with need, Marianne threw caution to the winds. 'Yes... yes I want you to take me,' she panted. '*Hurry...*'

Immediately he penetrated her and, as the two men began to fuck her in unison, it felt as though their shafts were touching each other in her depths. She heard herself sobbing and crying out incoherently as finally she was filled to the limit. And when Edward squeezed his fingers down and teased her clitoris she could take no more.

She screamed as her body jerked helplessly, impaled on the two men, constricted by their bodies from total freedom of movement but still spasming wildly as the most incredible orgasm imaginable took possession of her. For a few seconds she felt as though she'd lose consciousness, so overwhelming was her joy. Eventually she slumped between their sweating bodies, totally drained, but the men were still moving inside her, still climbing towards their own moment of release.

It was the doctor who came first, his testicles squeezing tightly against her buttocks as his stubby cock swelled even further and then erupted inside the warm cocoon of her bottom.

'Now you're mine,' Edward hissed, his stare fixed on her. 'Now you know what you really are and how much you need me.'

Marianne stared back at him through misty eyes, knowing the words he was uttering were the shocking truth. She was his, she did need him and she was horribly aware of what she really was – or at least, of what she had become. Finally, as though reading her understanding, with a grunt of triumph he stabbed his hips aggressively and ejaculated too, his hypnotic stare transfixing her while his cock pulsed and his copious seed flooded her.

Long minutes later he and the doctor withdrew, leaving Marianne limp and alone on the dishevelled bed, damp with perspiration. She could imagine what she looked like, and as Edward and his friend stared down at her she couldn't think of a word to utter in her own defence.

'Could you ever have believed she'd behave like that?' asked Edward.

'I'm shocked,' replied the doctor. 'I'm sorry, Edward, but I seem to have failed you.'

'It doesn't matter. From now on I shall attend to her myself. You've done your best. I remember you once telling me there are some things that doctors cannot cure. I fear that Marianne's lewd and wanton behaviour is one of them...'

Marianne awoke on the top of her bed, perspiration chilling her flesh. Clearly time had moved on, as it had begun to do during her recent visits to the past, and dawn was breaking.

She felt restless. Now she was away from Edward, back in the boring security of the modern day, she was in the mood for sex again.

She glanced at Steve sleeping quietly beside her. Easing back the duvet, she ran her fingers lightly over his chest. He always slept naked and, within a few seconds, she was lightly tickling his balls, watching the skin move beneath her touch. Encouraged by this, she began to massage his sleeping penis, and he moaned in his sleep, his hips twisting as he began to respond.

She was incredibly excited by the fact that he had no idea what was happening to him, and let her fingers play up and down the stem of his growing erection, feeling it engorge with excitement until it was standing up rigid and erect, yet still Steve slept.

Releasing her sleeping lover for a moment, Marianne put her hand between her thighs and slowly moved her fingers in circles around her clitoris. Her breathing was becoming heavier and her desire mounting. Turning back to Steve, she grasped his erection with one hand and lowered her body on to it, feeling the delicious hardness of him sliding up inside her. Instinctively her muscles tightened with a contraction that heralded impending release, and it was then that Steve's eyes opened.

'What on earth...?'

'Keep still,' she urged, bending forward so her nipples were near his mouth. 'Just relax and let me please you.'

'You might have woken me up first.' He sounded disgruntled.

'Isn't it more exciting this way?' she teased.

'Exciting for who?'

'For both of us.'

'I feel as though I'm being used.'

Marianne couldn't understand his reaction. 'Most men would love this,' she said.

'How do you know?' he asked.

'I don't know, but I imagine they would. I thought you were enjoying the fact that our sex life was more adventurous now.'

'I was, but that was before you went all peculiar on me.'

'Don't spoil it,' she begged him, feeling her excitement beginning to fade.

Almost reluctantly, he took a rigid nipple between his teeth and lightly caressed the end of it with his tongue. She wanted to beg him to be rougher with her, to nip at the sensitive flesh, to grasp the swollen mounds with his hands, letting his fingers dig deeply into her skin, but she knew she couldn't. At least the touch, however gentle, was an added aphrodisiac and once more hot desire flared in her.

Slowly she raised and lowered her hips again, still

rhythmically contracting her muscles around him, and his hips responded so he was soon thrusting up into her. 'I'm going to come in a minute,' he gasped.

'Not yet,' she begged. 'Wait a few more seconds. I'm nearly there now.'

She made a conscious effort not to grip him so tightly and slowed her pace. Immediately, some of the tension went out of his body and the moment of danger passed. Urgently she fed her nipple back into his mouth. 'Please, keep sucking,' she pleaded, and although she could tell he wasn't happy about it, he did as she asked. Soon she was tingling and the pressure of impending release grew almost unendurable. Certain that she, too, was going to come, Marianne speeded up the movement of her hips, rising and falling on his rigid shaft as glorious flashes of pleasure spread through her lower belly.

She was only just in time. As her climax swept over her and she threw her head back with a tiny mewl of delight, Steve shuddered and she felt him spilling his hot seed inside her until finally he was completely spent.

'Wasn't that good?' she panted.

'It was all right.'

He wouldn't look at her, and Marianne slipped off him. 'I thought it was a good way of waking you up,' she murmured dejectedly.

'It's a bit early, isn't it?'

'Oh, what's the matter with you?' she snapped.

'I don't know,' he admitted. 'I suppose it's you. You've changed so much and I can't get used to it. I still don't really understand what's going on.'

Marianne sighed. 'Nothing's going on. How many times do I have to tell you that?'

Steve rolled to the side, turning his back on her.

'I'm getting up,' she said impatiently. 'Do you want a cooked breakfast before you leave?'

'What time is it?' he asked, his voice muffled by the pillow.

'Six.'

'Great! I could have slept for another hour. I didn't need to get up at this time.'

'Well go back to sleep then,' she said, furious with his sulking.

'No, it's all right. I might as well get up now you've woken me.'

'Is that how you see it? That I "woke" you?'

'How else am I meant to see it?'

'I was making love to you.'

Steve shook his head. 'No you weren't, Marianne. We had sex, but that's not the same thing and you know it.'

They ate breakfast in total silence. When Steve left he kissed her perfunctorily on the cheek. 'See you soon.'

'When?' she asked.

'Two or three days, I'm not sure exactly.'

Marianne stared at him. 'You won't tell me, will you? You still believe I've got a lover.'

'I don't know what I believe any more. When I get back we must have a good talk about our future. Also, I'd like to have a look at this book of yours. By the way, when I went to the study just now there was a fax there from Angela. She says you promised to fax her some pages two days ago, but she's not received them.'

Marianne clapped her hand to her mouth. 'Damn, I forgot!'

'Perhaps you should spend less time daydreaming and more time getting on with your work,' he said caustically.

'Even Angela might lose patience with you in the end, you know. Then where will you be?'

Marianne didn't answer him, nor did she go to the front door to see him off. 'Oh, Edward,' she murmured, sitting at the kitchen table. 'What are we going to do?'

All at once she wanted to return to the past. She had no desire to write any more of her book or fax any pages through to Angela. All she wanted was to go back through the years and be Judith Fullick's companion again. Nothing in modern life was nearly as satisfying. Her everyday life had become mundane and boring, and her flesh craved the kind of forbidden excitement that Edward had tutored her in so well.

She did everything she could to conjure up images from the past and find a way back. She wandered from room to room. She sat in a chair, closed her eyes and visualised them all. She even went to the outhouse and sat, feeling slightly ridiculous, with her wrists in the iron rings, but it made no difference. She remained in the modern day, unable to get back to her lover.

'It isn't fair,' she muttered, returning to the house. 'Why isn't there a password or something that takes me straight back?'

Eventually she settled down to work, faxing pages of her first chapter through to Angela and then carrying on with the next chapter. The story still flowed well and she was pleased with the sexual dynamics between her hero and heroine, but they were a poor substitute for the real thing.

At eleven o'clock she was grateful to hear the doorbell ring. At least it gave her an excuse to temporarily leave her work.

'Hi,' said Sandra when Marianne opened the front door.

'Are you busy writing?'

'I was about to take a break,' said Marianne. 'Would you like to come in for a coffee?'

Sandra looked relieved. 'That would be great. After last time I wasn't sure whether I should call in or not.'

'I don't mind you calling in as long as you realise that sometimes you'll get sent away again,' laughed Marianne.

'You seem happier,' said Sandra. 'Is the book going better?'

'Yes, I suppose it is.'

'Steve was home last night, wasn't he?'

Marianne nodded. 'He popped back for one night.'

Sandra smiled. 'You must both be very much in love still. I don't think Graham would go to that much trouble.'

Marianne wondered what Sandra would say if she told her Steve had really come back because he'd hoped to catch her with a lover. There wasn't any point; it would only make her seem peculiar again and she was anxious to prove to Sandra that she was very normal. 'You know what men are like,' she said lamely.

'I vaguely remember,' laughed Sandra. 'Some of the magic wears off after five years of marriage.'

'Is instant coffee all right, or shall I grind some beans?'

'I really don't mind,' said Sandra, sitting down by the kitchen table. 'You know, this is a lovely room. I can understand why you don't want to modernise it.'

'Thanks, I…' began Marianne, but she stiffened as she saw Judith, and she wasn't alone.

Tabitha was standing naked at the old kitchen sink, shivering, with her bare feet on the stone floor. John was tethered in the same corner of the kitchen where Marianne had once been tethered, and he was naked from the waist down. His erection already looked painfully tight and

Marianne guessed Judith was inflicting some kind of punishment on him once again.

'Instant coffee will be fine,' said Sandra brightly.

'I'm sorry?' murmured Marianne.

'I said instant's fine.'

Marianne didn't know what to do. The kettle was on the worktop to the right of where Tabitha was working, and to her eyes the worktop no longer existed. Instead, there was a rough wooden table pushed against the wall. She couldn't think what to do. 'I tell you what, how about some squash?' she asked.

Sandra looked surprised. 'Well, I...'

'This lemon squash is delicious,' Marianne assured her, grateful that at least the table remained the same. There were already two glasses there and she took them over to the sink. As her fingers tightened around the old tap she felt herself brush against Tabitha, but Tabitha gave no sign that she knew Marianne was there.

Nervously, Marianne filled the glasses with water and then returned to the table, pushing one in front of Sandra. She was vaguely aware that Sandra was talking but the words were meaningless, because Marianne's attention was caught by the scene from the past taking place in front of her.

'I need some preserves from the cupboard, Tabitha,' said Judith, moving away from where she'd been standing next to John. 'You'll have to stand on the stool.'

Tabitha quickly dried her hands and, with difficulty, pushed a three-legged stool over to the cupboard. Then, with a nervous glance in John's direction, she lifted one foot off the floor and clambered on to it. Marianne realised this meant John was gazing at Tabitha's pubic mound, seeing it open up in front of him, and as she reached for the preserves her body was stretched tight, her back curved inwards and her large breasts arched forward.

Clearly satisfied with what was happening, Judith moved back to stand next to John. 'You can only take me if I'm sure you've learned better self-control,' she told him, and he bit his lower lip. A tiny drop of clear fluid dripped from the tip of his purple glans, falling to the stone flags. Crouching down, Judith let her tongue flick into the tiny slit and immediately John began to tremble.

'Please, mistress, don't do that,' he begged her.

'But you say you're as mature as a man now,' she reminded him. 'A man doesn't come until his woman's satisfied.'

Marianne wondered how long this torment had been going on. John's face was flushed, and his erection looked fit to burst. Obviously he'd already been kept waiting some time, but Judith didn't seem to be in any hurry to release him.

When Tabitha got down from the stool, Judith called her over, then sat the girl on the end of the kitchen table, directly opposite where Sandra was sitting. She pushed Tabitha's knees apart and then, as John watched, moved over to the sink, returning with a long curving carrot in her hand.

'I don't see why we should deprive Tabitha of her pleasure simply because you're learning to restrain yourself,' she commented.

'I don't want that inside me,' cried Tabitha. 'It's indecent.'

'Nonsense,' mocked Judith. 'And you're lucky we're so good to you.' She dipped the carrot into a pot of grease before slowly starting to insert it into her serving girl.

Tabitha squirmed, trying to inch away from the invading

vegetable, but Judith slapped her sharply. 'Sit still, you stupid girl! You know full well that soon you'll be enjoying this.'

Marianne thought it more likely that John's pleasure would come first. She could see he was struggling to contain his excitement as he watched the carrot disappearing inside Tabitha. When Judith began to rotate her wrist, Tabitha's whimpers of distress changed, and soon she was moaning despairingly. It was a moan that Marianne recognised. Despite what she'd said earlier, Tabitha was becoming very excited and when Judith began to massage the girl's abdomen with her free hand, Tabitha cried out. 'Oh, yes... yes!' she sobbed.

'Didn't I say you'd love it?' Judith gloated, urging the carrot inexorably deeper.

'I can't take any more,' cried Tabitha. 'It's filled me up!'

'I'll be the judge of that,' retorted her mistress. She turned to the tethered John. 'I'm sure you'd like to be filling Tabitha right now, wouldn't you? Look how she's responding. See how she's writhing so wantonly. Is this what she does when you're fucking her?'

Marianne was shocked by Judith's crude language; it didn't suit her at all. But the young gardener interrupted her thoughts.

'I'm going to come, mistress,' he groaned. 'I can't stand watching it no more.'

'In that case you'll forfeit your opportunity to pleasure me,' said Judith.

'I want to mistress, I want to a lot, but watching Tabitha like this – it's more than a man can stand.'

'Perhaps you should keep still, Tabitha,' Judith suggested. 'Maybe if you kept silent and didn't make your pleasure so obvious it would make things easier for John.'

'Oh, ma'am!' exclaimed Tabitha, and all at once her body convulsed as she climaxed.

Judith didn't even wait for Tabitha's last contractions to die away before leaving the girl and turning her attention back to the tethered gardener. 'You've done very well,' she said approvingly. 'Perhaps you would be able to satisfy me now. Let me see how ready you are.' Her hand closed around his shaft just below the swollen tip and, as her fingers gripped him, he shook his head despondently. 'Oh no,' he protested. 'Please, let go mistress.'

'I'm just making sure you're hard enough for me,' she said with a thin smile.

'I can't bear it,' groaned John, and his hips began to pump furiously.

Marianne watched, dry-mouthed and incredibly excited, as creamy fluid spat from his swollen cock, coating his mistress' fingers and dripping audibly on the floor below.

Judith waited until the last drops had fallen and then milked him tightly one final time. 'How dare you?' she hissed. 'Do you have any idea what kind of punishment my brother would inflict upon you if he knew what you've just done?'

'I'm sorry, I'm sorry,' he cried.

On the table Tabitha, clearly over-excited by everything that was happening, began to move the carrot in and out of herself without even seeking Judith's permission. Alerted by the sound of the girl's heavy breathing, Judith turned to glance at her. 'Have you learned nothing here?' she shouted. 'The pair of you will suffer for this.' She pulled Tabitha off the table and forced her to her knees in front of John. 'Start sucking him,' she ordered her.

'Don't, Tabitha,' cried John, but Tabitha, who always

protected herself first, ignored his plea and closed her lips around the tip of his glans.

Suddenly, Judith looked straight at Marianne. 'How long have you been there?' she asked. 'Have you enjoyed my little game? You look as though it's excited you.'

'It hasn't,' Marianne blurted hastily.

'Sorry?' said Sandra.

Marianne looked at her visitor in surprise. She'd completely forgotten she was there. 'What?'

'You said it hasn't,' explained Sandra. 'What did you mean?'

Marianne couldn't think what to say. 'You'd better go,' she said abruptly.

Sandra stared at her. 'Go?'

'Yes, I don't feel very well.'

'What's the matter? Do you feel dizzy? You've gone very pale.'

'I don't know what's the matter,' snapped Marianne. 'I'd like to go and lie down for a while, if you don't mind?'

'I'll bring you up a sweet cup of tea,' Sandra suggested.

'No!' Marianne was desperate to get back to the past. 'Don't you understand? I want to be left alone.'

Sandra got to her feet in a huff. 'There's no need to shout. I was only trying to be helpful. If you're ill you should see a doctor.'

'I'm not that ill,' Marianne said wearily. She wished the wretched girl would just go.

Sandra shifted uneasily, clearly wanting to say something. 'Steve's very worried about you,' she blurted at last.

'How do you mean, worried about me?'

'He thinks you need to see a doctor.'

'That's because he's paranoid,' said Marianne. 'He

seems to imagine I've got a lover. I don't know where he thinks I keep him hidden. In the outhouse, perhaps.'

'You really don't seem yourself,' said Sandra. 'You've changed since we first met you.'

'Just go, will you,' snapped Marianne, her voice rising. 'How many times do I have to ask you to leave?'

'All right, all right, I'm going,' said Sandra, nervously backing out of the room. 'I wish I'd never come now.'

'So do I,' said Marianne, but the moment the words were out she wished she could recall them, because Sandra looked absolutely stricken and she realised it was an unforgivable thing to say. 'I'm sorry,' she said hastily. 'I'm under a lot of stress at the moment, and...'

Sandra picked up her bag and hurried out of the house, slamming the front door behind her.

'That's done it,' muttered Marianne, but although she was worried, she wasn't as worried as she should have been because it had been necessary to get rid of Sandra. Judith wanted her back. She sensed they all wanted her back, and if she missed this opportunity she had no idea when the next chance would come.

Slowly she walked back into the kitchen. At first she thought that everything had been lost while she was getting rid of Sandra, but then she realised with relief that the kitchen had been transformed back to its state in the nineteenth century. Although Judith, John and Tabitha had vanished, the room wasn't empty.

With an inscrutable smile playing around his lips, Edward was waiting for her.

Chapter Twelve

Marianne advanced into the kitchen in a dreamlike state. Never before had she been so pleased to see Edward, and never before had he seemed so welcoming. 'Why did you go away?' he asked.

Marianne hesitated, looking down at the floor. She was once more wearing her rust-coloured woollen dress and rubbed her hands nervously against her thighs. 'I was visiting my cousin. She lives abroad with her husband but was here on a visit.'

'You'll never leave me again,' he said slowly. 'You did not have my permission to go.'

'Mrs Fullick said I might go,' explained Marianne.

'I pay your wages, not my sister.'

'You weren't here. There wasn't time for Mrs Fullick to get a message to you.'

'In that case you should not have been allowed to leave,' he replied. 'You know you're always meant to be here for me.'

'But I'm employed as your sister's companion.'

He shook his head. 'You and I know the truth of it, don't we? Why be coy when we're alone?'

She didn't answer him. She was almost consumed by her desire for this stranger from the past who'd entirely taken over her life. She waited, knowing he would understand how she felt and how best to deal with her. 'Come with me,' he said softly.

'Where are we going?'

'To the attic room.'

Marianne led the way, walking slowly up the stairs, her breathing constricted by rising desire and trepidation. She knew she would once more see something strange and terrible in the room and, to her shame, she couldn't wait to get there. However, she forced herself to walk slowly because she didn't want Edward to know how great her need was. In spite of this, she sensed he did know and that he was taking pleasure from it.

When they entered the attic, Judith was seated on a chair and Tabitha had been laid back over her mistress' knees. Dr Francis Proctor was seated on the floor between Tabitha's outspread legs, his hands playing with her sex, and the serving girl was whimpering, but whether with pain or excitement Marianne couldn't tell.

Edward drew her to one side of the room where they could watch what was happening. He held her tightly from behind, one arm around her waist and the other over her breasts, pulling her back against his body, trapping her so that there was no escape.

'What are you doing?' Edward asked his friend.

Francis turned his head. 'I'm anxious to see whether the breast exercises have worked. Also, whether or not she now controls herself better. While I examine her your sister will watch her nipples. Should they harden in an unseemly fashion then Judith will strike her with the whip. Tabitha knows this.'

'No doubt that in itself is enough to excite her,' murmured Edward, and the arm over Marianne's breasts pressed harder. Without thinking, she rubbed herself against him as a sweet ache began to simmer deep within her.

'Keep still,' he admonished.

Immediately she froze, then heard Tabitha's cries increase in strength. She saw that the doctor had unfastened his breeches and was rubbing the swollen head of his erection between the servant girl's sex lips, guiding the head with his fingers and massaging poor Tabitha's clitoris with it.

'Your nipples are hardening,' warned Judith.

'Then make him stop,' wailed Tabitha.

Marianne saw the doctor's spare hand creeping beneath Judith's skirt and she knew the pair of them were deliberately using the girl to increase their own desire. Ignoring Tabitha's plea, he continued to manipulate himself against her moist flesh.

'Her nipples are rigid, doctor,' said Judith, satisfaction clear in her voice.

'Then you know what to do,' he replied.

'No,' wailed Tabitha, but her protest was fruitless. Judith flicked the tip of a short riding crop down across the girl's breasts, and with every blow Tabitha screamed louder, her body writhing.

'Has that subdued her wantonness?' asked Francis, when the blows were over.

Judith ran a hand casually over the tormented flesh as Tabitha whimpered helplessly. 'Not really, they're as hard as ever.'

'They're not, they're not,' Tabitha protested, but Marianne could see the girl was obviously aroused. This time Judith let the crop fall over the girl's ribcage, and her breasts quivered violently with each spiteful blow.

'I don't think this is going to work,' said Edward coolly.

His friend didn't answer him, but now his hand began to move over Tabitha's hips, caressing her lower body, softly at first but then more harshly. Clearly filled with lust by Tabitha's moans and cries, he shunted his gnarled erection inside her and she wailed with the shock.

'Be silent,' said Judith, her face tight with disapproval. 'You are honoured that the doctor is willing to use you in this way.'

'Keep one hand on her belly,' Francis grunted. 'Make sure her pleasure doesn't spill.'

Marianne knew his instruction was impossible for Tabitha to follow. He was thrusting forcefully and Judith was sweeping the crop down indiscriminately over the tortured body, so the girl was being continually stimulated.

Marianne watched, feeling her own body responding as though she were Tabitha. She felt her muscles tightening in anticipation of pleasure, and then the doctor gave a guttural shout as his hips jerked and he emptied his sacs inside the servant girl.

'She's coming,' said Judith, pressing her fingers against Tabitha's lower belly. Marianne could see the tormented girl's muscles rippling. Tabitha's abdomen heaved frantically and her climax was forced from her.

Within a few minutes the doctor and Judith had changed places. This time Tabitha was lying face down over his knees while Judith applied the crop unmercifully. With every blow that fell Tabitha's screams increased, but at the same time, she squirmed against the doctor's knees. When Judith finished and threw the crop away Tabitha continued to squirm, clearly trying to obtain sufficient pressure on her clitoris for another orgasm.

Ignoring Tabitha's needs, the doctor pushed her to the floor, grasping Judith round the waist and dragging her to a corner of the room, lifting her skirts before falling to his knees and burying his face between her thighs. As Judith Fullick started to moan, her fingers buried in the young doctor's hair, Tabitha remained on the floor. She was sobbing with frustration and Marianne felt pity for her, because she knew Tabitha was no longer of any interest to the couple. They were now lost in their own pleasure and Tabitha, like Marianne on so many other occasions, would remain on the edge of release, her body filled with a desperate yearning that would not dissipate of its own accord.

The doctor brought Judith to several sharp climaxes, one following swiftly on the heels of the other, until she pushed him away. 'No more,' she gasped. 'Not yet.'

'Come with me,' Edward called to his friend. 'We'll take this one to my room.'

Marianne began to tremble as the two men gripped her arms and dragged her down the top flight of stairs to Edward's bedroom. Lifting her, Edward threw her into the middle of the bed. Then he pushed her skirt up and pulled off her undergarments. 'She paid a visit to relations without my permission,' he explained to his friend. 'This is her punishment.'

'Do you need assistance?'

'A little,' admitted Edward. 'In any case, I'm sure you'll be interested in seeing her response.'

'I'm sure I will.'

With casual indifference Edward flipped Marianne on to her front, but her skirts were still rucked up so that her buttocks were exposed. She heard Edward moving around the room, then the doctor put a hand beneath her belly, pressing upwards. Instinctively she lifted her hips, which enabled Edward to part her buttocks, and once more she felt the sensual sensation of oil being dripped into the valley between the cheeks of her bottom.

'Do you have the beads, Judith?' Edward asked his

sister, who had followed once she'd regained her composure and straightened her clothing.

Judith withdrew something from her pocket. By straining to look over her shoulder, Marianne was able to see it was a piece of twine that had round sewing beads strung to it at regular intervals, and now she understood what was going to happen to her.

Edward took the beads from his sister and began to ease them into Marianne's most private entrance. It was an extraordinary and humiliating sensation, making her feel full and tight and giving her an urge to bear down.

Francis Proctor stroked her belly lightly. 'Remain relaxed,' he instructed her.

'I'm getting cramp,' she gasped. 'My belly hurts.'

'It will pass,' he assured her, continuing to smooth the tense muscles. Once all the beads were inside her, Edward flicked his fingers over her buttocks and she jerked with surprise.

Then she was flipped on to her back. Her sex lips were parted and Edward cupped her there, pressing. She felt herself opening for him, becoming damp, and a few seconds later he placed a very fine strip of gauze over her aroused flesh. Then, with diabolical slowness, he began to drip the oil from the glass bottle onto her clitoris.

Marianne sighed with pleasure. The sensation was utterly exquisite. She could feel her orgasm approaching rapidly and she breathed deeply, preparing herself.

'I'll tell you when it's time for your pleasure to take over,' said Edward coldly. 'Until then, you will control yourself.'

Marianne sighed again, but this time with thwarted longing. For a few seconds the relentless drops of oil ceased and she relaxed a little, but then he tipped the bottle once more while Judith lifted Marianne's head, and she was forced to watch.

Soon the only sounds to be heard in the room were Marianne's cries of frustration. She could feel her clitoris swelling as her body opened. She was desperate to be filled, to have the yearning doused by Edward – but she had the feeling that this was the last thing on his mind.

'Her centre of pleasure is engorged,' remarked Francis Proctor, staring down at the oil-soaked cloth against which Marianne could feel her clitoris swelling. 'See how clearly defined it is.'

'Fasten it with a ring,' said Edward.

Marianne froze as she felt a cold ring of metal being pressed against her, gliding over the lubricated cloth and trapping her clitoris within its circle. Now she truly was helpless, her clitoris unable to withdraw as her climax grew imminent, and she gave a cry of protest.

'What's the matter?' demanded Edward.

'I don't know,' she confessed. 'It feels so good, and yet...'

'And yet?'

'I'm afraid.'

He smiled thinly. 'But isn't that what you like?'

It was, and she knew it was what he liked, too. He enjoyed watching her like this, struggling to control herself, afraid of what was being done to her and yet needing it more than she needed anything else in the world. With misleading gentleness, Edward started to massage her aching flesh whilst stroking the piece of thin muslin cloth until she felt the pressure building more tightly than before. Then he slipped two fingers inside her. He knew exactly what he was doing and she squirmed, knowing how dangerously near to coming she was. Then he added a third knowing finger and she went out of her mind with pleasure. Her body heaving, lost in helpless ecstasy, she allowed the forbidden pleasure to take over and revelled in the glorious sensuality of release.

When the muscle-wrenching contractions at last eased, she opened her eyes to see Judith standing over her, the birch twigs in her hand. Immediately Marianne crossed her arms over her breasts to protect them. The men, however, did not intend to allow her any escape. They seized an arm each, pulling them above her head to give Judith an easy target. The birch twigs cut down and Marianne knew how Tabitha had felt because the searing pain was a terrible shock after the delicious pleasure she'd just experienced. She cried out in protest, begging Judith not to repeat the blow. But she heard the men laugh and Judith raised her arm once more.

She thought she couldn't endure it, but then the vile pain began to excite her and she realised she was about to come again. Even as the convulsions shook her she wept with a mixture of shame and relief, because at least she'd survived and was still here. As for the shame, that was something she was becoming used to as she fully understood what Edward had made her.

With the routine established, Edward, his sister and the doctor relentlessly continued their insidious stimulation of Marianne, and every time they wrenched pleasure from her, Judith would use the birch twigs until even the pain was a source of arousal. Soon she'd lost count of the number of times she'd come.

She could hear herself crying out, but not in an attempt to make them stop. She was begging for them to continue, pleading for more as she became totally lost in the terrible perversions they were practising on her. Even through the mist of exhausted, slated lust she realised she was as much a part of this as they were. Without her co-operation it would not have been possible and the realisation seemed to free her.

'No more,' she eventually begged, as she watched Judith raise the bunch of birch twigs yet again. 'Please stop now, I need to rest… I'm exhausted.'

Edward shuffled on the bed and moved between her thighs. She felt his erection probing at her entrance and, with a sigh of relief, reached up to draw him inside her. 'Oh yes… yes please,' she mumbled, almost incoherently. 'Take me, fill me… I need you.'

She was so lost in the excitement of the moment her mind scarcely registered the fact that the door was opening, until she heard a completely unexpected voice. 'Marianne! In God's name, what are you doing?'

The doctor and Judith pulled her upright while Edward remained kneeling between her thighs and she looked over her lover's shoulder across the room. There, staring at the scene, his mouth gaping with shock, was Steve.

'What's happening?' he cried, beginning to back away from the bed.

'He's seen us,' Judith whispered in Marianne's ear.

Marianne couldn't believe the other woman was right. 'Wuh – what's the matter?' she asked Steve, then groaned as Edward thrust inside her, making her shoulders arch back.

'Who are these people?' Steve yelled. 'And you, what's happened to you?'

'I…' she stopped. She couldn't think of a word to say.

'You lied to me!' he raged. 'I knew there was something terrible happening but you denied it. Now see what's happened. It's too late, isn't it? They've taken you away from me.' With that, he finally found the strength to storm from the room, slamming the door behind him and turning the key. Only then, once he'd gone, did the room change and, with shocking abruptness, Marianne found herself alone.

Deserted by her companions from the past, she rushed to the bedroom door and began to tug frantically on the handle, but it refused to open. Not only was the door locked, it was also very well built and she knew she had no hope of breaking out.

She wondered exactly what Steve had seen when he'd burst in. Obviously he'd seen something, that much had been clear, but she couldn't believe he'd been witness to the absolute depravity of the scene. As he had no direct link to the past, she thought it unlikely that he could have seen more than a faint outline of figures, albeit figures from a different age.

Giving the door one final frustrated kick she turned her attention to the window. Flinging it open, she stared out and saw she had no hope of escape that way either. There was a sheer drop to the courtyard below, and it was a drop that could probably kill her. Even if she lived, she'd be severely injured. She wasn't sure why she was quite so desperate to escape, but there had been something about Steve's fury that frightened her. Seeing him emerge from the house, crossing the cobbled slabs, she waved her arms frantically. 'Steve! Steve!'

He looked up, shading his eyes against the sun. 'It's over,' he shouted. 'We're finished. After what I saw I never want you near me again.'

'I don't know what you're talking about,' cried Marianne. 'Why did you rush out the way you did?'

'I saw them! Those weirdoes all over you. It's

disgusting!'

'There's no one here,' she yelled. 'Let me out. We've got to talk.'

'It's this bloody house. It's possessed you, just like it possessed Judith Wells. Oh yes, Sandra told me about her.'

'You're mad,' cried Marianne, but he turned his back on her and went over to the old stables. When he returned he was carrying a can of petrol, and in an instant she realised what he intended to do. 'No Steve...' she cried, not wanting to believe what she was seeing. 'You mustn't. Where will we live?'

'You won't need to live anywhere,' he shouted back. 'You'll be dead. And I hope you rot in hell, you and your fucking phantom lovers!'

'Come up and talk to me,' Marianne begged, trying to calm herself, the enormity of his threat making her feel nauseous with terror. 'We can't keep shouting at each other like this. We can work this out.'

'We don't need to keep shouting, and there's nothing more to be said.'

She began to cry. 'Please, Steve, come up and talk to me! Don't do anything stupid! You'll only regret it afterwards!'

'I loved you.' His voice was full of torment. 'I loved you and trusted you. Didn't you stop and think of me at all?'

Marianne slammed the window shut, her mind in a total spin. She just had to get out of the house. But only a minute or so later she heard the key turn in the bedroom door and Steve was there. She watched him cautiously, and knew he was struggling to suppress his seething anger, as he locked the door and slipped the key into his pocket.

'I want just one answer,' he said. 'Did you ever think of

me when you were with him?'

'With who?'

'Don't take me for an idiot, Marianne,' he sneered. 'That man I saw. The same man who was in the drawing – the one who's taken you away from me.'

'No one's taken me away from you,' she said firmly, knowing she had to pacify him if she was to get out of the room safely. He had a wild look in his eyes, and was quite unlike the Steve she'd always known.

He looked longingly at her, as though wanting to believe her but unable to. 'I saw the way you were looking at him,' he whispered.

'Looking at who?'

'Stop playing games with me,' he shouted. 'I don't know who he was, I don't understand a thing about all this, but I know what I saw and I'll never forget it.'

'You're right,' said Marianne, abruptly changing tack. 'I should have been honest with you before but I didn't think you'd believe me. Now you've seen him for yourself it's different. I have been possessed, but against my will.'

'Possessed? Against your will?'

'By the man you saw, the one in the drawing. I think he lived in this house long ago and for some reason he wants me. I've tried to fight him but I felt so helpless on my own. Perhaps together we can banish him once and for all.'

Steve hesitated. 'What you're saying sounds totally unbelievable. And if I hadn't seen what I did, I'd have thought you needed locking up.'

'But after what you saw, you believe me, don't you?'

Steve wavered, and then nodded. 'Do you mean what you say about wanting to get rid of him?'

'Yes!' cried Marianne, putting her arms round Steve's

neck and pulling him towards her. It wasn't true. She didn't want Steve. In fact, she felt nothing for him any more. However, she had to make him believe that she did want him.

She kissed him, tugging at his shirt buttons and unfastening his trousers. With a groan of desire he buried his face in her neck. 'I want you so much,' he said huskily. 'Watching you with that man, seeing the way you were behaving, it drove me out of my mind. I want it to be like that for us.'

'It will be,' she promised. She was edging him towards the bed, but just before they reached it she was gripped from behind by a pair of strong hands, lifted into the air and thrown into a corner of the room.

Edward stood over her, his eyes furious. 'How dare you?' he demanded. 'Is your wanton behaviour now going to extend to other men?'

Terrified out of her wits, Marianne looked up at Steve. He was facing Edward with a look of rage and jealousy. Suddenly, he reached out and grabbed hold of the other man, but his hand passed straight through Edward's arm. Marianne realised that, although Steve could see Edward, Edward hadn't fully materialised for him. He wasn't flesh and blood, which meant Steve could do nothing but watch as he began roughly caressing Marianne's breasts.

'Let go of her,' Steve yelled. 'She's mine!'

Marianne felt a tug on her hair as Edward pulled her upright, his hands buried in the long curls at the nape of her neck. 'Yours?' he roared. 'You lost her the moment you moved into this house.'

'It's me she loves,' cried Steve.

Edward laughed. It was a terrible sound, full of such dark depravity that Steve recoiled from it. 'She may have loved you once,' he sneered. 'But that ended once I taught her what real pleasure is. She despises you now. You're pathetic. Even if she stayed with you, you'd never be able to satisfy her. Not after the things we've taught her.'

'I don't want to know about the things you've taught her,' cried Steve, clapping his hands over his ears.

'Haven't you noticed a change in her?' asked Edward, his voice silky. 'She's a disgrace; a brazen, lascivious young woman who needs constant discipline in order to control her unnatural lusts.'

'Marianne, come with me,' cried Steve, holding out his hand. She tried to move towards him but Edward's arm tightened round her waist and it was impossible for her to get free.

'I can't,' she exclaimed.

'Of course you can. He's only a ghost.'

'He's more than that to me.'

'I don't think you want to get away from him.'

'I do,' she shouted.

'You little liar,' whispered Edward. He pinched her nearest nipple until she howled with the pain. Then she gasped because, as the pain died away, already aroused by the fact that Steve was watching, she was shaken by a tiny orgasm.

'Stop it,' Steve begged her. 'Quickly, we've got to get out of here.'

'Even if she goes with you, she'll never belong to you again,' jeered Edward. 'I've put my mark on her and you'll have to live with that for the rest of your life.'

Marianne watched Steve's face as his brain registered what Edward was saying. After a few moments he looked at Marianne, but this time his expression had changed and there was no affection in it.

'He's right, isn't he?' he said miserably. 'He's changed you and you'll never be free of him. You like what he does to you. I've just seen that for myself.'

'I'm sorry,' whispered Marianne. 'I never wanted this to happen. I didn't understand what he was doing to me until it was too late.'

'Don't listen to her,' said Edward. 'I didn't change her, I simply showed her what she really was.'

'But I don't want to live without you,' muttered Steve.

'You don't have to,' said Marianne, struggling to escape Edward's grasp, terrified of what Steve was going to do. 'We'll move away. In time we'll forget all this.'

Steve shook his head. 'No, he's right. We'll never be free of him. There's only one solution.'

'What?' demanded Marianne, the crazed glint in his eyes filling her with a dreadful foreboding. 'What are you going to do?' But Steve didn't reply. Turning, he bolted from the room, again locking it behind him.

Edward manhandled Marianne over to the bed, throwing her down and roughly caressing her trembling body. 'We're well rid of him,' he said shortly. 'Your place is with me. You don't need him any more.'

His fingers moved delicately over her flesh, but just as she started to respond she smelt something burning and leapt to her feet. 'He's set fire to the house!' she screamed, and at that moment thick smoke crept under the bedroom door. Rushing over to the window and wrenching it open she saw Steve outside, the empty can of petrol hurled on to the cobbles. 'What have you done?' she shouted despairingly. 'What the hell have you done?'

'Let's see how the pair of you get on without this precious house,' he yelled up at her. 'He'll have a job to haunt you with his home gone.'

'Steve, get me out of here,' she pleaded. 'You haven't thought this through. Do you want me to burn to death?'

'What am I supposed to want?' he called back. 'Don't worry, if you're lucky Sandra and Graham might see the smoke in time to call the fire brigade, but I'd be surprised if they wanted to after the way you've treated them. You never cared about anyone but yourself, did you, Marianne? So why should anyone care about you now?'

She began to weep, screaming desperately at Steve to fetch help, but Edward pulled her away from the window and slammed it shut. 'Leave him alone,' he said contemptuously. 'What does it matter? Now you're free.'

She stared at him, at the brooding face. He could give her such incredible pleasure, but she knew there wasn't an ounce of kindness in him and she panicked, realising that if Moorhead House burned down she would never again be able to escape his clutches, no matter what Edward did to her.

Frantically she dashed back to the window and flung it open again. 'Help me!' she screamed at the top of her voice, but then Edward dragged her away again, pushing her on the bed. Smoke filled the room, and as Marianne's spinning mind tried to work out whether it truly was smoke or the mist that always preceded her journeys into the past, everything vanished.

Chapter Thirteen

When she opened her eyes she was lying on the moors. It was early evening and the wind was cool. Edward was standing nearby holding his horse's reigns. 'You've been sleeping,' he said.

Marianne gazed about her. 'I don't understand.'

'They're late,' he said casually.

'Who?'

'My friends from London.'

She frowned. 'I've never met your friends from London.'

Edward smiled. It was not a kind smile. 'No, but you're about to.'

At that moment three men arrived on horseback, dismounted and greeted Edward enthusiastically, before looking over to where Marianne was sitting amidst the purple heather.

'You didn't exaggerate,' said one. 'She's certainly a beauty.'

'And she has no living relatives?' asked a second.

'None,' said Edward smoothly. 'That was one of the reasons why I employed her.'

Marianne got to her feet, clutching a thin cloak around her. 'Why are they all looking at me like that?' she asked nervously.

'Don't feign innocence,' said Edward. 'You know very well why they're here. I told you I wanted to share you with my friends.'

The three men were advancing on her and in a blind

panic she began to stumble back away from them, but her ankle turned and she fell. The breath was knocked out of her and while she was still gasping, one of the men pushed her skirts up around her waist and unfastened his breeches.

'Edward says he finds it hard to control you,' the man leered, staring down at her and licking his fat lips. He dropped to his knees, his hardening penis bobbing obscenely from his breeches, and began to fondle her through her undergarments while, at the same time, another of the men knelt over her, unfastened himself, his erection sprang out and then he lowered himself over Marianne's face.

'Open your mouth,' Edward ordered abruptly. Instinctively she obeyed him.

As her lips closed around the stranger's gnarled cock and her tongue began to move hesitantly over the straining flesh she felt the first man's fingers fumbling at her sex. His touch was crude yet undeniably exciting, and soon she was sighing around the stalk that pumped back and forth between her stretched lips.

'You spoke the truth about her,' the man grunted to Edward, his voice thick with arousal as his hips drove back and forth. 'Such a sweet mouth to fuck!'

'Then take her, my friends,' said Edward calmly. 'Savour her to the full.'

Marianne wanted to protest, to say she didn't want these men, that it was only Edward she wanted, but she couldn't speak for obvious reasons. In any case, she was so excited by what was happening she wasn't even sure her protest would be true.

'What about me?' called the third man.

'Take her from behind,' said Edward.

Soon all three of them were possessing and invading

her, and despite the shocking depravity of it all she nearly went out of her mind with excitement as Edward stood watching, smiling enigmatically.

'You greedy little whore,' he said softly. 'You're loving this, aren't you?'

At that moment she felt her mouth filling up with hot sticky fluid and swallowed convulsively until every drop had gone and the man slumped away. The other two were still thrusting and they came within seconds of each other.

When they withdrew Edward pulled her to her feet, ripped off the cloak and removed her dress, leaving her with only her dishevelled undergarments for protection. 'Do you realise what you've done?' he asked angrily.

'I did what you wanted,' she whispered.

'You didn't ask my permission, did you?'

'There wasn't time,' she protested, then screamed as he raised his riding whip and curled it round her waist with full force.

'Once we're in London I shall really take you in hand,' he warned, tugging savagely on the whip and jerking her towards him. 'Believe me, in the end you'll learn to control yourself.'

'They'll love her at the club,' said one of his friends.

'The club?' Marianne didn't like the sound of that.

'I belong to a club in London – a very special club. We have nights when we can take guests of the opposite sex, although I'd hardly call them ladies.' His friends laughed. 'I think you'll provide excellent entertainment for all the members.'

Marianne shook her head. 'No, that's not how it was meant to be,' she cried.

He chuckled sarcastically. 'How it was meant to be?'

'That's not why I'm here. I wanted to be with you, like

I was before. In the house, with you and Judith. I don't want to go to London.'

Edward put a hand on her shoulder and turned her in the direction of Moorhead House. 'We've nowhere else to go,' he said quietly. 'And as for the others, their spirits died with the house. It was their only home. We have to move on.'

Marianne froze as she stared across the moors, barely hearing his words. Moorhead House was a charred ruin. Sandra and Graham were talking to a policeman, while close by sombre medics were carrying a covered stretcher to an ambulance. 'It… it's all gone,' she said, her quiet words barely audible above the wind.

'And that's exactly what I wanted,' Edward said triumphantly. 'Now you'll never leave me again. We're together for eternity.'

'No…' whispered Marianne, barely able to comprehend what she was seeing. 'I don't want to go to London with you. I don't want to be with you for eternity. I want to go home.' She waited for the words of denial to work, for everything to return to normal, hoping against hope that everything that had happened had been an awful dream, but she remained in her old undergarments with the wind raising goosebumps on her flesh.

'You can't return,' Edward insisted. 'Don't you understand, my dear? You died in the fire.'

Marianne felt her chin trembling, and then the awful scene around the charred and smoking house blurred as she began to cry. 'H-how can I be dead, when…?'

'Don't ask any questions,' he said. 'This is what you really wanted, you know it is.'

As she continued to weep, he pushed her into the shelter of some nearby bushes, laid her on the ground, pulled down her underwear and began to fondle her sex. He touched her lightly, gently, until she felt the liquid warmth spreading through her and her sex opened invitingly, longing for him. Never before had he been so gentle, so caring, and her clitoris swelled beneath his fingers.

'In a moment your pleasure will spill,' he whispered as he moved away from her for a second. Marianne closed her eyes, anticipating the delicious moment of release. Then, with no warning, Edward brought down the whip and she screamed in anguish, but as the scream died in her throat her body was racked by an incredible orgasm that shook her from head to toe, her pleasure triggered by the flashes of agony.

'You see,' said Edward. 'I'm the only man who can truly satisfy you. You need no one but me. Now get dressed. It's time we set off for London.'

Still weak from her orgasm, Marianne obeyed, and when she was dressed he heaved her up astride his horse before climbing up behind her. As the horse began to move Marianne remembered what Steve had said when he'd first seen the picture of Edward and Judith. She realised she was now heading for a life of excess and debauchery, a life that would be controlled solely by what Edward did or did not want. It was a terrifying thought.

The horse began to trot and Marianne was stimulated by the movement of the beast beneath her. Leaning back against Edward, she heard him laugh. 'I thought you might enjoy this,' he said.

'I don't have any choice,' she retorted. 'There's nothing I can do any more.'

'I don't want you to do anything,' he replied. 'All I demand from you is obedience.' As the horse broke into a canter and her body rose and fell against the saddle she sighed with relief, realising that at last she was totally free to enjoy herself in the ways she liked best. Suddenly London and the life she would have there with Edward promised to be the best thing that had ever happened to her.

'I'm sorry, Steve,' she murmured, 'wherever you are.'

Edward gripped her tightly around the waist with one arm. 'I never want to hear his name mentioned again,' he said firmly. 'Is that understood?'

'Of course,' Marianne conceded submissively, and she knew it would be no problem for her. Nothing would be a problem for her any more, for all those traumatic events which had taken place since she'd moved to Moorhead House had only been the means to fulfil her dark destiny.

Exciting titles available from Chimera

1-901388-20-4	The Instruction of Olivia	*Allen*
1-901388-15-8	Captivation	*Fisher*
1-901388-01-8	Olivia and the Dulcinites	*Allen*
1-901388-12-3	Sold into Service	*Tanner*
1-901388-13-1	All for Her Master	*O'Connor*
1-901388-14-X	Stranger in Venice	*Beaufort*
1-901388-16-6	Innocent Corinna	*Eden*
1-901388-17-4	Out of Control	*Miller*
1-901388-18-2	Hall of Infamy	*Virosa*
1-901388-23-9	Latin Submission	*Barton*
1-901388-19-0	Destroying Angel	*Hastings*
1-901388-21-2	Dr Casswell's Student	*Fisher*
1-901388-22-0	Annabelle	*Aire*
1-901388-24-7	Total Abandon	*Anderssen*
1-901388-26-3	Selina's Submission	*Lewis*
1-901388-27-1	A Strict Seduction	*Del Rey*
1-901388-28-X	Assignment for Alison	*Pope*
1-901388-29-8	Betty Serves the Master	*Tanner*
1-901388-30-1	Perfect Slave	*Bell*
1-901388-31-X	A Kept Woman	*Grayson*
1-901388-32-8	Milady's Quest	*Beaufort*
1-901388-33-6	Slave Hunt	*Shannon*
1-901388-34-4*	Shadows of Torment	*McLachlan*
1-901388-35-2*	Star Slave	*Dere*
1-901388-37-9*	Punishment Exercise	*Benedict*
1-901388-38-7*	The CP Sex Files	*Asquith*
1-901388-39-5*	Susie Learns the Hard Way	*Quine*
1-901388-40-9*	Domination Inc.	*Leather*
1-901388-42-5*	Sophie & the Circle of Slavery	*Culber*
1-901388-11-5*	Space Captive	*Hughes*
1-901388-41-7*	Bride of the Revolution	*Amber*
1-901388-44-1*	Vesta – Painworld	*Pope*
1-901388-45-X*	The Slaves of New York	*Hughes*
1-901388-46-8*	Rough Justice	*Hastings*
1-901388-47-6*	Perfect Slave Abroad	*Bell*
1-901388-48-4*	Whip Hands	*Hazel*
1-901388-49-2*	Rectory of Correction	*Virosa*
1-901388-51-4*	Savage Bonds *(Feb)*	*Beaufort*
1-901388-52-2*	Darkest Fantasies *(Feb)*	*Raines*
1-901388-53-0*	Wages of Sin *(Mar)*	*Benedict*
1-901388-54-9*	Love Slave *(Mar)*	*Wakelin*

All **Chimera** titles are/will be available from your local bookshop or newsagent, or direct from our mail order department. Please send your order with a cheque or postal order (made payable to *Chimera Publishing Ltd*) to: **Chimera Publishing Ltd., PO Box 152, Waterlooville, Hants, PO8 9FS**. If you would prefer to pay by credit card, please email us at: **chimera@fdn.co.uk** or call our **24 hour telephone/fax credit card hotline: +44 (0)23 92 783037** (Visa, Mastercard, Switch, JCB and Solo only).

To order, send: Title, author, ISBN number and price for each book ordered, your full name and address, cheque or postal order for the total amount, and include the following for postage and packing:

UK and BFPO: £1.00 for the first book, and 50p for each additional book to a maximum of £3.50.

Overseas and Eire: £2.00 for the first book, £1.00 for the second and 50p for each additional book.

*Titles £5.99. All others £4.99

For a copy of our free catalogue please write to:

Chimera Publishing Ltd
Readers' Services
PO Box 152
Waterlooville
Hants
PO8 9FS

Or visit our WebShop at:
www.chimerabooks.co.uk